KISSED BY DEATH

VEGAS IMMORTALS: DEATH AND THE LAST VAMPIRE

HOLLY ROBERDS

Cover Design: Holly Roberds

Editors: Jolene Perry & Christie Hartman

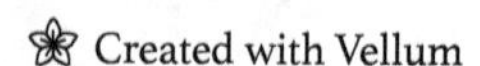

BOOKS BY HOLLY ROBERDS

VEGAS IMMORTALS

Death and the Last Vampire

Book 1 - Bitten by Death

Book 2 - Kissed by Death

Book 3 - Seduced by Death

The Beast & the Badass

Book 1 - Breaking the Beast

Book 2 - Claiming the Beast

DEMON KNIGHTS

Book 1 - One Savage Knight

Book 2 - One Bad Knight

LOST GIRLS SERIES

Book 1 - Tasting Red

Book 2 - Chasing Goldie

THE FIVE ORDERS

Book 0.5 – The Knight Watcher

Book 1 - Prophecy Girl

Book 2 - Soulless Son

Book 3 - Tear in the World

Book 4 – Into Darkness

Book 4.5 - Touch of Hell

Book 5 - End Game

* For recommended reading order, visit www.hollyroberds.com

To my family, friends, and fans who always believe in me, even when I forget to.

1

"Everybody thinks it's every woman's dream to find the perfect man. Actually, every woman's dream is to eat anything she wants and not get fat."

"What happened here?" The British voice was edged with both shock and dismay.

"What?" I cast a glance around at the hotel suite I lived in. It looked as it had for the last five days. I stood and crossed the room to Timothy. Which required I deftly tiptoe over stacks of plates, takeout boxes, and piles of dirty clothes. After gorging myself a couple times, I decided I didn't need to hoover everything down. So abandoned cake pieces, half-eaten burgers, and cold French fries decorated the platters.

"Mother of pearl, Vivien, this place is positively disgusting." Timothy must have been really shocked to use that kind of language. Despite appearing to be in his late twenties, Timothy's actual age was closer to five thousand. And he only reverted to old-fashioned curses when particularly aghast.

Not that it was too hard. He was the most fastidious, proper (not to mention the tidiest) person I'd ever met. Next to him in his perfect suit, not a gelled hair out of place, tablet in hand, I resembled a hobo. My rocking lounge wear was comprised of lime-green sweatpants, two sweatshirts pulled over each other, and fuzzy socks. Well, one sock.

Where did that other bugger get to?

I studied my surroundings a little closer. "Yeah, I guess I should take a time-out from watching reality television and pick up a bit."

The Asian man looked about with open astonishment. "Why haven't you let in the maid service to handle this?"

"What? And invite *his* spies in? No, thank you." To show I didn't need help, I grabbed a stack of takeout boxes that had only started to smell, and delicately perched them on the already full trash bin.

Okay, maybe I needed a little help.

Timothy began muttering to himself. "No, maid service won't do. We'll simply have to burn everything in here to get it properly cleansed."

I stuck a hand on my hip, officially offended by his offense. "It's not that bad."

He must have left the door open because Miranda walked in. "Whoa, that's pungent." My friend covered her nose, joining Timothy in his horror. Her fro of tight curls bounced when she reared back. A portion of her hair was braided over one ear, giving her a seriously badass vibe. She wore her uniform, having just gotten off her shift. Miranda was the new head of security of the Sinopolis Hotel, and she'd stepped into the role like a total boss. And yet, she scanned my pad with disbelief.

"What?" I threw my arms out. "It's not that bad."

Miranda gave me the onceover, her expression

becoming more pained from behind the hand still covering her nose. "Did you throw a party and not invite me? It looks like you invited a ton of people over and ordered from every junk food place available."

"Not all restaurants, but most of them," I corrected. Then with a grin, I said, "Miranda, while you've been busy with your new job, I have been living the dream."

Timothy and Miranda exchanged a wary look.

"I can eat whatever, and however much I want, and never get fat." I threw up my hands in triumph and did a booty dance.

Neither of them joined in with my victory dance.

Miranda spoke first. "Um, Viv, isn't that because you drink blood now, since you're a vampire and all?"

I stopped mid-booty shake.

Timothy cleared his throat. "That's why I'm here. You need to feed." His tone was careful, as if worried he would spook me. Too late. I was spooked.

Suddenly, I was a torrential cleaning machine. I yanked out a trash bag from under the sink, then started throwing takeout boxes and entire cups and plates into it as well. "I don't need it. I don't need him."

Ever since I woke up a vampire with no memory of who I was a month ago, I'd needed to feed on blood every day to survive. But when I made a deal with the devil—or I guess more accurately, with Death himself—my needs changed. I did it to save Miranda's nine-year-old son. And I would do the same thing again in a heartbeat. But that didn't mean I was ready to come to terms with the new arrangement.

I had fed from the god of death, and now only his blood would sustain me. And because of our blood bond, Grim could control my will whenever he damn well wanted to. While he hadn't treated me like a slave or a drone yet, I knew the dark side of that power. The master vampire who turned me had used me like a tool for his bidding. And if I learned one thing early in life, it was that power corrupts.

"You haven't seen him in five days," Timothy pointed out.

"Did Grim send you here?" If his majesty thought he'd snap his fingers and I'd come running, he'd better guess again.

"No."

"You're lying."

Timothy let out an exasperated sigh. "Well, you've ignored his calls and texts when he's done everything from cordially invite you to dinner, to threaten to pull you by the hair to get you to see him."

I didn't understand the dynamic between those two. Though he was a god like Grim, Timothy acted more like the Alfred to Grim's Batman. Except Timothy was far too young to be Alfred, and Grim wasn't a vigilante. Just a beast.

I glowered at Timothy. "And now he's sent someone to butter me up because he's too afraid to come see me. He knows if he showed up at my door, I'd kick his ass." For good measure, I threw some pretty intimidating karate chops into the air.

But that wasn't entirely true. Even on my best day, with all my vampire strength and speed, Grim was a god and able to rip my head clean off with little effort. I'd seen him do it to a number of vampires, or sekhors, as he called them. The first time he used the word, I thought he was calling me a sucky whore.

And I was the last one in existence. I stopped myself from thinking about that for too long. Sekhors were around aplenty in ancient Egypt when everyone was worshipping Grim as Anubis, but then the vampires went crazy with boredom and bloodlust. They tried to take over the world. So the gods wiped out all of the sekhors, since human-turned vamps couldn't handle immortality without going batshit insane.

My brain stumbled and paused on that thought.

Was that where the myth about vampires turning into bats came from? So far I hadn't figured out how to sprout veiny wings, but I could make annoying high-pitched squeaking sounds.

Long story short, Grim wasted all the bloodsuckers. And until he met up with my fangs a couple weeks ago, he hadn't seen a vampire in five thousand years. Dude was not happy about it.

But the two of us destroyed the master vampire and his little army, and Osiris gave me special dispensation to continue with my undead existence. On the condition I help Grim discover who resurrected the vampire bloodline.

So, my choice was to either unearth a conspiracy plot amongst the gods, or have my head ripped off. Sure, I could play Scooby Doo to save my neck. I was, after all, a bounty hunter in my previous life. Piece of cake. Mmm, cake.

"Do you want to take this one?" Timothy asked Miranda in a sidebar.

"Yeah, I didn't realize how bad things had gotten," Miranda said. "Give us a minute."

"No problem, I'll get someone to take care of...this." He cast a last glance around with fearful dread before stepping out, his phone already to his ear.

Meanwhile, I furiously jammed the trash to its limits with junk. I pulled out another bag and left the kitchen to tackle the living room.

Miranda dropped her hand and came as close as she

could without knocking over my impressive skyscraper of pizza boxes. "Vivien, sweetie, you need to eat."

"If you were paying attention, you'd notice that's all I've been doing." I crammed a throw pillow I'd spilled spaghetti on into the waste bag.

"You get what I mean. You can't live off human food anymore, and Timothy said you haven't been to the penthouse in five days. I know you're in pain."

A plate hovered above the trash as I stopped to glare. "I am not." Yes, every movement made my very atoms feel like they were being scraped against a chilled cheese grater. But she didn't need to know that.

Miranda took advantage of my pause, taking the garbage bag away from me. "You are wearing two sweaters, and I'm betting you have at least one pair of leggings on under those sweatpants." She gave a pointed look at the piles of blankets that swallowed the couch.

Ha! Showed how much she knew. There was a pair of pajama pants between the leggings and sweatpants.

I'd heard about vampires staying at the temperature of a corpse. But nowhere in the lore did anyone capture the fact that when I didn't get a decent meal, I'd become as cold as a witch's tit in a frozen hell after a blizzard. Miranda didn't even know about the many heating pads hidden amongst the blankets, and I didn't enlighten her. Out of my makeshift cocoon, it hurt to move. It hurt to stand still. Everything in me pounded with thirst and need, making me weak as a kitten, and my head might as well have been stuffed with cotton. At least being hungry now didn't make me want to lunge at Miranda and rip her throat out anymore.

Similarly, ever since Grim's blood hit my lips, my desire for human blood disappeared in a magic puff of smoke. I once heard when someone started drinking top-shelf liquor, they couldn't stand cheap swill anymore. After drinking blood from a god, there was no going back to human. I couldn't even if I wanted. I only desired...needed Grim's blood.

Nope. I don't need him. I don't crave him. Not in any way whatsoever.

"Not to mention," Miranda went on, hands on her hips, "you look like death."

I crossed my arms. "I am dead. Or undead. And I don't need him."

"So you're going to die from a case of stubbornness?"

"I'm testing a theory. If I eat enough human food, maybe I'll magically turn back into a human, just like in a fairy tale."

Miranda's brow arched. "We read very different fairy tales." Then she licked her lips and dropped her arms, as if preparing herself. "What are you really afraid of, Vivien?"

"You think I'm afraid?" My laugh came out a bark. "I'm not scared of anything." I'd survived on the streets as a vampire for two weeks on my own without killing anyone, destroyed the master vampire, and literally laughed in Death's face. I was a straight-up badass. No, I was Taylor Swift—Fearless.

Miranda straightened and said in a firm tone, "Great, then you'll have no problem going to him tonight and getting what you need. Now get in the shower," she said, pointing to the bathroom. "Pull your big-girl panties on and go see him."

"But—"

Miranda's face darkened, and she pulled the scariest weapon out of her arsenal. Her mom voice. "No buts, missy, you do what I tell you or I'll show you what they taught me in Special Forces." Only slightly less scary, Miranda was ex-

Army, but the Special Forces bit was new to me. I trudged off to the shower, throwing only one mournful glower over my shoulder to let her know I wasn't happy.

I stepped out of the bathroom, barely warmed, despite trying to burn off my skin with scalding water. When I emerged, I saw Timothy had made fast work of my rooms. Not one but four cleaners rushed about the place, tossing garbage, cleaning surfaces, and vacuuming. Miranda sat perched at the kitchen counter, drinking a cup of tea.

A satisfied smile spread along Miranda's mocha-colored face. "There now, don't you feel better?"

I had to admit, a thorough scrubbing did me good. My hair had transformed from a dark, scary rat's nest to thick, smooth auburn waves. Strangely enough, I felt more fragile now that I'd cleaned up. It was as if my loofah scrubbed away both the grime and the lie I told myself that I'd never need to face my dependency on someone else's blood again. I'd put on some heavy black eyeliner. It was the closest thing to war paint I had, and it helped cover up my vulnerability.

I wore a crop top, leather pants, and pulled on a bulky, bright blue faux fur coat. The combo would appear to be a style choice, rather than functional. My teeth chattered when I didn't feed, no matter the hundred-degree weather of a Las Vegas summer.

"Do I pull this off?" I asked with a little spin. "I named the coat Cookie Monster, obviously." Not only was it the same shade as the beloved puppet, I too possessed a voracious sweet tooth.

"It's Vegas," Miranda said. "If you wore a green spandex suit and walked on stilts down the Strip, no one would look twice."

"You're right," I said, pulling the coat closer around me. "People will think Cookie Monster is pimpin'."

And in Vegas, one could totally get away with wearing a pimpin' jacket.

"Wait, do people say pimpin' anymore?" I said.

"Nobody has said pimpin' since the nineties," Miranda pointed out.

"Oh god, what will it be like when I'm thousands of years old, dropping outdated slang like a fuddy-duddy? Like Timothy?" I shuddered.

Timothy rolled his eyes before clicking off his tablet. Pretty sure the guy would expire if he wasn't beep-booping on his little iPad. Then he pushed me out the door. The deadlock slammed shut with an obnoxious clank.

I turned to Miranda, who'd been ejected along with me. "Did I say something?"

"Constantly." Despite her dry accusation, there was no real judgement.

Beneath the spirit of a tough-as-nails mom and ex-Special Forces soldier was a sarcastic hellion after my own unbeating heart. When Miranda stumbled upon me and a far scarier vampire in an alleyway, I'd saved her. I'd convinced her not to kill me because she owed me her life. But then she turned around and saved my ass. We had a mutual save-each-other's-butt thing going. I liked it.

I'd never had a genuine friend before. But I now understood what everyone was talking about all these years. She cared about my well-being, made me laugh, and partnered up with me for hijinks. Even fewer people would get tangled up in a supernatural battle against vampires. But Miranda jumped right into the fray with me.

While Miranda was clued into vampires, she did not know Grim was the god of the dead. She knew something was off about her new boss. But I doubted she'd jump to the conclusion that gods walked amongst mortals. And I was forbidden from telling her. As in, I literally couldn't; Grim used the blood bond between us to bind my will so that I could never tell Miranda. So, of course, I immediately tried to tell her. But in my hundred attempts, every time I either tried to form the words or write them down, an invisible grip would tighten around me, preventing me from revealing that fact.

Probably for the best. Miranda had enough to come to terms with after finding out vampires were real. Not to mention I'd almost killed her son. I still wasn't sure how Miranda could stand to be around me, even though Jamal was as right as rain now, if not suffering from a minor case of anemia. She said that wasn't me, it was the master vampire controlling my will, so it didn't count. That was true, but part of me wondered if she was biding her time to kill me. Though she had ample opportunity over martinis at girls' night. Maybe she was plotting to steal my Netflix password before chopping my head off. Clever girl.

Miranda and I took the elevator down to the lobby of Sinopolis. The pyramid hotel was the epitome of exclusive wealth and a hub to the high rollers. When the doors opened, tropical flowers, fresh soil, and water filled my senses. In the center of all the onyx tile and gold accents was an honest-to-god oasis.

Miranda kept pace with me as I approached the private elevator to Grim's penthouse. I raised an eyebrow. "Acting as escort?"

She gave me a terrifying smile. "If I need to twist your arm to get you in there, I will."

I stuck my tongue out at her. "I'm a scary, strong vampire. I'd like to see you try."

Miranda pushed me. I flailed and stumbled, barely saving myself from splatting on the tile floor.

"Whoa, not cool," I complained, rubbing my arm. "I think you bruised me." If I had even a drop of blood, I would have been as tough as a brick house. Which was her point exactly.

"Yeah, super scary and strong. Now get your butt on that elevator," she said, pointing at the call button. I pressed it, but not without considerable grumbling. Timothy programmed the buttons to recognize my fingerprints, or lack thereof.

They opened with a bing. Dread pooled in my stomach. I stepped inside and turned around, pushing in the gold circle that would send me to the top of the pyramid hotel. Where he was waiting.

Miranda gave me the thumbs-up as the doors closed. Though the second they shut, I wanted to pry them back open. But the elevator had already started its ascent. I backed up to a corner and shut my eyes, trying to psych myself up.

"You are strong, independent, and don't need anyone. You are just here for a quick bite." I couldn't even laugh at my joke. "You will not be affected by his presence. You will have a dignified meal, slam, bam, thank you man for the blood, and be on your way."

I silently added. *And do not, under any circumstances, let him know he turns you into putty.*

2

The elevator doors slid open with a loud ding that made me cringe. I stepped into the penthouse. Grim lived at the very top of the pyramid-shaped hotel he owned. A single light was on in the kitchen, off to the left, and I made out the silhouette standing over by the wall of slanted windows.

He looked out the windows at the colorful lights of Vegas's biggest attractions. He didn't bother to turn around, though he must have heard me enter.

In slacks and a black button-up shirt, his broad shoulders and back held the menace and power that always surrounded him like a mantel. He didn't turn as I took a few steps closer.

Something inside me trembled. Was it because I was weak, near starving, cold as a corpse? Or from the fury that I had to submit to the power he held over me? Either way, I hated it. I would have destroyed myself rather than drink from *him,* if it weren't for Timothy and Miranda intervening.

If it killed me, it would be death on my terms. I couldn't think of a more ironic outcome.

"Sorry I'm late for dinner," I said, taking a stab at levity.

He didn't respond or turn around.

My defenses drained away as his blood called to me. Beckoned to me like a rushing river of ambrosia. I knew I'd been depriving myself, but now my body screamed as it fully experienced the throes of the starvation I'd been putting myself through.

Satisfaction...satiation was within reach.

The god of death's voice came out as a low, throaty rumble that sent a shiver up my spine. "What must I do?"

I continued my careful, measured approach, though part of me still wanted to turn and run. I got two steps before I stopped, trying to resist the need pounding through me.

"Should I break your door down? Throw you over my shoulder and force you to feed?"

I took another step.

"Is it better I let you continue your hunger strike until you've withered away to nothingness?"

Half a step this time.

An extra layer of danger lined his tone now. "Accept that you will drive me to madness by making me wait, unable to know how you are?"

I stopped, only a couple feet away from him. Still, he did not turn around.

Put on the spot, I felt compelled to give an excuse. "I was...busy." Even that sounded lame to my ears.

Grim turned to look at me, half of his face cast in shadow. The other half shimmered with dancing neon lights from the strip. I didn't need to breathe, but he still somehow took my breath away. Those deep mahogany eyes were dark with power, the dark scruff around his full lips more pronounced, and thick black hair fell into his eyes. All the expensive, refined clothes could not hide the savage force of him.

Then he grinned. No, it wasn't a smile. He was baring his white teeth at me, in warning. Any sane human would be scared out of their wits, but if they only knew what he really was. The god of the dead. Known in ancient Egypt as Anubis, also called the Grim Reaper, and now known as Grim Scarapelli. He had more secrets and history hidden underneath this hotel than I had atoms in my body.

Everything about him pulled me like a powerful magnet. His heat called to me, and I wanted to be enveloped by it.

But I wasn't a fish, and he wasn't a hook and line. I dug my heels in and scrounged up some of my own power.

I tapped my foot and set a hand on my hip. "Are you going to be fussy all night, or are we going to do this? I have places to be."

Grim fully turned toward me and arched a brow. "Oh?"

I expected him to move closer, but he didn't. Bastard. He was going to make me come to him.

I swallowed hard and closed the distance between us. "Yes, I am very busy and important."

Grim canted his head before giving me a slow onceover. Another shiver raced up my spine. "Admit it, you missed me."

His words surprised me. The god of the dead was toying with me.

I gave him a half shrug. "Sure, in the way someone misses a cow because she wants a glass of milk."

Energy rolled off him in an intense wave. Gold sparked in his eyes.

"I missed you," he murmured.

Grim's answer shocked me. There was an underlying tenderness to his words I didn't know him capable of.

Despite my resentment, I wanted to mold myself against him, drag my tongue along his neck and bite into him right there. I was so hungry, and even from a few feet away, his delicious scent wrapped around me. But I refused to lose control no matter the pain it caused me.

"You miss having your little bloodsucking slave around? Mad I won't stick around to let you puppeteer me?"

His expression flattened, now deadly serious. "I would never treat you like that."

I was done talking about this. There was nothing Grim could say that would convince me he would not use me, however he saw fit. He had the power; he would take it. And I would do everything I could to throw a wrench into that plan, or more likely, a dozen wrenches. Maybe even stick a banana in his tailpipe.

The little men running my brain madly punched buttons and pulled levers.

We need orders, sir. All the dials appear to be on the fritz. Are they broken?

She doesn't know whether to be amused or aroused by that last bit of imagery, Jenkins.

That's messed up, sir.

We aren't here to judge, Jenkins. Just do your job and get her focused on feeding. If this old girl doesn't get blood soon, we'll all be out of a job.

The tiny men in hardhats were right. The fact was, I was here to feed, and that's what I was going to do. Before I could think any more, I reached for him. My hands fumbled as I tried to pull Grim's shirt collar back, my fingers stiff with cold. I felt as awkward as a teenager about to have her first kiss.

Whoa, not the same at all. Don't even think that.

"Wait." Grim grabbed my hands, stopping me. Then he

took a step back. "I like this shirt. I don't want blood to get on it." He untucked the garment from his pants, flashing me a strip of bare flesh. A much-needed bit of heat snaked through me. His eyes remained trained on me as he unbuttoned his shirt in a lazy, unhurried fashion.

I did my best to look anywhere but at him, but I couldn't help watching each button slip out from the slits of his shirt. Hard muscle exposed itself to my eyes bit by bit. Then Grim slid the shirt off his sculpted shoulders, revealing his bare upper body to me. I'd fed from him twice and knew that skin tasted how it looked. Like salted butterscotch. My head turned fuzzy and light.

Because I'm near starvation. Yes, right, it has nothing to do with him.

The god of death was just that, a god. He looked like every painting, sculpture, and perfect rendition of what mere mortals thought worthy of reverence and worship.

His gaze was still fastened on me when he finished. It took a moment for me to realize he was waiting for me to approach him a second time. Cocky bastard.

If I weren't starving...

The heat emanating from him drew me in again. Canines elongating, I dipped my head to where his neck met his shoulder and bit into him.

Blood welled into my mouth, and I couldn't help the groan that escaped my throat. My fingers dug into his arms. Like the last couple times I'd tasted Grim, it was like biting into an apple that opened the gates to the universe.

His life-giving liquid slid over my tongue and down my throat. A rich, dark, honey nectar. When I'd fed from humans, my body warmed up at the core, gradually spreading outward. But when I drank from Grim, heat came like bright, hot stars bursting inside of me.

It was pure power, and I wanted to drown in it. I travelled past planets, beyond stars, until I was floating in space. The galaxies were spinning, expanding as if in some chaotic yet perfect never-ending dance. I, too, was part of this ballet of elegant entropy. I was both everything and nothing.

It scared and excited me to where I thought I would burst.

Then the expanse narrowed until it was only Grim and me. Something brushed against my mind, like a memory or a promise. But it didn't matter. Only this present moment, with the two of us, mattered.

I heard the steady rush of his blood leading to his heart.

Thump. Thump.

Unable to help myself, I molded my body against him. My hands ran up his arms to his shoulders.

Thump, pause *Thump.*

His heart had skipped a beat.

A part of me bucked against the intimacy, and the other part wanted to continue down the rabbit hole, touching and tasting, to see how many times and how quick his heart could skip.

"Enough," he said, low and soft.

Satiated, I released him, sucking in a gasp of cool air I didn't need. It was then I realized Grim held me up in his muscular arms, as I'd turned into a boneless puddle. Grim slipped his hand under my legs to cradle me, then carried me over to the couch before gently setting me down. I registered the brush of his fingers as he pushed hair back from my face. I let out a contented mewl.

When had I taken off my jacket? The furry blue coat lay on the floor, like a sleeping pet. Heat now radiated from my skin. His warmth, now mine.

At the beginning, I'd intended to drink in a controlled

manner. I planned to resist latching onto him like a feral, starving child. But with his blood running through my veins now, I didn't give a flying fairy.

I was a rainbow unicorn riding cloud nine on a rad surfboard.

"Fuck," I said on a soft breath.

"Better now?" he asked, sitting on the couch by my hips.

I flung an arm over my eyes, suddenly feeling so terribly vulnerable, I was on the verge of tears. The relief his blood gave me rocked me to my core. And being in his arms was like coming home.

"Yeah." My words came out shaky, but talking would keep me from breaking down. "I knew I had been depriving myself, but holy blood bags."

"You will never do that again."

I lifted my arm at that. "What?" The crescent shape of teeth marks on his neck had already almost finished healing. A rivulet of crimson slid down his collarbone and it took everything in me not to lunge forward and lap it up with my tongue.

"You will never go that long without feeding, simply to spite me," he said.

I pushed up on my elbows and glared. His bossiness was killing my buzz. "Oh please, like I did it just to spite you."

"Then why did you?"

"Because..."

I don't want to need you. I don't trust you. I don't trust myself.

All my reasons caught in my throat, each reason more loaded than the last. And explaining any of them would be like handing him the end of my rope. With only a slight tug, he could completely unravel me.

So I didn't explain. Instead, I pushed Grim away and stood up. Though I was still a little dizzy, I tried not to let it show as I leaned over and grabbed my coat. "Thank you for dinner. My compliments to the chef." I meant the words to come out with more levity, but they were dry and biting.

As I turned to go, the truth pressed against my tongue and teeth, dying to come out.

I had missed him too.

No, I missed his blood, I insisted to myself.

The denial skated over my core, then flung off a ramp. Dammit.

Deep down, I knew Grim was more than a meal ticket. One of us was fire, and the other ice, though I was never sure who was which. All I knew was I desperately wanted one of us to melt into the other.

Nope. Scratch that. That was the blood talking.

I reminded myself he possessed total and complete power over me. He'd enslaved me to his blood. No one held that kind of power without abusing it. He'd treat me like one of his reapers—pull on my leash, strangling me, as soon as I stepped out of line.

Grim's phone buzzed in his pocket as I pressed the elevator button. When he picked it up, I didn't need my sensitive vampiric hearing to pick up the yelling over the phone.

I recognized Timothy's cultured British accent, though he sounded panicked. "He's gone."

"Timothy, what's happened?" Grim was on full alert now, tone rigid and spine straight.

"I don't know how it's possible, sire, but he's gone."

"Calm yourself, man." Grim barked the command, taking control of the situation. "Who is gone?"

"Amit. Amit is gone."

Grim was a man of few words and even fewer facial expressions, so when he paled, alarm flashing in his eyes, I knew Timothy's cause for panic was legit.

If Death himself was worried, it stood to reason we should all be a wee bit terrified.

3

I threw my shirt back on, not bothering to fasten it back up, and stepped into the elevator with Vivien. She filled the small space with her intoxicating scent of leather and sugar, and something that was sensually hers alone. Raw sexual impulse and need rioted in me, but I closed my iron fist around the urge, controlling it.

There were three buttons in the elevator, a gold, white, and black one. The top gold button led to my penthouse, the white one was for the lobby, and the bottom black one would take us far below Sinopolis. I pressed both the button that stopped at the lobby and the black button beneath it. But when the doors opened to let Vivien off at the main level, she didn't step out.

Vivien didn't look at me or make a move to leave. She simply clutched her jacket to her bare midriff and waited for the doors to close.

When they started to close, I threw a hand up, stopping them with a jolt.

"I'm coming with you," Vivien said without looking at

me, an argument already rising in her tone, though I'd yet to say anything.

The doors began to close again. I stopped them a second time, allowing her ample opportunity to exit, though my senses screamed there was no time.

She went on. "Osiris only let me live to help you uncover the conspiracy meant to upset the gods. From what I just heard, this is serious, which means I'm officially on the clock." Shooting me a glance, she added, "I'm done sitting on my ass."

I allowed the doors to close this time.

Next to her, my mind drifted. I remembered the way she shivered when she drank from me. The way the furry jacket slid off to the floor, baring her shoulders.

Like jerking the wheel of a car, I redirected my thoughts. I must focus on the task at hand. I'd deal with Vivien later.

Because if she thought she could run away instead of facing the reality of our new relationship, she was mistaken. The sooner she accepted we were now connected by a blood bond, the better. Unfortunately, there was no time to manage the dealings of our delicate alliance.

A situation far more grave had arisen. A situation almost as impossible as a vampire appearing after thousands of years.

When the doors opened to my antechamber, I gestured, inviting her to exit before me. Despite the urgency of the dire situation, I could not override the decorum hard-wired into me. She made haste, walking into the great hall made of sandstone.

Massive columns lined the room, hieroglyphics etched in them. The ancient Egyptian murals lining the walls looked as fresh as if someone had painted them last week. All were depictions of my sacred duty. As if I could forget it.

Timothy paced back and forth between my seat on the raised platform, to the doors to the side that were now wide open. The doors were twenty feet high and led to Amit's chambers.

Timothy's hair looked as though it had been tortured by his agitated fingers, causing it to stick up in all directions.

Without saying a word, I strode past my aide, but Vivien stopped behind me. I turned to see her regarding the entrance with apprehension. Then I remembered she had snuck down here and witnessed my judgement of a soul. The woman in question had not received a favorable judgement. I'd denied her entrance into the afterlife, and she instead faced the worst fate possible.

Vivien likely knew I kept something terrible behind these doors. But I had no patience for her fears.

"Are you coming?"

Vivien jumped as if I'd snapped her out of some memory. Then she threw her shoulders back and followed me into the side chamber.

The humid heat of a swamp mugged me as we entered. Amit's sanctuary was near endless to the naked eye. To a mortal's eye, it would appear to be an endless jungle. I rolled my sleeves up and began searching through the lush foliage for Amit.

"Amit," my voice boomed through the space.

"I've already tried that, sire," Timothy said, irritation clear in his voice. He stayed near the entrance instead of following us in. Though Timothy had all my faith, a part of me still hoped he was wrong, and Amit would appear. I needed to confirm he was missing for myself.

"Who's Amit?" Vivien asked in a hushed tone next to me. Her eyes darted all around as if she weren't sure what to think. I could only imagine the space was disorienting to her. Magic helped bridge time and space to create this perfect sanctuary for Amit.

"He is a god."

"Like you?"

"Yes, and no." I pressed farther into the sanctuary. Vivien stayed close, making her way along the jungle floor. Pushing back a branch, I explained. "Amit does not have a human form like I do. He preferred to grow old and strong in his god-likeness."

"God-likeness?" she asked, ducking under the branch before I released it.

"You witnessed my god-likeness when I fought my brother and then again with the horde of sekhors."

"Oh, the scary, half-jackal, half-man, half-beast form you changed into?"

I didn't pause to correct her understanding of fractions. "Yes. Amit's god-likeness is that of a giant crocodile."

She snapped her fingers. "I knew it! This place reminds me of a massive lizard habitat mashed up with a swampland."

If Amit hadn't been missing, I might have laughed.

We came to the edge of a body of water, knowing it to be fifty times deeper than it appeared on the surface. I bent to one knee and dipped a hand in the warm, murky pond of water. "Yes, Amit requires a specific environment to thrive, one with an abundance of water and heat."

"Why does he live in here?"

I twisted to face her, keeping my hand in the water. The liquid teemed with life. I could feel the pulse of life force from plants, fish, even the bacteria that was hard at work producing methane, sulfur, and carbon dioxide. "He is crucial to keeping the balance of the universe."

"Oh yeah?"

"When someone is brought to me, I weigh their soul and if they have not lived an ethical life, their soul is destroyed."

"How does one destroy a soul?"

I stood, shaking the droplets off my hand. The reality of the situation was sinking in. My senses searched the reservoir, but there was no trace of Amit. Then I leveled a look at Vivien. "By feeding the tarnished soul to Amit."

"Whoa, that's heavy. So, did he run away or something? Tired of dining on the souls of the damned?"

"He eats nothing else, and he could not have left without our noticing." And yet, it appeared he had somehow managed.

"Because...giant damn crocodile?"

I nodded. "Precisely."

As if on cue to confirm my suspicions, one of my reapers appeared. The sleek black dog's eyes glowed gold. Ddot had brought me a soul for judgement.

"Oh hey, little guy," Vivien cooed. Ddot pressed against Vivien as she smoothed her hand over his head in vigorous pets.

"So what makes you think he's not here?" she asked, while coercing Ddot to lie down so she could scratch his belly. My reapers never acted with such indignity before Vivien showed up.

I unsuccessfully suppressed a groan. "Could you please not treat my reapers like common canines?" Word had traveled amongst the ranks that my sekhor would scratch behind their ears.

"Amit could be in that giant pond," she said, ignoring my request.

"First off, I checked. While the pool brims with life, there is a distinct lack of the god's presence."

"You got all that from just touching the water? That's

kind of cool," she admitted, crouching down to scratch Ddot's stomach with extra vigor.

"Second, my reapers would never chance entering Amit's chambers. Even when they aren't carrying souls for judgement, Amit would eat one of them to get the aftertaste of a soul. If Ddot is here," I gestured to the reaper who was now licking Vivien's hand in appreciation, "he does not feel in danger of being eaten." I dragged a hand over my face, tension setting up in my back and shoulders. "Which means Amit is well and truly gone."

Vivien stood up and wiped her hands of errant fur against her thighs. "So, what happens if Amit isn't here to devour the souls?"

Our eyes locked. "Nothing good."

"I believe I have discovered something, sire," Timothy called, still at the chamber's entrance. He did not care to be in Amit's abode. I wasted no time hurrying over. Vivien was right behind me, and Ddot stuck close to her.

"What is it?" I asked my aide.

"You should see this security footage." Timothy's lips were a thin slash as he angled his tablet toward me.

Four people wearing ball caps were wheeling out what looked like a giant, petrified Amit out behind Sinopolis, where they loaded him into a container attached to a semi.

"Is that...?" Vivien's words trailed off in wonder. "It looks like a massive statue of a crocodile."

"Yet Amit is two times that size. They've somehow managed to both shrink and freeze him."

The thieves wore matching generic khaki uniforms.

"You weren't kidding," Vivien breathed. "He's a big boy. The size of a house. He looks like a statue, though."

My stomach rolled, then twisted. "They've done something to him. I'm not sure what, but Amit would not be taken without a fight." My frustration mounted. Despite my claim, there was no evidence of a struggle in Amit's habitat.

At one point, a security guard stopped the four-person crew. Two Asian men, another lanky man with light-brown skin, and a shorter woman with blonde hair who barely covered five feet. When the guard approached, the short woman took point, gesturing to the crocodile. They said something and the security guard shrugged then returned to his rounds.

"At least there is a witness to question," Vivien said, pointing at the guard.

I watched the crew close up the doors and take off with Amit.

"How did they get him out?" Vivien asked. "I thought the elevators require fingerprint recognition. Plus, there is only one lift that goes in or out of here."

Timothy and I shared a look. I answered. "I don't know how they overrode our security measures, but there are more than a dozen exits from this level. They are simply hidden from plain view."

Vivien cast a look around as if she could discover the secret doors with a glance.

With a few more taps on the tablet, Timothy brought up a hidden lift that was in the far back corner of the habitat. Sure enough, the thieving crew used the lift as if they'd done so a thousand times. The short female was the one to press the button.

"Why is this lift so big?" Vivien asked, pointing to the screen as they returned to the lift with a now-petrified Amit in tow.

Since Timothy became wholly absorbed, furiously typing on his tablet, presumably to discover how the woman bypassed security, I answered. "We sometimes import endangered flora or fauna into Amit's habitat. He enjoys the stimulation and growth, and we've managed to rehabilitate the numbers of many animals and plants before re-situating them in the wild again."

Vivien's eyebrow arched. "Death is an environmentalist? Who'd-a thunk?"

Shooting her a sharp smile, I said, "Perhaps I do it to make sure I have plenty to kill later. A hunter wants to ensure his hunting grounds are teeming with life to reap."

She tsked, a knowing smirk pulling at her mouth. "Now, now. Don't pretend on my account. Death is nothing more than a harmless, cuddly teddy bear who wants to save all the little flowers and bunnies in the land."

"Try to cuddle me and find out how harmless I am," I growled. My eyes swept up and down her, conveying the damage I would wreak on her given half a chance.

Vivien's pupils dilated into dark pools. She seemed unaware of her fangs lengthening. I pressed my tongue behind my teeth, bracing against the sudden need that pounded through me, making it hard to think.

"Ah, here we go," Timothy said, breaking the moment like a pane of glass. Vivien jerked. I swallowed a disgruntled growl. "The security log shows that," Timothy continued, his surprise and shock now trained on Vivien, "you were the one who entered and left."

Vivien reared back with a scowl. "What? No way. I had nothing to do with this. I don't even know where that entrance is. And why would I steal Amit?"

"No one is saying you did any such thing," I said, unable to keep the amusement out of my voice. "Someone remembers that unique feature sekhors shared—their distinct lack of prints."

Vivien relaxed.

With a terse nod, Timothy said, "Yes, they could have replicated the effect in a number of ways, I suppose."

"Call Ms. West," I said to my aide. "We need her back here. Tell her our security's compromised and there has been a theft."

"Is that...wise?" Timothy asked. "She is human."

"And has already proven herself more than capable of handling supernatural situations without asking too many questions while getting the job done. Seeing as she broke into my penthouse, I would consider her more than apt at discovering how these thieves trespassed. She does not need to know the particulars about Amit."

Armed with his mission, Timothy left to handle his duties.

I turned to Vivien. "I fear you are correct in your initial assessment. No matter who is responsible for this theft, someone is yet again attempting to upset the balance. We have to find Amit as soon as possible."

Though Vivien was right, she wasn't smug about the confirmation.

"What happens if we don't find Amit?" she asked again, following me back out to my antechamber.

I leveled a serious gaze at her. "We have to find him. Any alternative is simply unacceptable."

"Okay, don't tell me," she said with a huff. "I'll go hook up with Miranda and see what I can find."

We stepped into the elevator, and I pressed the button to the lobby. "No. There is something else you must accompany me on."

"Something more pressing than finding the gigantic crocodile god you use as a garbage disposal for the evil souls that don't get to graduate to the afterlife?"

I suppressed a sigh. "I need you to attend a ball with me."

Vivien blinked. "You're kidding."

"I'm afraid not." Despite myself, I could not hide my distaste. "It has been a century since my family has gathered, and now there is an insistence for a soiree tonight. Our presence is required."

"And you were going to tell me this when?"

I gave her a hard look. "If Timothy had not persuaded you to visit me this evening, I would have come for you myself."

Did I imagine a shiver went through her? I must have. And I also must have imagined that flicker of desire in her eyes which accompanied it. Vivien had made it clear she could not hate me more. And if I'd learned anything throughout my existence, it was that hate and resentment could endure an eternity.

"I assume when you refer to your family, you mean a bunch of gods are throwing this bash?"

I nodded. "While we all run various hotels on the Vegas Strip, rarely do we gather."

"So then why the sudden need to throw a fancy party?" Her nose wrinkled. She was unaware of how adorable the expression was.

I licked my lips slowly. "I daresay that has everything to do with you. Word has spread by now that the sekhors have made a resurgence, and that one alone remains. They wish to...meet you."

"The way you say it makes it sound like they're sharks looking for some chum."

"You are not far off." I lowered my voice. "Though sharks feed to nourish themselves, they don't tear other fish apart for sport."

"Oh goody," she breathed in apprehension. Then she straightened her shoulders and tilted her chin up as the rebel in her arose. "So then, why are we going to play Cinderella for a night when we should be out looking for Amit?"

"Because," I said, refastening the middle button on my shirt. Her eyes caught on the movement. "I can guarantee whoever is behind this conspiracy, if not Amit's theft, will be in attendance."

Her jaw went slack as realization dawned in her eyes. "Right, so while they think they're at a dog show, there to judge the size of my teeth..."

"We shall be questioning them in turn."

Vivien's green eyes brightened with interest. "Now, this I can get on board with." She rubbed her hands together like an evil villain.

How, in the most of stressful, dire moments, did Vivien still make me want to crack a smile or chuckle? I daresay it was a supernatural power of hers. Perhaps the same one she used on Osiris, so he'd condone her continued existence.

Returning to the task at hand, I said in a warning tone. "And Vivien, the dress code is strict."

A mischievous grin spread over her face. "I'm good at following the rules."

Vivien didn't dress to impress. She dressed to shock and antagonize. While she bared her flesh and shapely body, she sprouted invisible lethal spikes the moment anyone got close. I could just see her now, re-donning the latex suit and kitten heels she'd worn at my night club. The others would see it as an invitation, and I could not abide it.

I turned to face her. "This is no joke. These gods, my family, will be there, probing for any chink in your armor, then do everything to tear you apart. It is important when we show up that we present ourselves in a manner that is..."

"Yeah, yeah, yeah, I get it. You want bulletproof Cinderella."

My fingers wrapped around her arm. Not with bruising force, but a gentle firmness. The feel of her skin beneath mine sent a fresh wave of emotion through me. She'd been away from me for too long.

"This won't be like the Wolf Town Club. My family will do everything to find fault in you. They will dig into the crevices of your character and your past until they have scraped out your most sacred, private, and vulnerable parts, then display them under lights like a set of rare jewels."

Her sea-green eyes rounded, boring into mine. I couldn't tell if she hung on my every word, or if her thoughts were elsewhere.

"A bunch of sociopathic, backstabbing piranhas. Got it." There was a tremor of uncertainty in her voice as she pulled her arm away. Did I successfully put her on guard, making her nervous for the coming event? Or perhaps something else I'd said or done set her off balance?

Vivien's fingers touched the hand I'd wrapped around her arm. She paused, then pushed my fingers away to take a step back.

Right. Vivien had made it clear my touch was unwelcome.

I ran a hand through my hair and averted my gaze. "Yes, well, Timothy will arrange for attire and assistance to be sent to your suite to help get you prepared."

Before she could respond, I turned on my heel and left. Part of me wanted to turn right back around and demand she tell me what she was thinking, but I couldn't rush things. We were already in for an eternity together, Osiris willing. We had time to get used to the new arrangement.

It was unclear whether I could spend forever allowing her to dance around the edges of whatever *this* was. Or succumb to the yawning need that demand I push her beyond her limits, the way she did to me.

An unbidden voice rose from deep inside me. *Push.*

4

The smell of swamp, and something sharp, like citrus, filled my sensitive vampire senses. After Grim's abrupt departure, I took a quick detour to the lift the thieves used to get in and out of the antechamber. Timothy returned and agreed to take me, though he complained I should be getting dressed.

My hands ran along the caged steel walls searching for a clue.

"What are you hoping to find?" Timothy asked, his foot tapping with rhythmic impatience.

"Maybe someone dropped something. Like a business card with contact info, along with a signed confession."

I ignored Timothy's snort. I'm not sure what had his panties more in a bunch: Amit gone missing, or this upcoming soiree.

I found squat. The lift led to the hotel's underground parking garage where we'd seen the culprits load up a truck. After five minutes, Timothy declared he was pulling the plug. We needed to prepare for the ball.

He did *not* think it was funny when I bippity boppity

BOOPED his nose. Ushering me back to my rooms, claiming he had business to take care of, Timothy assured me everything I'd needed to get ready was already delivered to my suite.

Had I known that meant he'd sent a whole damn team of makeup designers and hair stylists, I would have found a pumpkin patch to hide in. A fashion coordinator wheeled in two racks of dresses behind me. Armed with hair curlers, mascara tubes, and six-inch heels, the stylists cornered me.

At first, I considered snarling and biting at them like a rabid animal to get them to back the truck up. But damned if I wasn't a little excited to get this show on the road.

Not because I wanted to attend a ball. Who says ball, anyway? He should have said gala, or benefit, something more modern.

No, I was excited for the mission. The hunt was what drew me to bounty hunting in my previous life. I was like a dog with a bone ferreting out information and hunting down a skip. My profiling skills had gotten pretty keen. As an amnesiac, I still noted accents, behavioral data, and anything that could tell me about the people around me. Once I knew enough about someone, I could figure out their habits and routines, which made it a piece of cake to corner someone on the run.

Even in high school, my peers would hire me to get dirt on their ex. It was honest work. I would drag the ugly truth out into the light. And while I could have been a PI, the daredevil part of me thrived on the legwork and danger involved in bounty hunting. Private Investigators had it too safe.

So, instead of snapping my jaws at the beauty team, I dutifully sat down at the massive suite vanity and took a bracing deep breath, signaling they could begin.

Somewhere between getting my hair curled and eyebrows lined, I video-called Miranda, and set my phone down where I could see it. She answered from a seat in the hotel's security office. No doubt, still trying to track down the team that snatched Amit.

"Whoa, are you being attacked? Do you need help?" she asked.

"Har har," I said. "I'm going to a function with Grim, and Timothy sent these..." I was about to say rabid hyenas, but when the man doing my makeup reared back and gave me a pointed look while evilly swirling a makeup brush in a pot of pink something or other, I reconsidered. Blood bags. "... err, helpful stylists to get me ready."

"What function?"

"A family function."

"Like a reunion?"

"Yeah, that also happens to be a ball."

"A ball?" There was a pause, then a stifled chortle. "Like a ball, ball? Where Cinderella gets dressed up and loses a shoe?"

This. This was why I liked Miranda. Despite her scary badass demeanor, we often ended up surfing the same bizarre brain waves.

"Hi Vivien." Jamal's face filled the screen. He shared the same shade of brown skin as his mother, as well as her wide nose, but where her eyes were near black, hard and calculating, his were a soft, expressive light brown.

I couldn't help the smile that sprung on my face. "Hey J. You keeping your mom company?"

Miranda wrestled the phone back from her son. When the camera shifted around as they fought for control of the phone, I got a good view of the mottled scar on his neck. My fangs had done that. Looking at it still sent stinging shocks of shame and remorse through me.

It still amazed me either of them wanted anything to do with me.

"I couldn't leave him at home without a sitter," Miranda explained.

"Yes, you can," I heard Jamal chime in behind her.

The kid was ten years old, and in my opinion, able to take care of himself for one night—said the childless vampire, who thrived on a lack of supervision. But Miranda wouldn't hear of it. I didn't know if that was because she was a widowed single mother or an ex-soldier with control issues. Or maybe she knew the things that went bump in the dark could bump a little too close to home.

Miranda ignored her son's insistence he could take care of himself. "Though why Mr. Scarapelli is losing it over a giant, petrified crocodile is over my head. I don't suppose you know why." She said the last bit as if she already knew I had a raging clue what was going on.

I wanted to tell her why Grim was freaking out. Even with these dolts, pulling at my hair and mushing wet products on my face, I wanted to say the enormous crocodile is a god who eats souls, and we need him back, stat. I gathered the words in my mouth, ready to spill the beans.

Instead, a puff of air escaped my lips. A frustrated mewl followed.

"Fine," Miranda raised her hand, feigning hurt, "you don't want to tell me either, you don't have to."

"Believe me, I really want to tell you, I just...can't." Because Grim gave me a direct, will-controlling order never to reveal gods. Damn him. "But someone at this ball is likely behind the theft. Have you got anything new on the criminals?"

I should have given her more time to investigate, but I couldn't wait. This shindig started in less than an hour, and patience wasn't my virtue.

A hand pinched my cheeks together, forcing me to pucker up so a stylist could smear lipstick on me. These three had zero interest or respect for the very important conversation I was having.

Thankfully, Miranda was looking away at something, and missed my angry puffer fish impression. "Still working on it, but I managed to get a hold of our security man and get a quick rundown of what happened. He told me the movers said the crocodile was part of an old, lame magic show at Sinopolis. The woman said she was told it was an old, useless relic that needed to be tossed out to make way for the new."

Wow. The double meaning in that was scathing. Someone was sending a message, along with the middle finger, as they waltzed out of the hotel with a captive croc god. I wasn't sure who should be more insulted, Grim or Amit.

"Well, thanks for letting me know. Maybe the tip will come in handy tonight."

"Hey, Viv?" she said, stopping me from ending the call.

"Yeah?"

"You're looking a lot better. I'm glad you finally had something good to eat. Did you get any dessert?" she asked, her lips curling up in a devilish grin.

Instead of answering, I glowered back at her through the video as best I could, but someone yanked at my hair, forcing a yelp from me. "Text me if you find anything else."

"Will do, Cinderella. Just don't get drunk and lose your shoes."

She hung up while I still grumbled something about chucking a shoe at her.

INSTEAD OF MEETING Grim at his penthouse, there was a limo waiting for us. He stood outside it in a tuxedo that fit him like a damn glove. With his broad shoulders, tapered waist, and impossibly sensual, dark features, there was only one word that kept coming to mind.

Yummy.

I blamed Miranda and her joke about having "dessert."

Yes, yummy, because you drink his blood, I insisted to myself. It's like literally looking at breakfast, lunch, or dinner.

The tiny men in charge of running my brain piped up. *"Sir, she's trying to cross wires here. Should I try to reprogram her thoughts to fit the wishful thinking?"*

"Jenkins, you damned fool. We keep the lights on, we can't remodel the place."

Grim caught sight of me. He froze as if struck by lightning. I'd shocked him before with some of my getups. But it was nothing compared to the ensemble I was now wearing.

Thank god my stylists had brought two racks of dresses, because I dismissed most of them without a thought. When I spotted the one for me, my stylist smiled, albeit with surprise. Apparently, she'd been warned about my unique sense of fashion.

The elaborate jeweled bodice pressed my breasts up so well, even I thought I could pose for the cover of some bodice-ripper novel. The hand-stitched A-line gown fell around me in magnificent ruby-red waves. Gold stitching complemented the jewels of the top, then transitioned into the ornate floral brocades down the full skirt. Everything about the dress was royal, near gothic luxury. My favorite part of the ensemble was the spiked headpiece that resembled a lethal halo. Without conscious effort, I raised my chin higher and rolled my shoulders back.

The rubbernecking from passersby in the lobby only confirmed what I'd felt. I was standing before the god of the dead as a queen incarnate.

Granted, it took a team of four people to get me this polished. Even my eyebrows were perfection, down to the last hair. I may not be a goddess, but in this attire, I felt every bit as powerful and magnificent as one. And I'd need any edge I could get.

Grim continued to scrutinize my appearance in a lengthy head-to-toe examination.

"So I take it I pass the bar standard on this one?" I asked, raising my arms and looking down at myself as if seeing the dress for the first time.

I half-expected Grim to loosen his collar, or stutter out a compliment, but no. This was Death. His lips tightened as he gave me one last up-and-down and then simply said, "It will do."

"Wow, don't gush." I tried not to feel slighted that all I'd gotten was a mere pat on the back when I deserved a prize for looking like an elegant, fierce deity.

Asshat.

Instead of answering, he held out a hand to help guide me into the limousine so I wouldn't step on my dress. With a sigh, I took it, letting him help me into the car with my behemoth of a dress. After being hyped by the style team, I'd felt like I was on my way to a Disney castle, but as the limo door shut behind us, it now felt like I was on my way to my own funeral.

5

The stretch limousine pulled away from the curb. Two flutes of champagne sat next to an open bottle of Dom Pérignon on ice, but neither Vivien nor I reached for it.

A smothering silence descended on the vehicle. The urge to stare at the vision that was Vivien was almost too much. The only way I kept my eyes averted was by bringing her into my mind's eye as she had emerged from Sinopolis.

People around her slowed to gape. The magnetic glow she emitted as a sekhor intensified, and it took everything in me to stay rooted to my spot by the limo. Vivien had morphed into an unearthly creature that had stepped straight from a renaissance painting of either heaven or hell, and I couldn't figure out which. Then I remembered Lucifer was a fallen angel, and realized that fit her best. An avenging angel from hell.

"Will Timothy be there too since he's also a god?" Vivien asked, interrupting my thoughts.

I jerked, but quickly recovered. "Yes, he will meet us there. And you will also see Bianca again."

Vivien's shoulders dropped a few inches in clear relief. Bianca was an oracle and had met Vivien before. Though Timothy and I had kept Vivien's existence a secret, Bianca called me out of the blue, demanding we meet. She'd had a vision about Vivien, and warned me to never let Vivien out of my sight.

Vivien took to Bianca almost immediately. But it wasn't surprising. Many flocked to the goddess, with her old Hollywood elegance—Bianca favored the forties—and kind heart.

"Though she'll be late," I added. "As is her way. She thinks it's fashionable, or makes an entrance, or some such thing."

"And we're what? Going early?" Vivien toyed with the edge of her dress. I couldn't tell if it was a sign of boredom or a nervous tick. Did she have any concept of what we were about to step into?

"Of course not." I frowned. "We will arrive right on time."

Vivien crossed one leg over the other, flipping the dress up slightly, catching my eye. "Don't go to many parties, do we? You should have taken a page out of Bianca's book."

I leaned forward, resting my elbows on my knees, looking up at her. "You forget. Sinopolis is the most exclusive party scene on the entire Strip. Perhaps I thought it best that we arrive at the same time as everyone else so they will be distracted greeting each other in a flurry, rather than solely focused on you."

She snorted. "Aren't I the big attraction?"

"You are. And while we have a moment, it's best we go over some rules."

She groaned and rolled her eyes. "Here we go."

I ignored her obvious displeasure. This was important.

"One, you will not tell them anything about our relationship."

She shot me her best deadpan stare. "What relationship? The one where I'm supposedly your slave, or the one where you're the equivalent of a farm-to-table meal for me?" Before I could respond, she added, "I'm not going to be all dramatic and tell them how you wanted to kill me when you first met me."

"Don't be absurd," I said, waving a hand. "I still want to kill you."

"Har har."

I pressed on. "Two, divulge as little about yourself as possible. I'd advise against sharing anything about your occupation and name from your previous life, though I'm sure that information is already known." I had done my best to shore up all crevices and cracks that my peers could sink their claws into, but I knew it wouldn't be enough.

"Three, do not let them inside your head. They will do everything they can to undermine your confidence to test if you are worthy or not."

"Worthy of what?"

"Worthy of existence."

She crossed her arms. "Great, just great. At least tell me there will be an open bar."

I sat back. "On that front, we can both be grateful."

Though even that posed a danger. The number of times someone had spiked the punch with some magic side effects had rid the use of any community punch bowl, but they could bribe a server.

"Don't worry," she huffed. "I'm not going to act like a gigantic screwup and embarrass you."

My head swiveled toward Vivien. I shot her a quizzical

expression. "Why do you think my concern is being embarrassed?"

"Isn't it?" She grabbed the champagne flute and tossed its contents back in a neat swallow.

"No," I said, slowly, "but this isn't the first time you've come to that conclusion."

As if unnerved by something I said, she grabbed the other flute and sank the second champagne. An expression flitted across her face. I almost didn't catch it. But it was as if there were some memory she was trying to shake off. "Well, I guess you seem like such a proper guy, you don't seem to like when I rock your boat."

"Not because I am embarrassed. You are simply..." I searched for the fitting word. "Unpredictable."

She cheered me with the empty glass. "Don't I know it. Never know what I'm going to do or say next, I tell ya."

"But make no mistake, the others will not respond well to any antics. Sekhors have not been allowed to exist since the ancient times and many of my brethren will consider you a threat. If you give them reason to think that, they may do something rash whether or not I am by your side."

"Aw, I'm going to blush."

She reached for the open champagne.

"Are you worried about me, G?"

"Yes." Maybe she could shake off the seriousness of the situation. But there was genuine danger, like she'd never faced, and I couldn't treat it so cavalierly. If something happened to her...my chest tightened.

Vivien paused, as if caught in my gaze, bottle still poised in the air.

"I will do everything in my power to protect you," I went on. "But there are a number of rules—specific etiquette among the gods you know nothing of, and I haven't the time to educate you. One wrong move and everything could go horribly wrong, not for you, but for me. And if I'm compromised, who knows what the others will do to you."

She resumed pouring the champagne with a new intensity. I was deadly serious, and she knew it. Good. She should be afraid. But the damn fool woman was unlikely to heed my warnings. Still, I gave her a moment to let what I'd said sink in.

Her crystallized soul, the one I could never reap, filled the space with that dazzling glow. The blood bond had only intensified the magnetism of her essence. Had I been a lesser god, I would bend her to my will in all manner of ways. None of which she'd find too unpleasant. My eyes drifted to her full, red lips for the barest moment.

Vivien's throat moved up and down as she swallowed. "Do you remember what I said to you after the last time you kissed me?"

"Never again."

Luminous sea-green eyes bewitched me, while her words were weak and thready. "And then you said..."

That tight feeling in my chest moved to my gut and warmed. "The next time it happened, it would be because you begged me to."

Vivien leaned forward. Her eyes tracked me like laser beams, drawing me to her. The way she slowly licked her lips made my mouth dry up like the Sahara. My heart pounded in my chest despite how everything else in me had gone completely still.

"Well, I think I have something to ask you."

We were only inches away. Heat between us rocketed with invisible sparks.

"Yes?" I drew out the word, expectant yet oh so patient.

Then she pointed just past my feet. "Can you hand me the cork? It fell down there."

The sexual haze shattered like a pane of glass, its remnants littering the limousine floor.

I blinked once, then twice, before scooping up the cork and handing it to her. As I sat back, she flashed me a big grin, showing off her fangs. Then instead of picking up the glass she'd already filled, she put her lips straight to the bottle and tipped it back, staring at me with what I imagined was her best rendition of a deranged animal. An elegant, well-dressed, deranged animal.

While Sinopolis was a masterpiece of onyx glass, gold antiquities, and lush foliage, the Florence Hotel was a vision in cream marble and ionic columns. I led Vivien to the canal that ran through the inside.

Vivien smirked at me even as I led her into the boat. "A pre-party gondola ride? Isn't this move a little hokey, even for you?"

I handed the gondolier a card that served as our invitation before sitting down and leaning back. As the ferryman pushed off, I watched Vivien try to hide her delight at riding on the "inside boat," as she called it. Her eyes were round, and a smile played at the corner of her mouth as we floated down the artificial channel. She ignored the people who not only stopped to stare at us, but the several bystanders who pulled out their phones to snap photos of us. While I was usually the subject of such attentions, even I knew the people around us could not tear their eyes away from the woman next to me.

Vivien turned to me. "Are you trying to make sure we

show up fashionably late now, after I outed you for being a goody two-shoes?"

Our gondola thrust into the darkness of a cavernous opening. Light shot by and a strong wind rushed through the tunnel. We might have been careening in the dark at hundreds of miles per hour. Vivien gripped my knee, and I resisted the urge to pull her up against me.

It was imperative I never push her. Though that stunt she pulled in the limousine made me want to grab her beautiful face and kiss her until her knees shook. Instead of reaching for her, I wrapped my fingers around the edge of the boat.

Soon enough, the gondola slowed as we approached a well-lit stone pier. Majestic candelabras flanked a large ornate door. Before she could protest, I stood and wrapped my hands around Vivien's waist and lifted her up onto the stone platform, then stepped up next to her. Without another word, our ferryman slid back into the darkness, leaving us alone.

"Remember what I told you in the limo. No one is to be trusted, and be careful what you do and say in there."

The angel from hell saluted me. "Aye aye, captain."

I'd give it five minutes before all hell broke loose.

6

The grand doors opened by themselves, as if by magic. Grim took my hand, escorting me into a whole new world.

We walked out onto a landing at the top of a grand set of marble stairs. The rich scents of expensive perfumes, roasted lamb, and cinnamon surrounded me.

A hush fell over the crowded room as everyone turned to face us. Looked like everyone had arrived early so they wouldn't miss the floor show. Displayed on the landing, I felt like a prize pig at a fair.

However, the vantage point gave me an equally fair view of the ballroom.

The ballroom was packed with attendees. Two long water troughs spanned the length of the room on either side. They brimmed with blue lotus flowers. Several live, long-legged, wading birds were poised among the blooms in the false ponds. Baroque-style moldings curled up the cream walls to the arched ceiling. Next to the dance floor was a ten-person orchestra.

The scene was breathtaking...or it would have been if I'd had a breath to take.

Fragrant roses, calla lilies, and orchids decorated the marble ballroom in grand arrangements. Despite the delicious fragrances, a sour patina coated my tongue. I couldn't let my nerves get the best of me.

And while the grand hall was the epitome of opulence, the guests were a whole other ballgame.

I had to ask myself an important question—had I accidentally stumbled into a carnival?

There were dresses and suits as dazzling and unique as those worn to the Met Gala, but a lot of the outfits pushed right into the bizarre.

A rail thin, frail-looking goddess wore what I could only describe as a giant blue dot that came down to her knees. A god donned a white plastic suit with a collar that went up past his ears. One voluptuous, brown-skinned goddess wore a ballgown composed of black feathers that made her look both elegant and powerful. Had I imagined the feathers flapped as if alive?

Another god wore a plaid mask that covered the top half of his face and elongated up into long bunny ears. Okay, those bunny ears definitely twitched. A shiver of the heebie-jeebies raced down my spine.

Many of the outfits reminded me of Picasso paintings with strange sharp angles and bursts of color.

More arresting than the high fashion was the blatant display of power here. Gowns and suits were accented with auras of ice and fire that surrounded their shoulders, hands, or heads. My stomach churned. I would have killed for a Tums.

It was then I noticed even Grim had added to his attire. A mantle of power fell over his shoulders in thick black clouds that evaporated into wisps. A skull emerged from the smoke before sinking back into the inky mass before another surfaced in a swirling dance of death.

Holy blood bags, I was in way over my fucking head on this one. Panic skittered under my skin, urging me to hightail it and run back out and jump into the canal and swim away if need be.

Not that Grim was likely to let me leave.

The gods' scrutiny nearly drowned me in tension, making me want to shift my shoulders. But I knew better than to squirm. My training from not one but two lifetimes ago kicked in. I raised my chin and narrowed my eyes as if I owned the room.

I didn't know gods, but I knew elitist snobs. Show them an inch of your underbelly and they'd tear you to shreds.

With a slight tug, Grim guided me down the marble staircase. Without music, our footsteps resonated with a cringe-worthy echo throughout the ballroom.

We weren't even halfway down when the murmurs started. The hairs on my body rose as an electric zing raced along my skin in warning. Power pressed against my skin from all around me. Though I was a tough-as-nails, immortal vampire, the last vampire, anyone in this room could easily set the bloodsucker numbers back to zero.

One foot in front of the other, old girl. For once, I was grateful my heart didn't beat. If it could, it would have been pounding like a jackhammer.

Instead of greeting anyone, Grim led me out to the empty dance floor. "Can you dance?" he murmured.

"I take it you don't mean twerking," I murmured back. Then gave him a quick nod of confirmation.

Grim worked to suppress his look of exasperation at my last comment. Despite there being no music, he firmly but gently guided me into a waltz. I fell into step with practiced ease.

His exasperation gave way to surprise as I matched his pace with the elegance of a Disney princess. Though his face was such a mask of calm control, I doubt anyone would notice the subtle shift in his expression.

Panic still raced along my skin as all eyes were trained on us.

But Grim's whisky-colored eyes held me, and a sense of safety wrapped around me. Then the orchestra readied their instruments, and the music began. Immortals paired off to dance around us, and the invisible spotlight fell away. Relief swept through me.

"You could have warned me," I said, thankful for the cover of music to speak to Grim without being overheard.

"About?" He guided us flawlessly across the floor.

"How extra everyone dresses. I should have glued a live goose to my head or something."

Gold drowned his eyes. His powerful body perfectly framed mine, his hands warm and dry against my cold, clammy ones. "You are by far the most brilliant creature in this room." His words were husky as he attempted to keep his voice low.

I swallowed down my nerves, skittish for a whole other reason now. "Yeah, but did you see the woman in the yellow fur-lined gown that goes over her head as a cap and spans, what, ten feet around her? They're looking at me like I'm some kind of lame slob who didn't get the dress code memo."

Grim attempted to hide a smile and failed. "That isn't why they are staring at you. I told you that when you became sekhor, your soul became trapped in your body. But what I didn't share is that your soul underwent such an intense metamorphosis that it hardened like a diamond, and to an immortal's eyes, you glow. They stare because they haven't seen anything like you in thousands of years, and your very being calls to the gods. Long ago, before the uprising and subsequent war, gods and sekhors partnered because of this natural attraction. And your glow is intense, a siren's call to any god in range."

Right before I was about to make a face, I caught myself. Not for one instant would I allow myself to appear confused in this place. Instead, I plastered on a smug, supercilious smile as he stepped back and spun me. "You and Timothy aren't affected," I said through my teeth, when he drew me back in his arms.

Another twirl and this time he drew me in so our faces were so close I could see the color of his eyes shift like molten gold. His dark smoking mantle fell over me, but it was silken against my skin. My mouth went dry, and I grew dizzy. It wasn't from the dancing.

Something about this, being by Grim's side, felt far too right. Again, the nagging sensation of a forgotten promise tugged at me.

"I assure you, that isn't true," he murmured. His eyes dropped to my lips as if caught in the same liquid moment as me. There we stood on the edge of something so intense, terrifying, and exhilarating I couldn't decide if I should hurl myself over the cliff side or run the opposite way.

I wanted to close the distance and taste him. Fill that gaping emptiness inside me with his touch. Heat spread through me, though I hadn't fed from him in hours.

A man's voice broke in. "Grim, it has been far too long."

We separated, and a chill swept through me, chasing away the warmth. What had I almost done? I needed to get a grip on myself. I stepped away from Grim, clutching the edges of my dress, in what would appear to be a graceful pose. Really, it was an attempt to calm my shaking hands.

The approaching god appeared to be in his mid-fifties with salt-and-pepper hair. Handsome, with a cocky smugness, he reminded me of George Clooney. A heavy mixture of sandalwood and coconut suntan lotion accompanied him, which would explain his deeply bronzed skin. He struck me as someone who spent most of his days poolside.

Red silk robes fell at his feet and hugged around his throat like a turtleneck. Chains of jewels fell over his shoulders and chest. Two long golden snake cuffs curled around his arm. Their emerald eyes glowed. I suppressed a shiver of revulsion. I hated snakes. Maybe I'd watched *Indiana Jones* one too many times, or maybe it was the brief fling I had with a guy who bred snakes. He'd insist I hold them every time I went over, and even once wanted me to let him bang me with one of his slithery friends wrapped around my neck. Umm. No thank you.

In this getup, I would have taken the man before me to be a king from an eastern country.

Yeah, you're a sexy silver fox and you know it.

The woman wearing the black-feathered gown was with him as well as a lanky young man with ice-blue eyes and slicked-back bleach blond hair in a white suit. Even his shoes were white. They were a perfect dichotomy of black and white standing next to each other. All three bowed before us. I was about to mimic them, but Grim squeezed my arm, stopping me.

"Seth," Grim said, with an almost imperceptible nod. "Marcella, Idris."

"And this must be your sekhor," Seth said when he arose, with a light Greek accent. A merry glint shone in his eye as he took my hand and kissed the back of it. I kept with my chick-made-of-ice routine.

"This is Vivien," Grim said by way of introduction.

The three of them bowed again, but Marcella shot me a look of unbridled hate just as she dipped her head.

Oh goody, I've already made an enemy.

"I haven't seen one of your kind in many thousands of years, my dear," Seth said, not having released my hand yet.

All his focus was pinned on me, and I felt his power wrap around me like a boa constrictor. If he wanted to, could he close it around me and squeeze me to death with it? I worked not to squirm under his attention and met his eye with a silent impertinence of my own.

How dare you look into my eyes for so long, peasant.

Seth's eyebrow jumped as if he could hear my thought. But no, I found when I thought something specific, it came through loud and clear on my face. It was a gift.

I thought of what Grim must have seen on my face only moments ago.

Maybe I should return the gift...

Seth continued, "And might I say, I'd almost completely forgotten what it was like to behold the glow of a sekhor."

"While some of us have never forgotten," Marcella muttered.

I wasn't psychic, but I could read her thoughts through her eyes. *Stab stab stab.*

With a lighthearted laugh, the younger god with ice-blue eyes moved Seth aside to take my hand and kiss the back of it as well. Tattoos covered the backs of his hands, disappearing up under his sleeve. They also traveled partway up his neck from under the white shirt. "And some of us are not old enough to have forgotten."

Idris winked at me, and I instantly became less tense.

The lights dimmed, causing me to look up at a colossal chandelier that floated as if by magic. It morphed from a bright yellow light to moody violet. The music changed to a more contemporary song as gods continued to dance nearby. The atmosphere became more intimate, and I felt it would be easier to get lost in the crowd now, though Grim said it wasn't likely with my glow.

Edward Cullen, eat your heart out. I sparkle too.

Following my gaze to the chandelier, Seth said, "Yes, gods throw the most over-the-top parties. Can I get you a refreshment, my dear?" Then he snapped his fingers as if in realization. "Oh right, you brought yours with you."

The mantle around Grim bristled. He was not amused.

On the bright side, it seemed to lessen the boa constrictor hold of Seth's power around me. As if there wasn't enough room in this ballroom for both of them to flex.

The smile I gave Seth didn't reach my eyes. "As a human, I was accustomed to BYOB. But now I see, instead I should have brought my sense of humor for tacky jokes."

Idris's eyes widened as he coughed into his fist to hide his laughter.

"Oh, she's a wild one, isn't she, Grim?" Seth said, appraising me with a keener interest.

"You don't know the half of it," a woman said as she joined our little group. Wearing a slinky emerald gown, the lithe woman moved with the fluid gait of a super-model. Her dark hair was slicked back in a way that I'd only seen high-fashion models pull off as sexy. Amongst her own kind, Galina's pupils were now vertical slits in brilliant green eyes, resembling a cat's. Made sense, Galina's true name was Bast, goddess of cats.

Maybe if Seth pushed, she might scratch his eyes out. That would liven up the party.

I had only briefly met Galina, but I knew she'd helped Grim find me when I'd been kidnapped by the master vampire.

She stopped to stand between Grim and Seth. Grim seemed to relax ever so slightly with her nearby. My feelings had a confusing reaction to his sudden ease near the drop-dead gorgeous goddess.

Allies, good, I insisted to my inner cattiness that began sharpening its claws.

"Looks like this sekhor is a match for your stunning wit, Seth." Then, pressing a manicured finger against her lips, she pretended to think. "Oh wait, that would be any female on the planet Earth." Then she shared a knowing smile with me.

Okay, claws fully retracted now. I was all for team Galina.

"Ah, Galina, still flirting with me?" Seth leered at her.

"Only in your dreams," she assured him, with a dismissive wave of her hand.

"That you are," Seth said, looking her up and down.

What a creep. But it looked like Galina had no problem holding her own with lecherous men.

"Ugh," she said, with a noise of disgust, "I'm getting a drink." Then, as she walked by me she gave my arm a slight squeeze and added, "and a shower."

I had half a mind to follow her to the bar.

"Grim, may I speak with you? In private?" Marcella asked, her voice tight. Her focus fixed on him with a dark ferocity.

"Oh Marcella," Seth said, waving his hand at her. "Why ask in private, when we all want to know the same thing.

Perhaps we could silence the room so we can all hear the answer."

Then, as if by magic, the room went quiet. Everyone stopped and turned to face us. My stomach squeezed in alarm, feeling like a piece of raw meat dangled in a fish tank of piranhas.

The merry sparkle in Seth's eye hardened. "Why did Osiris allow you to take a sekhor?"

"Perhaps he likes me better than you," Grim said, the edge of his tone sharp as a blade. "After all, you did try to kill him."

The urge to back him up with a woot and an "oooh burn!" was strong. But did I really want to end up in the middle of a fight between gods? Nope. I kept my mouth shut. Not only did I impress myself, I impressed the little dudes running my brain.

Jenkins, it's a bloody miracle.

It is, sir, that it is.

"I didn't try anything," Seth hissed. The emerald eyes on his snakes glowed, and their bodies shifted around his arms.

Idris held his hands up. "Hey, old fogies, that was a long time ago. If we pulled out every old feud in here, there would be no time to party, am I right?"

That was when Timothy arrived, along with Fallon, another god I'd met before. Now that he wasn't trying to kill me, I could appreciate how striking the handsome black man was. His hooded, bedroom eyes were even more compelling. While one was dark brown, the other glowed a brilliant blue. A large pair of light gray wings were folded behind his navy suit.

One wing flickered. Right. Not costumes. Those wings were the bona fide real deal. Again, I felt like an ant in this lion's den. But like...an irritating, bitey ant that could annoy the bigger beasts until she was smushed.

"Yes, it is such a pleasant party," Timothy said crisply. "It would be terrible to be rude to our hosts." Timothy was already the epitome of put-together and fashionable on a regular basis. Now he wore a brilliant purple suit with vertical lines of gold-stitched hieroglyphics. Timothy pulled the outfit off like a *GQ* fashion trendsetter. On closer inspection, the hieroglyphs were shifting, crawling down his suit like codes of the Matrix.

"Especially when the host has not yet been introduced to everyone," a woman said in agreement. The crowd parted to reveal the owner of the voice. A woman in what appeared to be her mid-fifties stood there in white and gold regalia. With silver hair pulled up in an elegant twist, the woman was the epitome of graceful aging. Her opalescent gown shimmered with power. I instantly both wanted her to be my mother and to never disappoint her.

I had to push down my sudden need to find macaroni and make art for her to put on her godly fridge.

Seth receded into the crowd, looking only mildly put out.

This time Grim bowed, and I followed suit along with the rest of the room. Her fingers tipped my chin up, forcing me to rise.

"So, this is what all the fuss is about," she said. Fine lines surrounded her eyes, making her appear sage and calm.

"Isis, this is Vivien, my sekhor."

When Grim said her name, a slight pulse of light surrounded her.

"Indeed. And pray tell, how is my husband, Anu?" she asked.

"Guarding the gates to the afterlife as always."

Her lips thinned. "Hmm." Then to me, she said, "Never marry a workaholic, dear. Unless you are an independent woman capable of entertaining yourself for centuries on end."

Was I allowed to marry? Or did she mean if I married Grim? Was either even allowed? I knew better than to voice my questions out loud. And besides, being enslaved to Grim through a blood bond was more than enough commitment for me.

Laughter tittered through the crowd and, once again, everyone went back to chatting, dancing, and drinking. Isis took her leave, but Marcella pressed forward.

"Anu," she said, her voice strained. Marcella had used a nickname for Grim's ancient name, Anubis. She looked on the verge of beating me to death if he didn't give her a minute.

Grim turned to me, a silent question on his face.

"Go, I'll be fine."

"Of course, she will," Idris said, shooting me a grin. "Leave the kids to get the party started."

"Not likely, young one," Fallon said, stepping between us and giving Idris a playful shove. They fell into some age-old banter just as Timothy said next to me, "Drink?"

"Immediately."

7

I had barely closed the doors to an adjoining drawing room when Marcella laid into me. "What is this, Anu? How is this possible? How could you bring her here?"

"I understand you are upset, Marcella."

"You have no idea how I feel," she snapped. Feathers on her dress bristled and flapped in agitation. "You are the one who killed all the sekhors, wiping them out, and now here you are with one on your arm."

"Events transpired in a way I could not have foreseen."

A literal flame sparked in Marcella's eyes for a moment. "You are playing with fire, Anu. And if you know what's good for you, you will get rid of her before you suffer the ultimate price."

Before I could say anything, Marcella turned on her heel and walked back out to the ballroom.

"She's not wrong, Anu."

I turned to see Fallon leaning against the door frame, hands in his pockets, massive wings tucked behind him. Among our own kind, his left eye glowed a brilliant blue.

"She is upset." I walked over to a gold and mirrored cart that held several decanters. I plucked one containing a purple liquid and removed its top. Inhaling, my senses filled with violets, crystalline waters, and someone else's laughter. I set the decanter back down, replacing the glass stopper.

Pushing off from the door jamb, Fallon entered the room.

"Have you truly considered the danger you have put yourself in, Grim?"

Ignoring him, I picked up a second decanter, this one a bright pea green. A whiff of this one and tingles shot up my nose and raced through my extremities. Anise, fresh cut grass, and the jolt of ten shots of espresso.

Fallon came to stand next to me. "I know you are god of the dead, responsible for sorting and keeping the souls of this realm in order." Then under his breath, "Not to mention for keeping our wily kind in line." Then he turned to meet my eye. "But I fear you've cracked and are acting out."

My spine stiffened as my mantle of power spread another foot. I shot him a sharp look. "Don't be ridiculous, Fallon. I am as in control as ever. I am not in danger of anything. Vivien cannot pose a threat if she does not know the truth about her kind. She does not know that she could become more powerful than any of us by drinking too much of my blood, and I assure you, I would never allow her to take more than she needs. Besides, she is not one to seek power. Of that, I have become sure."

Realizing my tone softened as I spoke about her, I reached for the decanter of amber liquid and poured myself several fingers of scotch. A bottle like this would go for well over $150,000 for the humans, but I knew many other gods had plenty in their basement keeps as I did. Some bottles even dated to the very early 1800s, making them the most aged bottles on the planet. I drank the smooth, peaty liquor and enjoyed the familiar comfort of its burn. I did not need the influence of godly ambrosias clouding my judgement.

Fallon took the green bottle and poured himself a glass before walking over to one of the tufted, high-backed chairs. He sank into the seat, wings nestled behind him, as he threw one leg over the other. He said, "For a sharp fellow, you sometimes shock me with your density, old friend."

My glass paused, inches from my lips.

Fallon had set his drink down to thread his long fingers as he regarded me with slight amusement. "You are in danger because of your feelings."

I scoffed, then let the drink finish its course down my throat.

"Grim, you've held yourself on such a tight leash since Qwynn, punishing yourself for neglecting your duties. Flogging yourself for letting the men and women feast upon the flesh of the pharaohs you were sworn to protect."

Cold washed over me. In the Victorian ages, interest in ancient Egyptian culture had a resurgence. And with the trend, it had become stylish for the rich to hold 'mummy unwrappings' in their homes. Then they would dine upon the flesh of the pharaohs, with the notion it would grant them health and long life.

It was an absolute abomination of the highest caliber, and I'd let it happen on my watch. So wrapped up in the opium, pleasure-seeking lifestyle with Qwynn, I failed to put an end to it. Then, when I finally pulled myself from her bed and our wild parties, I found it was my own wife who had been orchestrating such atrocities.

Fallon continued. "Ah, you cannot hide your surprise, but do not worry that I know about this. It is a very few who know how Qwynn pulled the wool over your eyes. Your ex-wife was deceitful, manipulative, and vied for her own pleasure as she was always wont to do." Fallon shrugged.

Then, leaning forward, Fallon's wings spread out of the chair. "But this sekhor, she is already making you vulnerable in the eyes of the others. They either believe she will drain you dry, subsume your power, and go for them next, or..." He trailed off, his eye glowing brighter as if to make sure he had my attention. "They see her as your weakness. Your feelings for her are clear in every move you make, every time someone speaks her name, or looks in her direction. Your possessiveness is palpable."

I rotated the glass in my hand and gave him a cool smile. "Ah, but such possessiveness is natural to have toward my sekhor. She is bound to me, and I know many are now fearful I will use her as a weapon against them. They would not dare interfere if they valued their safety and freedom. It is the nature of the blood bond. She is bound to me, my possession."

Fallon unthreaded his fingers to point at me. "See, right there. You give yourself away, Grim. It is plain as day. She is not a possession to you. She is more than that. Marcella sees it too. The others have seen you obsessed, enamored, and furious with Qwynn, one of our own. But until this evening, we have never seen you vulnerable."

Having enough of Fallon's assessment, I rolled my eyes. "That is ridiculous. She does not make me vulnerable." Even as I spoke the words, though, something tugged at my gut as if my body recognized the mistruth.

Hadn't I been concerned about falling into the same extremes with Vivien as I had with Qwynn? But because I knew that road, I was certain not to take it.

Vivien and I were bonded, and we'd find a way to work

in simpatico.

The part where I assured her she would eventually beg me to kiss her was merely a game. Games were nothing. Harmless ways to pass eons of time.

My words came out low. "I told her that her soul would atrophy and corrupt over the ages. She would become power hungry with vampiric hubris. I told her it was inevitable."

Fallon said nothing, though there was a question underlying my words.

Something tightened in my gut.

"I never trusted taking a sekhor and forming a blood bond. Granting anyone immortality is against my nature. It has always been my job to ensure the order of death. And with time, I saw how the sekhors soured, coming to both hate our kind and humanity. Their bloodthirsty war only solidified my belief that immortality should not be granted, only born into. But now that I know Vivien...I can't see her fulfilling the fate I predicted."

Fallon sighed. "You've always seen things so black and white. It's understandable, what with your duties, judging souls into group A or B."

Looking into my glass, as if the answers could be found at the bottom, I said, "When the others came to me, begging me to clean up house, they told me everything I wanted to hear. Their immortality had driven the sekhors mad. And when I saw the tainted glow of the vampires in the throes of battle, I was further convinced we should never have meddled with mortals. All must meet their eventual end."

When he didn't respond this time, I met Fallon's hard gaze. "Was I wrong?"

Licking his lips, Fallon seemed to deliberate over his next words. "We have lived to see many a millennium, and there are even things I wish I could forget. We were at the height of our power, and the sekhors were not treated as partners in immortality. Though it was a divine bond, neither side could resist, we treated them as servants, slaves." His voice lowered. "Most of our brethren were not benevolent. Many found amusements in torturing the vampires. They would force the sekhors to feed on their own families, ravage towns who prayed to the wrong gods. The sekhors were dogs who did our dirty work. Not to mention the sexual atrocities I'd heard tale of after the fact... Thousands of years later, witnessing the crimes of humanity, I began to understand the patterns and the full impact of our crimes against the vampires. No, brother, I don't believe it was the passage of time that soured the sekhors. It was us. We drove them into the darkness."

"Why didn't you tell me?" My words came out raspy.

Not only had I turned a blind eye to what happened, I'd killed all of them. An entire race. A select few gods pleaded with me, begging me not to. They swore their sekhors would not turn evil and to spare them. But blood filled my eyes from the war with a horde of the oldest vampires, and their words fell on deaf ears.

Fallon leaned forward in his chair, focusing on a spot on the floor. "I'm not proud of everything I've done, Anu. I could blame the standards that others set, or willful ignorance, but the fact of the matter is I viewed them as less. When the gods motioned for a vote of the extermination of all sekhors, it cost me nothing to go with the flow. When you came for my sekhors, I had no trouble handing them over for disposal. So focused on making my own way, the vampires were of little consequence to me. Where I was once angry with Osiris for stripping us of our power for the sake of humanity, I now understand why he did it. It's not immortality that corrupts. It's power. Or so it seems to corrupt everyone...but you. For many a century, I've carried the weight of those regrets, rightfully burdened. I did not think it was wise to burden you along with me."

Regret clenched around my being as Fallon confessed everything. I'd been a fool. Easily manipulated as the others played my prejudice, as if it were their instrument.

Fallon went on. "You know, she is a reminder to everyone in there. A reminder of either the terrible sins of our past, or a reminder of what we could be again." Fallon stood with his glass, tipping it at me before taking a sip. "Doesn't help that Osiris gave you special compensation to once again prove that you are special and above the rest of us."

"I cannot help that."

"Of course you can't. The god is the very root of that saying the humans use...what is it? 'He works in mysterious ways?'"

I could not disagree. Osiris was the most powerful of us and he was sure to keep a distance from all of us, so we never knew what to expect from him. While Seth was the god of chaos, Osiris's unpredictability far outweighed Seth's erratic acts.

Timothy strode into the room, then slowed as if taking in the heavy atmosphere. He looked back and forth between Fallon and me. "Everything all right?"

Before Fallon could answer, I set the glass back down on the mirrored cart with a loud clink. "Of course. But I fear I've left Vivien to her own devices too long."

With a quick flick of his wrist, Fallon threw back the rest

of his drink. “Indeed, and the wolves are hungry tonight. Best not to let them play with her too long.”

The thought of anyone playing with her ignited a fiery rage inside me. I would never let what happened repeat itself. Vivien was not a plaything or a tool to be used.

I was out the door in an instant.

8

Timothy disappeared to find Grim after I assured him I was fine for a couple of minutes on my own. The buffet table would make an adequate babysitter.

I would have thought becoming a vampire would have precluded me from nervous noshing, but nope, here I was again, popping mini eclairs, chocolate-covered strawberries, and dear god, what was this?

"It's dosa," the goddess next to me explained. Her accent suggested she spent considerable time in France. Her stunning dress was entirely composed of crystals complete with a headdress bigger and pointier than mine. Her jet-black hair swept back in a complicated updo. A supernatural rainbow sparkled from her eyes like the light reflecting off the glitz of her dress.

She must have seen my look of confusion at the dish in front of me.

"It's like a crêpe." She paused. "You do know what a crêpe is?" Her question was delicately put, but I plainly heard the 'are you an idiot?' sentiment underneath. It had been a long time since I'd dealt with so many passive-aggressive a-holes. But it was just like riding a bike.

A bike you wanted to pedal off a cliff.

Now the question was—ignore her, or bitch-slap her?

"This isn't like any crêpe I've had." Nailed my attempt to sound like a helpless simpleton, in one take. I resisted the urge to look around for my Oscar.

Hopefully, my unassuming Elly May Clampett impersonation would make me more approachable. I needed these gods to talk to me. Sure, I was scarfing down cream puffs, but I was also here on a mission.

So far, I'd learned half the immortals here hated my guts. And the other half regarded me as an exotic zoo animal. I still had no clue who would want to steal Amit.

Gun to my head, I'd say Seth did it.

Maybe I only thought that because he was an arrogant prick...

Until I could prove it, I'd rub elbows with the walking chandelier next to me to see what I could find out.

The goddess's sympathetic smile was saccharine and cyanide. "Dosa is made of beans and lentils, but it is better with the chutney in the bowl next to it."

Hmm, she wasn't a total loss.

I reached for the spoon, dishing some chutney on top of the dosa. "Thanks."

"So you and Grim, have you known each other long?"

I bit into the dosa just as she asked the question, and shrugged one shoulder in an inconclusive answer.

Yum. Next-level crêpes. I was feeling more worldly already.

"I'm sorry, I'm being so rude. I'm Lydia."

The princess didn't think she was being rude. She wanted me to know her name.

When I finished chewing, I said, "I'm Vivien." First wiping my fingers on a napkin, I reached out a hand to shake hers. I even did it in the fancy way where I left my hand a limp fish, hanging there to be touched.

Disgust passed over her face in a blink of an eye before she smiled wider as if it would excuse her from touching me.

Maybe she thought my fingers were sticky? Or maybe this was one of those rules? Like she couldn't touch me without Grim being present, and it was part of some weird immortal code?

Or maybe she was just a biatch.

Only one way to find out. I forged ahead, wanting to do a little digging of my own. "I understand you gods don't get together often."

A secretive smile sprung to her lips. "No, but everyone thinks you are quite the spectacle." Again, her underlying tone let me know she didn't agree.

I mean, I was pretty awesome, but I didn't expect everyone to know it. I needed to get this convo on track to finding out who would want to screw over Grim.

"You've known Grim a long time?" I actually had no idea how gods socialized, but no time like the present to find out.

"Oh, for eons, but I don't know him as well as I'd like. He's always so busy with work. He rarely slums with us demigods." Lydia gestured to a group of gods standing in a mini circle, casting blatant glances of interest my way. Suddenly I was in high school all over again, getting tested by the bored, beautiful, rich kids with the self-esteem of dirt.

Like Idris, they seemed younger. Several gods, especially those in Grim's circles, seemed to be closer to thirty or older. Not only did these demigods appear to be in their early twenties, but I also recognized the vicious juvenile gleam in their eyes. I'd bet my left boob Idris was a demigod too. Not the rightie, though. Never the right boob. That one was my favorite.

I focused in on the pertinent bit of information I'd learned. There was a hierarchy system among the gods. People crossed lines for love, money, and power. A demigod could be gunning for power, and running amok, stealing enormous crocodiles and such.

Like those high school kids, these demigods were still practicing being entitled. The other, more mature gods I'd met knew their superiority and communicated that confidence in their every movement. They didn't need to prove themselves, like the young'uns here. I wanted to ask more about the difference between demigods and full gods, but I didn't want to chance looking ignorant. I'd ask Timothy later.

Lydia leaned in, her voice conspiratorial. "Forgive my impertinence, but the others wanted to know." She meant her posse that still hovered nearby.

I raised my eyebrows expectantly.

She stepped closer. "Do you think him too much to manage?"

My lips quirked in a sideways smile. "Grim can be cantankerous and bossy at times, but he's lightened up considerably since meeting me."

Lydia cleared her throat with a nervous, almost pitying laugh. "No, I mean, is he too much for you to..."

I waited for her to spit it out.

"...service," she said finally. "Based on his reputation, we assumed he puts you to work...often." With a mirthful glint in her eye, she poked her tongue against the inside of her cheek, making extra sure I understood her full meaning.

Muffled giggles exploded from the nearby group.

Yeah, I got it. To them, I was Grim's slave. They assumed my primary duty was blowing him before fetching his pipe and slippers. And they wanted me to suck and tell.

In my silence, Lydia forged ahead. "It's just that there has been much talk about his...size and sexual appetite. But of course, that comes from Qwynn." She rolled her eyes. "And Qwynn will say anything for attention and loves to stretch the...truth, if you know what I mean."

I slid another oyster onto my plate, stalling.

I couldn't help the pinch I felt at hearing about Qwynn blabbing about Grim's massive member. The thought of them banging made me feel queasy.

With a light squeeze to a wedge of lemon, I doused the mollusk in juice.

There were options here. Number one. I could punch Lydia in her bitch face.

Number two, I could have fun with this—tell Lydia that Grim liked a good ole hamster up the butt among other fetishes. Maybe balloons and feet? I mean, if this was a party, shouldn't I have a good time? And my idea of a good time meant screwing with nosy bitches.

The slick briny oyster slid down my throat. Yep. After all these years, I still hated them.

Surprising myself, I went with option number three. Meeting Lydia's taunting smile with a condescending coolness, I went with the truth. "I can't say I've had the pleasure of sucking his dick. Ours is, how best to describe it, a business arrangement."

At the last moment, my gut instinct had kicked in. I was hyperaware not to expose my jugular to anyone in this room, and suddenly I didn't think it was a good idea to make Grim vulnerable either. Even if I thought it would be funny.

Pretty sure I would also cause a bigger ruckus by breaking Lydia's pert little nose.

At first, Lydia feigned disappointment, then her expression turned to pity. "Oh, I'm so sorry to hear that." The words were exaggerated unnecessarily.

Don't touch it, Vivien. Don't fall for the bait.

"Why?"

Dammit.

The hint of a smile at the corner of her lips told me she was happy I bit on her hook. "Oh, I just mean to say, if you're his sekhor, that he would have if...I'd think he'd..." She pretended to bumble with her words, while getting her full meaning across. "It is expected that a blood bond be sealed with the intimate act. It's no secret Grim's boudoir skills are world-renowned. And seeing as he never bonded with a single sekhor, even when the rest had done so, I figured his disgust for sekhors had changed. But if he hasn't bedded you, he must not have gotten over his revulsion of your kind."

He's the only one who's never taken a sekhor? I'm his first and only blood bond?

Regaining my composure, I said, "Did it occur to you it might be my choice not to be...intimate?" I parroted her word choice.

Her laugh tinkled like little, irritating bells. "Oh, of course. How silly of me, I'm sure that's it. I just recalled him once describing sekhors as disgusting creatures unworthy of a god's blood. It makes sense. He wouldn't take one to bed with those sentiments. But you put me right. It must obviously be of *your* choosing." Her insincerity was as syrupy as molasses.

When I set my plate down, it clacked against another platter. The oysters were obviously bad. I felt sick.

Why did I suddenly want to stalk over to Grim and rip his clothes off and ride him in the middle of this ballroom to stake my claim? I could show these entitled jackasses I did what I wanted, when I wanted, with whomever I wanted.

"Then again," Lydia said, "after sealing the bond, some gods felt sekhors were better suited for...simpler tasks. We don't have rocks for you to split to build our temples anymore, so what does Grim have you do?" She sipped demurely from a glass of violet, bubbling liquid.

My fangs elongated, cutting my lip as all the muscles in my body tensed. So, I was too dumb and incapable to be Grim's slut?

Oh, this chick had just about pushed me past my limit.

"Oh dear, I've upset you." Lydia's worry was about as real as Pamela Anderson's boobs. "Just because it's expected a god would take his sekhor to bed doesn't mean anything is wrong with you."

Something in me snapped. "Our relationship isn't like that. But I can't see how bad I'm doing if you've known him for, oh, how many centuries, and he won't lay a thirsty bitch like yourself? So we must be in the same category of revolting."

Lydia's face tightened with anger. I'd hit pay dirt with that strike.

Sure, call me the dirt beneath your feet, honey, but I'll drag you down to my level.

A familiar melodic voice broke in as Bianca appeared at my side. "Lydia, it's so good to see you. I still see you are overcompensating for your status with gaudy, over-the-top taste."

Relief swept through me. I didn't realize how on edge Lydia had gotten me. The bitch had riled me up, and I cursed myself for letting it happen. I was better than that.

Her passive-aggressive claws should have no effect on me. I blamed it on a lack of recent practice, but I'd done a lot to get away from this kind of crap. Yet here I was, entrenched in entitled a-holes.

At least when I tracked down skips as a bounty hunter, my marks had the decency to call me names to my face. Far preferable to this underhanded bullshit.

Bianca linked her arm through mine and led me away from Lydia and her cronies. While many of the gods were dressed in outrageous, expensive attire, Bianca seemed to blow them all away with her graceful, old Hollywood elegance. Her champagne pink dress swirled around her, floating, as if defying gravity itself. Her diamond blue eyes and soft, secret smile sucked you in, making you think you were the only person in existence. The only thing that was missing was a tiara from this Grace Kelly princess.

"You dismantled her nicely enough," Bianca said with laughing eyes.

"It's a pecking order similar to that of a prison. Like going up to the biggest guy and knocking him out on the first day." I regretted not doing just that to Lydia. Or Seth. Or Marcella. What was she doing with Grim, anyway? Was she desperate to get in his pants, too?

Bianca's lips parted, showing her pearly whites in a brilliant smile. "I see this isn't your first party with the upper echelon."

"I wasn't always this amazing, ball-busting vampire you see before you."

"Hard to believe," she said, snagging a champagne off the tray from a server who passed by.

I was wrong about this ball. The politics of this crowd were too thick for me to cut through and ferret out potential suspects. Maybe if everyone wasn't so damned obsessed with me, I could get some information. Instead, I felt like a circus freak and no matter what I did, I came off like a grinder monkey.

Then I spotted Grim making his way back through the crowd toward me. His face had been a mask of cold, hard indifference all night, but now there was something else in his eyes. Worry? Fear? As if he'd heard something that put him on edge.

Good. It was a comfort to know I wasn't the only one rattled.

Seth stepped in front of me, blocking my view of Grim, and held out his hand. "May I have this dance?"

I thought for sure Bianca would tell him off like she had the others, but her arm slipped away from mine. From her regretful and resigned expression, this was one of those obligatory games I had to play.

Dammit to hell. What I wouldn't give for a case of leprosy, right now.

With a tight smile, I nodded and slipped my hand into Seth's so he could lead me onto the dance floor.

9

Another slow song began as Seth led me into a waltz.

Blood bags. I wished for something more upbeat and louder, so I could focus on the dance and not the slick, conniving man in front of me.

Would the orchestra perform a rendition of Cardi B's 'WAP' if I requested it?

Grim stalked along the perimeter of the dance floor, ignoring everyone around him. His eyes trained on me. They'd turned dark, and I wished I knew what he was thinking.

"How are you enjoying the party?" Seth asked, never missing a step.

Great, small talk. I should have shoved a cupcake or something in my mouth to keep from having to talk. Instead, I grinned and bore it. "It's very nice."

He sucked in a sharp breath as if I'd slapped him. "Oh, very and nice. Both damning, tiresome words meant to convey you are having an absolute dull time and are not impressed by the pomp of gods." Then he chuckled. "That's alright, my dear." Seth directed us farther into the crowd until Grim could no longer stay in sight unless he walked through the middle of the dance floor. It felt as though a tether to my safety had been cut. I had a feeling that's exactly how Seth wanted me to feel.

Well, joke was on him if he thought he'd cornered me. Because with that safety went my patience. I was done pussyfooting around.

"What is your problem with Grim?"

Before he could help himself, Seth's jaw slackened in surprise. Catching his own reaction, Seth chuckled. "Indeed, you are as perceptive as you are bold. I will have to watch you." A sharpness entered his eyes. He wasn't kidding about that last bit.

I waited for my answer.

"We gods all have long, complicated histories. Mine is especially complicated with Anubis."

With a quick glance into the crowd, I saw Grim's eyes flash as Seth called him by his original name. Still, I kept my expression neutral. Damned if I didn't need to spend more time reading up on mythology to prepare myself. Though this morning I did not know I had any other commitments other than bingeing *Real Housewives*.

Seth's laugh was much lower and darker this time. He'd caught my surprise, though I tried to hide it. "Or perhaps you could say it has to do with Anubis acting as Osiris's lapdog, keeping an order many of us had no say in."

"Is that what you want? Power?"

"Don't you?" he shot back. "You think Grim won't assert his will over you and dominate the way he does with the rest of us?"

Inside, I reeled. My instinct was to go to Grim's defense,

but I shared the same belief. Ugh. I hated it when I had things in common with sleazeballs.

Seth slowed our pace. "We gods, we all play a role in the continuance of this world. Grim has dominion over the souls, the most powerful source of energy that draws all of us to Vegas, simply to be near the warmth of that hub. And yet, we're supposed to be caretakers for humans. We make this world, not to our liking, but for their benefit."

"Looks like you gods do well for yourself," I said, indicating the grand surroundings.

"Indeed, but I believe even you know what it is like to live in a gilded cage."

Then Seth's face flickered into another's. It was the face of a man I knew, and if my heart could still beat, it would have stopped. I gasped as pain and shock stabbed through me. I stumbled back and out of Seth's arms in the middle of the dance.

Grim was at my side in an instant. "Are you alright?"

"It's purely my fault," Seth answered for me. I couldn't find my voice, it had frozen in my throat. "I stepped on her foot. I'm a clumsy fool. We haven't had one of these parties in so long, I've verily forgotten these old promenades."

But Grim wasn't looking at Seth. He was waiting for me to answer. To tell him if anything was wrong.

"I'm fine," I said, my voice only slightly scratchy. "He stepped on my foot."

Grim didn't seem convinced, but he didn't get a chance to press.

"While I have you, Grim," Seth barreled on, "I would like the honor of the official introduction."

Though I sensed Grim wanted to protest, I got the vibe this was one of those bullshit 'decorum' things again. I don't think he could have said no.

Grim took my arm, and we followed Seth, though I was still reeling. We climbed the few stairs up to a dais.

Seth raised a glass of champagne and the room stilled and quieted. "It is rare we get together. Seeing as many of our parties end in veritable disputes." Seth laughed good-humoredly, and the crowd did the same.

I didn't like this. Being on display like a piece of meat.

"But we have an occasion more than just reconnecting. We have a guest of honor." Seth swept an arm toward me, and there was a smattering of polite golf claps.

"It can't be easy for Grim to deal with the fetid souls of humans." Seth wrinkled his nose in distaste. "For gods to spend their days caring for insignificant mice may seem noble to some, while others feel humanity to be a mistake altogether." A titter of laughter went through the crowd. Too many hungry faces nodded in agreement with Seth.

"But our fearless leader, who has always been the martyr, always the one to defend the humans and their freedoms, has finally bound himself to another." Seth clapped Grim's back, though Grim's stiff posture and cool face showed he did not enjoy the affection.

In the crowd, I spotted Bianca and Galina. Bianca looked uneasy, but she could have been mirroring my discomfort. Galina stared at Seth with unerring focus, like a cat about to pounce.

Even Timothy and Fallon had a stiffness in their posture that only added to the writhing mass of nerves in the pit of my stomach.

Seth reached down, trading his champagne for a sizable velvet box.

"So to honor your newfound bond, many of us wanted you to have this." Seth spoke to us as he handed the case to Grim.

With a crack, the jewelry box flipped open to reveal a jewel-studded dog's collar. I even caught on the nametag the engraving, Grim's Bitch.

Grim's body didn't so much as shift as it exploded into muscle, sinew, and black inky fur as he turned into an eight-foot-tall beast. Grim's god-likeness was a monstrous jackal. Saliva dripped off his thick fangs as he let out a bloodcurdling roar.

Gods on all sides of the room surged toward the platform, at each other's throats. Ice, fire, power, and light shot everywhere. Everyone had chosen a side, and I was at the center of the storm.

Grim's massive jaws closed around Seth's head, but Seth had shifted too. He pushed Grim off with a high-pitched roar of his own. Eyes fiery red, and a long snout, he was a mix between an aardvark and a dog, with a long, forked tail and gray fur. Seth's god-likeness made Grim look like a stately being. The hideous monster fighting Grim had me wishing I had a torch and pitchfork on hand. I felt the weight of several malicious eyes pinning me.

Aw shit, I was in way over my head. I caught Timothy's wild-eyed gaze as he mouthed the word "run." Then the hieroglyphics ran off his suit as they came alive. He took hold of the chains of glyphs and used the corporeal writing like whips and chains. Timothy beat back the crowd surging forward.

A hand wrapped around my arm and jerked me back, away from the chaos.

Idris. "We need to get you to safety." Not knowing what else to do, I followed Idris behind a curtain to a door that led to a secret library. He clicked the door shut, then turned around with a sigh of relief.

"Well, that was a shit show."

I'd been overwhelmed by the unexpected explosion and mass of angry gods, but now I'd gained my footing.

"I need to go back out there," I said, moving toward the door again. "Grim needs backup."

Idris held up his hands. "Whoa there, darling. Cool your jets. You are no match for that mob of gods. They all want to tear you to pieces." His face tightened with worry. "They still might, if they get to Grim."

"Grim can't die," I said. Grim had told me gods couldn't die.

"Ah yes, but there are far worse things they could do to him."

I remembered how Osiris tortured Qwynn in a fiery prison for creating a master vampire and trying to upset the balance of the gods. She talked about power like Seth had. I filed that away for later.

Still, I couldn't leave Grim out there. I gathered my skirts. "Well, that's my food source out there, and there is no way I'm going to let anything happen to him."

Idris blocked my way to the door. "I want to help you."

I didn't have time for this. The cacophony rose as if the entire next room were being smashed to bits. And here, I was doing nothing. More monstrous roars shook the walls.

"You'll need enough strength to fight off the gods and keep your head." Idris loosened his tie and unbuttoned the top few buttons of his shirt before pulling his collar to the side. "Drink from me. You'll have the strength of not one, but two gods. None of them will be able to stop you."

I blinked. "You're saying the more god's blood I drink, the more powerful I'll become?"

Idris gave me a strange look. "Yes, of course. Didn't Grim explain that to you? I'm surprised he didn't insist you drink heavily beforehand, in case something like this," he waved his hand at the door, "happened. For your own protection, at the very least."

Sonofabitch. Of course he hadn't told me. Grim played everything close to his chest, and he wouldn't want his little puppy to realize she could pull back on the leash.

A yowling scream came from the next room. My pissiness at Grim evaporated. Was that him? Was he hurt?

Idris's concerned blue eyes were fastened on the door. "He's outnumbered in there. I don't know how long he'll last."

Idris was earnest in his appeal, but something didn't sit right with me. Drinking from Grim was such an intimate experience, I couldn't imagine sinking my teeth into someone who was a stranger to me. Or really anyone else, if I was being honest.

When I didn't make a move, Idris released his collar and took a step back. "I understand. You don't know me, and there's no time to build trust. If you won't help him, I will. Stay here, where it's safe." His tone wasn't damning, but each word landed like a brick.

Idris pointed to the corner. "Hide behind those drapes. If Anu or I make it, we'll come for you. If not..." Another thundering crash, and I jerked. More yowls and screams of pain shook the walls.

My stomach flip-flopped with anxiety. Time moved too fast. I couldn't think past the fears crowding around me. Grim being swallowed up by the crowd, as they tore him to pieces.

Idris turned to go, but I grabbed his arm.

I couldn't do nothing.

"Fine." I didn't like it, but I couldn't sit in here like a useless China doll. I was a scary vampire, after all.

My hands wrapped around the back of Idris's neck. I

paused, fangs hovering over his pulsating artery. The hesitation was involuntary as the voice in my gut grew louder, telling me to stop.

The door blew off the library and there stood Grim. He was in human form again, his dark hair hanging in his eyes. An almost palpable rage swept into the room with him. Other than the wild fury he wore, he stood there stark naked. Black clouds rolled off him as if he were a one-man hurricane. They began to fill the room.

"Get away from him," he said, a hundred demonic voices layered over each other.

Overwhelmed by seeing Grim, well, all of Grim—I stood frozen in place, but Idris backed away from me as quickly as if I were a fire.

Idris bowed low, keeping his eyes down. "Sire, I'm so glad you've come, she demanded to drink from me. If you hadn't come—"

What a little shit!

"Silence," Grim's voice boomed. Furniture rattled in the room as several books fell off the shelves. "We are leaving. Now."

He left no room for debate. What scary naked god of the dead said, went.

10

Vivien followed me back out through the destroyed ballroom that had vacated of all gods. Food, booze, and blood spattered the floors and walls. I was half-tempted to set fire to the place. But before I could break out the matches, Isis headed us off.

"Anubis, I wish to speak with you before you go." Her face was set like the hard marble surrounding us.

I did not answer, but I stopped.

Vivien grabbed a velvet tablecloth that was relatively clean off the floor and handed it to me. I didn't bother telling her that any modesty amongst gods was always false. Yet I wrapped it around my waist.

"I had no idea Seth would make such a production," Isis said. "Had I known, I would have, of course, intervened."

"Is that all? Are you done?"

Isis bowed her head and took a step back. "I have a private car waiting for you both."

At that, a valet stepped forward to escort us.

Isis remained bowed as I strode away from her. Vivien kept up despite her long train. She even kept it from dragging on the detritus on the floor. I should have assisted her, but I needed to escape this place. Not to mention, the only solution circling my mind would be to rip the bottom half of her dress off.

Once we were out of earshot, Vivien shared a piece of her mind.

She always felt compelled to share.

"Wow, you dismissed her like she was nothing."

"What would you have me do?" My jaw was tight even as I spoke. I still had a volcano's worth of eruptive violence in me, but I tamped it down with all my might.

"I don't know. Tell her you know it's not her fault? That Seth is the massive dickwad here. Thank her for the bomb party?"

The tension traveled to my temples. I pressed a finger to one side of my head to ease it. "She offered words as a substitute for preventative action."

"Oh, is this one of those Grim Reaper, god of the dead things?" Vivien grabbed more of her dress in her arms to ascend the short staircase as the valet led us up to a discreet back exit.

Vivien looked like a five-year-old, trying to keep the fabric off the stairs by pulling it around her knees. Earlier, she'd been the epitome of decorum and grace, but now she was back to full hooligan mode.

"One of my reaper things? Why yes, it is." I couldn't help the annoyance creeping into my tone. "I've judged an unfathomable number of souls and after their horrific, short-sighted, or sometimes outright selfish behaviors, they plead for forgiveness, thinking a few puny words could make up for the impact of their actions. Isis was the host and therefore responsible for ensuring the comfort and protection of her guests."

The valet opened a door into a tunnel road where a single black limo was parked, door already opened.

"Is Seth dead?" Vivien asked, softly, since our voices echoed in the cavernous space.

"No. Killing another god is an impossible feat. But I made him feel the pain of my...disappointment." Then shooting her a sharp look, I added, "And soon I'll have to a pay a visit to Idris to make my displeasure with him known as well." My last words came out in a sneer.

Vivien opened her mouth, but I gave her a look so menacing she must have thought better of it. Her jaw snapped shut, and the valet moved to help her into the car, careful to load her dress in with her. She'd chosen to sit on the long side bench as usual while I slid into the back seat, smoothing my hair back. The leather felt cool on my bare back and legs. The tablecloth was still wrapped around my waist for Vivien's benefit.

Fury and remnants of panic still raced through me. First, Seth with his outrageous display of public disrespect toward my sekhor—he wanted a scene, well, he got one. And then when I walked in on Vivien, about to sink her fangs into that slimy twerp's throat, I nearly lost it all over again. As it was, I was still seeing red.

Dark clouds of power continued to roll off me, so I took a deep breath so as not to congest the vehicle. The trip back to Sinopolis was quick and when I directed Vivien to the private back elevator that opened up into the library of my penthouse, she didn't fight me. I disappeared only a moment to change from the tablecloth into a pair of slacks. Throwing on a button-up shirt, I didn't bother fastening it.

When I emerged, I found Vivien sitting at the gleaming black marble island in the kitchen. She'd removed her shoes and jewelry, and the corset-like bodice lay on the stool next to her. She unfastened her updo, causing her auburn hair to tumble out from the spiky halo in waves.

Tonight, she'd been magnificent. Golden, imperious, and untouchable as she waltzed amongst the gods with the certainty she belonged. No ordinary human could have done as well.

Yet here in my kitchen, divested of the armor, she looked softer, inviting. Vivien no longer reminded me of an avenging demon from hell. Now she resembled a fallen angel, all tousled and still glowing, though she couldn't see it. In the privacy of my penthouse, there was only intimacy and safety with her near. Tapped like the sap from a maple tree, my violence drained away. I wanted to pull her into my arms and sink into her softness.

Vivien hadn't noticed me standing there yet, or if she had, she didn't turn around.

But she was not my lover, and I could ill-afford the indulgence of such thoughts. Not with the fate of all the souls on my shoulders. My ex-wife taught me that emotion-fueled actions came at a cost. And when one was the keeper of all the world's souls, any cost was too high a price.

Steel strengthened my spine. "I don't know what you thought you were doing, but your behavior was unacceptable."

She stopped fluffing out her now freed hair to drop her jaw. "*My* behavior was unacceptable?" she sputtered. "I'm not the one who started an all-out brawl, destroying an entire ballroom and ending the party."

Rolling up my sleeves as I crossed the kitchen to grab a glass, I explained. "My transgressions were warranted. Seth insulted my sekhor and me. I could not let such impertinence stand or others would think me weak." I grabbed the decanter of my favorite scotch and poured three fingers' worth. "But what you were about to do would have been a massive disaster for both of us." Coming to stand on the other side of the island so I could face her, I took a long drink of the smooth earthy liquor. But it did nothing to numb the fire building inside me again.

Vivien snorted in frustration. A cute sound, if the subject matter weren't so grave. "Is this one of those 'you don't know the rules, Vivien, so you don't know what you fucked up' situations?"

I set my glass down a little too hard with a loud clink. A crack shot up the side of the glass. "You tell me, Vivien. Because from where I stand, the moment I leave you alone with another god, you are more than willing to sink your teeth into his veins. Here I thought you found the idea of relying on my blood repellent. Perhaps you find Idris a more attractive prospect."

The glass shattered under my grip, and the amber liquid spilled onto the island. The idea of her being attracted to that insouciant, conniving little upstart made me want to rip off both of their heads.

"What do you care? Is it because you don't want to lose a valued piece of property?"

"You know that's not what I think of you."

Her voice rose. "Then why did you do it? Why did you bond us with blood? Was that the only way to save Jamal? Binding my will to yours? Surely there were other ways to protect the balance. Jamal's life is still finite, while I'll be enslaved to you for eternity. It doesn't seem balanced at all."

She was right. The deal had not been a fair one. Yet I forced Vivien to trade an eternity for a mere eighty or so years of Jamal's life. Nausea swelled inside me. I could not explain it. In the moment, I knew she would agree to anything for the boy, as much as I knew she would regret her bargain.

But the impulse had been so strong that it had almost come from outside me.

As a vampire, Vivien always attracted me, but in those tunnels, her magnetic pull was irresistible. A gravitational field all its own. It was like my entire existence had been headed to that one point where her fangs sank into my neck, binding us together.

Vivien tilted her head with a deadpan expression, and her eyes touched on the mess of scotch and glass. Then, her eyes met mine with a silent question. *Are you happy with yourself now?*

I wasn't. I was a monster, disgusted with myself. Fallon said I was the only one uncorrupted by power, but I'd abused it to enslave Vivien to me. I was no better than the others, who selfishly used and abused their sekhors.

Then Vivien said in a calm tone, "I was trying to help."

My jaw clenched so hard it hurt. The notion I'd nearly lost her to that pissant demigod stung as deeply as finding her in another's bed would have.

I picked up the largest pieces of glass before throwing them into the nearby trash. Then grabbed a kitchen towel and threw it over the leftover mess. "Who, exactly, were you trying to help?"

She threw up her hands in exasperation. "You, ya big doof."

I paused.

Vivien avoided eye contact, instead distracting herself by removing the spiky halo and setting it down next to the rest of her jewels. "You were in there, outnumbered by a lot of angry gods who are apparently pissed about my existence, which I'm still not totally sure why, by the way. But Idris pulled me out of the way when you shifted into angry jackal monster guy. The second he got me to safety, I knew I needed to get back in there and help. So I told Idris, but he assured me I'd be dead in a minute."

Idris had been right to remove her from harm's way. If Timothy, Fallon, or even Bianca had been closer, they would have done the same. I would have done my best to protect her, but my rage had been entirely focused on Seth. I might not have had the wherewithal to protect Vivien, even as I promised. Shame and revulsion slapped me, realizing what the emotion-fueled outburst could have cost me. The very one I was trying to protect.

Vivien went on. "I told Idris I didn't care. My meal ticket was in there, and I needed to get to you. Make sure you were okay." Her excuse of protecting me because I was her food came out flimsy and weak. "Idris told me if I drank his blood, I would be supercharged enough to fight by your side and not get killed."

Shock zinged through me like a lightning bolt. Vivien was only going to drink from Idris in order to protect me.

I must have stared for a long time because Vivien squirmed. "What? Say something. You're freaking me out."

I blinked, and shook my head. "Sorry, I simply don't know whether I am more stunned to find that you were so eager to come to my aid, or furious at Idris's attempt to con you." My fists clenched shut as I suddenly knew exactly which emotion to deal with first. "He will be dealt with accordingly."

Vivien splayed her hands on the cold black marble and gave me a penetrating look. "What would have happened if I drank his blood?"

I told her the truth. "Our blood bond would have dissolved, and he would have taken hold of your will."

Vivien frowned. If I'd learned anything, Vivien adamantly opposed being controlled or manipulated, and Idris had attempted a weighty con. But had I done anything different?

Perhaps she desired another pairing than with me. Maybe Idris was a more attractive immortal to align herself with. Someone who didn't take himself so seriously.

"That weaselly son of a bitch," Vivien growled. The tightness around my chest loosened as thoughts of Vivien bonded to Idris melted in the fiery ire I saw in her eyes.

THEN SHE THREW up her hands. "Okay, so I didn't think it through. When I get overwhelmed, I get impulsive. I mean, when I find out my skip is a serial killer, not only do I get wound up and spooked, I leave him alone with my drink and then stupidly sip it. Then boom, I wake up a vampire. And tonight, all I could think about was jumping into the mix to help you. I definitely didn't think about the possibility of him controlling my will. But," she paused, "would drinking his blood have at least helped me power up to fight off the other gods?"

I didn't answer.

"Grim?"

Everything in me bore down against the truth. The secret she could not know. The reason the other gods viewed her as a threat.

"Hello, earth to Grim. Would it have helped?"

"Yes." I couldn't stop myself. For all I wanted to conceal this from her, the truth seemed to arise of its own accord without my permission. "Vivien..."

Don't say another word. You cannot tell her the more she drinks of a god, the more powerful she would become. It is forbid-

den. It could cost you everything. She can't be a danger if she doesn't know how to exact harm.

In the end, my need to protect Vivien won out. If any of the others knew, if Osiris knew, I had told her the truth why I had to exterminate all the sekhors, she would be in danger.

Vivien had been watching me intently, as if sensing I was about to divulge something of great importance.

A presence drew my attention over her shoulder.

Latsyrc, one of my reapers. As Latsyrc came into view, Yelram and Nylorac also apparated at his side. Then three more, five more, twenty more reapers were there. All their eyes glowed a bright golden hue. Each of them carried a soul, ready for judgement.

Vivien turned to look over her shoulder, following my gaze.

Before I could stop her, Vivien got up and went to them. My reapers closed the distance as they all vied for her attention. She smoothed her hand over their willing heads and soft black coats.

"Why are they all here? I've never seen so many at one time before."

My hands curled around the marble as dread flooded my chest and stomach. "I thought I had more time," I murmured.

"Grim?"

Releasing the countertop before I broke that, too, I joined Vivien. Several reapers sat at attention by my feet. I wasn't sure what possessed me, but I ran a hand over Esor Eitak's head. Esor Eitak closed his eyes, enjoying the touch.

"They are carrying souls, and they have brought them to me for judgement." I sighed. "My reapers can only carry one soul at a time and they all have reached capacity."

"You mean every one of them is carrying a soul and can't pick up any more?"

"Precisely." I let my fingers drift up Esor Eitak's soft ear. The reaper leaned into me. "And now it must fall to me."

Vivien stopped her petting frenzy. "What must fall to you?"

"I must relieve them of the souls they carry, so they can collect more. It's imperative the reapers continue their duties."

"What are you going to do with them? Pop them in a genie's bottle or something?"

The corner of my lips twitched. "I'm afraid no such solution is available. No, I must be the one to carry them until Amit is recovered."

"Carry them?"

"Yes, I will hold them within my being."

"You can do that?"

I stepped back and took a deep breath as I held up a hand. The golden eyes of my reapers sparked and glowed more intensely around me as I grabbed hold of the souls inside of them. They had already ferried the worthy souls over to the afterlife with Osiris.

But these remaining spirits were in need of judgement, or they were the damned, meant to go directly to Amit. As I absorbed the souls from my reapers into my being, a bitter sourness engulfed my mind and heart. I closed my eyes as I went inward. I had to make room for the souls, which required a great deal of shifting my internal power so that I could encase them. I needed to separate them from my being. Once I'd finished binding them in the energy equivalent of an amniotic sac, I opened my eyes. All the reapers had gone. I found myself braced against a chair, drained of energy.

Vivien stood there, transfixed. Fear, worry, and awe warred on my sekhor's face, while her mouth parted. "Holy fuck," she breathed. "We need to find Amit."

A tickling sensation ran from my nose to my upper lip. I reached up, and my fingers came away wet with black blood. With a deft pull of my handkerchief from my pocket, I cleaned the rest away.

A wave of nauseating power rocked me from the inside. I ran a hand through my hair and took a steadying breath. Shutting my eyes, I willed my power to balance.

I'm in control here.

When I opened my eyes again, indecision, or maybe hesitance, flitted across Vivien's face. "That seemed...not good."

"Yes, well, it certainly isn't a pleasant, or usual, part of my job." My voice came out as a croak, so I went over to the kitchen and got myself some water.

Cool water slid down my throat, helping to calm my internal state.

"How long can you keep that up for?" Vivien asked.

As I refilled my glass, I said, "For a time." I set the glass down, needing to brace myself on the counter for a moment. Pressure swelled and moved inside of me. No matter how much water I drank, it would not wash away the tainted souls now trapped inside me.

"That's not very specific," she countered.

After draining the second glass, I turned to her. "In truth, I don't know. I've embodied souls like this before, but never for an indefinite period."

She took a few steps toward me, her hands flying about. "Well, what if they were just left to roam about until we found Amit and we could get everything sorted out? Then you could grab them and take care of it."

A wry smile tugged at my lips. "Unfortunately, that is not an option. To leave souls disoriented and adrift would be like releasing a poison gas upon the earth. Raw, dark power would not only further twist the souls themselves, but that of the living beings. It's too dangerous to have that much tainted energy go free. And I can only imagine what my brethren would do. I imagine many would attempt to harness the power of those souls to become more powerful."

"Maybe that's been the plan all along," she said quietly. "Take you out of commission and let chaos reign."

I didn't respond. The gears were turning too quickly in my mind. She was right.

"And seeing as Seth seemed to be a fan of creating chaos..."

I saw where this was going and shot her a sharp look. "Don't go near Seth, Vivien. I'm serious. Our focus is on finding Amit."

"But if we follow him, he may lead us to Amit."

"I said drop it." Too late, I realized my words came out a roar that shook glasses in the cabinets. I wasn't sure if the display of power had come from my fear for her, or the pent-up energies of the dark souls writhing inside.

Vivien paled before the storm clouds rolled into her eyes. Sticking her hands on her hips, she asked, "Is this the part where you force my will?" There was both a challenge and a warning in her voice. If I took her will, she intended to make me pay. But that wasn't my intention at all.

Pinching the bridge of my nose, suddenly tired, I said, "No. I need you to know that is Seth is dangerous, and he's already painted a target on you."

She rolled her eyes. "The collar was just a dumb move to get you to lose it."

I dropped my hand. "What happened when you were dancing together?"

Vivien averted her gaze as she pretended to adjust her dress. "Nothing, he stepped on my dress."

"You have the lying capabilities of a four-year-old."

At first, she reared back in surprise. Then she stuck her tongue out at me.

Before she could say something else combative, I invaded her space, lifting her chin with a knuckle. "Fine, don't tell me. But Seth knows your weakness now and he will continue to exploit it, if nothing else but for the sheer joy of it." I stepped back, my shoulder sagging as the weight of the souls dragged me down. I needed to rest and regain my strength if I was going to keep them contained. "I must excuse myself. I need rest."

Vivien nodded. "It's morning, but strangely enough, I don't feel tired. I'm going to see if Miranda is in. Maybe she'll have something on Amit."

It was difficult to focus on her words, though I was entranced by her mouth. She, too, seemed distracted.

Vivien walked to the elevator, in bare feet, not bothering to grab her shoes or jewelry. Had this been a different time, a different circumstance, she would have been leaving in a tousled disarray for other reasons. But we wouldn't be sharing breakfast or rolling in my bedsheets.

The doors closed, and she was gone. I put my desires in a—what did she call it? A genie's bottle?

But who knew how long that would hold before it shattered under the pressure?

11

I trotted down to the lobby after a quick stop at my room to change into black jeans, a white crop top, and a leather jacket in case I got cold again.

Seeing Grim absorb those souls was more than concerning. It was downright fucking scary. Not because his death mask flickered as he did it—his face morphing into a skull and sucking darkness that communicated annihilation to every cell in my body—but because it was like watching him toss back a bottle of poison.

The urge to grab his arms and shake him until he stopped nearly pulled me off my feet. But who knew what would have happened if I touched him while he drew the souls into him? Breaking his concentration didn't seem like a good idea.

Anger shook me. If he thought he was getting brownie points for being a damned martyr, he'd have to get them from somebody else. If he wanted to commit suicide to save the world, then it wasn't my problem.

Except I could only drink his blood and I needed him to survive.

No, that wasn't true anymore. I could make a blood bond with another god.

When Grim was a thin thread away from throwing a violent tantrum over what I'd almost done with Idris, I'd been tempted to push back.

Dancing on the tip of my tongue was the declaration I regretted not biting Idris. Maybe he'd be a better partner, a better meal, a better kisser...but even just thinking about the lie made my stomach twist in sour knots.

Ever since I'd made a deal with Death, I'd wanted to punish him. I'd raved to Miranda and Timothy he would screw me over the first chance he got. Then Seth said all the things to me I'd been thinking about the last several days, and I balked at his predictions.

Dammit. My feelings were getting the best of me. Sure, Grim hadn't abused the power...yet. But it was only a matter of time. Right?

I may not want Grim to have control over me like he did, but the terrifying truth was, I wouldn't prefer anyone else. Sighing, I resigned myself to the fact I needed to save him, even if it was from himself. I would find Amit and then we'd iron out the rest of our...situation.

Annoying feelings bubbled up, whispering all kinds of nonsense.

Maybe you can trust him. Maybe he won't use you. Maybe he won't control you.

My throat constricted. I didn't know if I was making excuses because I had to believe it to spend the rest of eternity with him or because I wanted him. Oh yeah, I wanted Grim. I wanted the god of death so bad; I knew it was only a matter of time before I slipped up and ended up begging him to kiss me. Just like he predicted. Bastard.

What started out as intense lust, a death wish like no

other, had morphed into something more. At first, I saw him as a tyrannical, scary god, bent on killing all vampires. But after seeing him amongst the self-indulgent assholes of his kind, I realized how different he was from the rest. Grim cared about protecting humanity and their souls. There was ferocity to his protectiveness, meant to keep the rest of the gods in line. And that required he appear to be in complete control at all times.

Blood bags. I respected him.

His job was never-ending, and it exhausted me just thinking about all he juggled. Not for the first time, the loneliness of his position struck me. The moments where I cracked through his intense demeanor, earning a smile, or a moment where he let his guard down, felt more precious than gold and was more addictive that cocaine.

I made a mental list.

Step one. Find Amit.

Step two. Cling to any and all scraps of dignity.

I frowned. I knew the first task would be easier because Amit actually existed.

After texting Miranda, she wrote back that she was hard at work trying to track down the culprits. But she needed a hefty caffeine fix since she'd been at it all night and was at the hotel's café.

The best thing about being sequestered in a casino as a vampire was I could come and go and not have to worry about sunlight. Like the rest of the hotels on the Strip, most of Sinopolis was devoid of windows to keep people unaware of the time so they could spend more time plugged into their addiction, whether it was gambling, drinking, partying, or whatever.

Perkatory wasn't more than a coffee stand with some café tables, sectioned off from the lobby by a surrounding wall of lush plants. I really wanted to know who named it Perkatory. Never in a million years would I give Grim credit for a coffee/purgatory pun. No, someone else had to have come up with it.

A deep line creased between Miranda's eyes as she studied her laptop screen, hand gripped around the tallest cup of coffee I'd ever seen. Knowing Miranda, the cup was likely brimming with straight shots of espresso with only one sugar packet dumped in to cut through the bitterness.

Wanting to see if the caffeine had reached her heart yet, I slammed into the seat across from her, hoping to give her a jolt. Miranda only brought the cup to her lips, never taking her eyes off the screen. "You'll have to do better than that if you want to catch me off guard."

"What, are you just used to bombs going off when you were in the Special Forces, so nothing phases you? Or is this like a mom thing where kids are so loud and unpredictable your senses are just dullened at this point?"

Instead of answering me, she said, "Hey Aaron, can you get my friend here a triple shot caramel Frappuccino with extra whipped cream?"

The barista, who was mere feet away, heard her request. The barista had shaggy blond hair that brushed his shoulders and a crooked nose. He shot me a dazzling, confident smile and said, "S-s-sure." His words came out in a stutter.

It was still too early for the partiers to get up and go for their morning java, otherwise there'd be a line a mile long. At 6:30 AM, no one milled about.

"Can you put sprinkles on the top?" I asked Aaron.

"L-l-l-like a cupcake?" Aaron said. Now that I'd heard him speak twice, I knew his stutter was a permanent companion of his.

"Aaron, you just became my new favorite person. How did you know?"

With a mischievous smile, he pointed at my necklace. The charm was a tiny pink cupcake covered with sprinkles and a cherry on top. I used to live above a bakery. The necklace was a gift from the owner, since I bought sweets from her like it was my job.

In my secret heart of hearts, I wished I could make cupcakes and cookies. When I'd lost my memories, I'd been adamant I was a baker. But turned out, my talent for causing oven fires trumped any baking abilities.

"Clever boy," I said, shooting him a finger gun of acknowledgement.

I couldn't peg Aaron's age, if he was in his early twenties or late thirties. He reminded me of a California dude, the kind that surfed all day long. There was a carefree ease to the barista, and it was hard to pin the age of people who stayed young at heart.

Turning back to Miranda, I asked, "So any new leads?"

"Not yet. I spoke to the security guard." Her lips pursed. "He got all defensive that he didn't know they were stealing. But I explained it had happened on his watch and now that I'm head of security, I won't tolerate anyone just waltzing off with Mr. Scarapelli's belongings."

Geez. I wasn't even the one responsible, and I felt cowed by her verbal whip. The only way she could have made it any worse was by saying how 'disappointed' she was. If I worked for her, I would start jumping through some fire hoops to impress my boss, and make damn sure I didn't get on her bad side.

I leaned back in my chair, stretching out my back. "To be fair, it's not like a massive crocodile was on display anywhere in the hotel."

What I wanted to say was the poor guy couldn't know there was giant croc god in the basement, but I couldn't tell Miranda that. *Blood balls.*

Miranda looked up at me. "It doesn't matter. If an employee sees something being removed from the premises, they should know how to check with the proper channels to ensure nothing is being stolen. There is a hole in the security system, and I intend to plug it up."

I made a face. "Way to constipate the system. Go you."

Aaron walked up to us with my drink. Having overheard what I said, he laughed.

"Don't encourage her," Miranda cautioned him. "Pretty soon she'll believe she is the funniest thing in the world, and then she'll really be impossible."

"Excuse me," I drawled out. "I *am* the funniest thing in the world." My hand raised, inviting Aaron in for a high-five, who met it with a laugh.

"I l-l-like her," he said.

A woman wearing gigantic sunglasses, in a crumpled Versace dress, stumbled up to the coffee stand. I could smell the expensive booze radiating off her from the night before. "Latte," she croaked. "A big one. The biggest one."

Aaron shot me a wink, then went to tend to the woman.

Mirada shut her laptop and drummed her fingers atop it. "So, are you going to share about this ball you attended? Or do I have to drag it out of you?" A sly smile played at her lips.

Blood bags. What to say and what not to say.

I was dressed like a goddess, mingled amongst the snootiest, most terrifying powerful immortals on earth, Grim nearly ripped everyone's heads off, losing his clothes in the process, and I almost bound myself to a conniving bastard who wanted control of my will, for only god knew what.

Literally. Only that god knew what he wanted with me.

Instead, I settled on, "I think I know who stole Amit."

Miranda perked up at that. "Really?"

"There was this douchewad at the party. He has a real axe to grind against Grim, and me, apparently."

Miranda gave me a sardonic, expectant look. "What did you do to him?"

"Nothing," I said, raising my hands in defense. "I swear, never even met the guy until last night. Maybe he's prejudiced against vampires?" I sipped the sugary drink. Ah. Maybe if I drank enough of these, my heart would start pumping again.

"What's his name?"

"Seth. He's a real ballsy asshat." I remembered how his face had morphed into a familiar face from my past and before I knew it, I'd pushed my sugary drink away from me.

Using the knowledge that the gods all owned hotels, it didn't take long to find him on social media. Miranda leaned in as we took a little tour of his life. Seth owned the Menaggio Hotel. The man was the master of selfies, always sporting that smug smile that inspired a horde of women and men alike to comment on how hot he was, or what a baller he was. It was all *Yolo, don't hate the player, hate the game*, and *just call me daddy*. Yuck.

After some scrolling, Miranda sat back. "Do you have any proof?"

"It's more of a gut feeling."

Miranda tried to hide her expression, but she wasn't fast enough. She had zero confidence in me.

"Hey man, I've learned to trust my gut," I protested.

"Great, but you need proof and a trail to follow." She tapped her finger on the laptop.

Picking up my drink again and tipping it at her, I said, "True."

"Oh god, what are you planning?"

Playing with the straw, I said, "They should get rid of the straws. It's terrible for the turtles. I'm surprised Grim is so blasé about massacring the gentle creatures of the seas."

"Viv."

"And I bet other animals get screwed by the straw game too, but somebody went to bat for the turtles. If it were some cute fuzzy otters, I'd bet everyone would stop in a hurry. I'm sure the blob fish are also suffering. Have you seen a blob fish?" I made a retching sound.

"Vivien. What. Are. You. Planning?"

I took a long sip even though my stomach was still all churny and yucky, thinking about the face Seth flashed me last night. Miranda never lost focus. Damn her.

"I'm going to follow him."

"Oh boy. This feels like a bad idea." She smoothed her hair back at her forehead, flattening her curls as if trying to find something she could control.

Geez, did Grim already text her and tell her to head me off at the pass or something? *Rude.*

Before Miranda could poo-poo my idea any further, I shouted out, "Hey Timmy, what's shaking?"

Sure enough, Timothy was back in his normal suit. I still remembered how epic his display of power had been with those chains of glyphs. I knew Grim was the god of the dead, but Timothy and I hadn't had the conversation yet about what his deal was.

Grim's aide stopped short when I called him. If I didn't know any better, I'd say he seemed flustered or embarrassed. His eyes flitted to the counter where the Patrick Swayze look-alike helped that poor partied-out woman, before he walked over to Miranda and me.

"Morning, ladies."

"Glad to see you're alive," I said, looking for claw marks, bruises, or missing limbs. No evidence of the brawl was visible. Timothy could handle his own in a fight. Not that I was too surprised.

Miranda fought side-by-side with him against vampires before and later told me said he fought with the precision and accuracy of an assassin.

"And you." He nodded. His eyes flicked back over to the coffee station before meeting Miranda's eyes. "Any luck with the investigation?"

All he got in response was a grunt of frustration from her.

"Timmy, tell me something," I said, surveying my nails. They were still shiny and pristine from my whirlwind makeover, and I wondered how long that would last. "This mega croc that has gone missing—"

Timothy shot me a warning glance. Though I couldn't imagine why he was worried. He knew I couldn't say anything, even if I wanted to.

"Doesn't it require a certain environment?"

He shifted his weight to his other leg.

Come on, Timmy, work with me.

"That statue," I exaggerated the word, "was kept in a hot, humid location. Wouldn't it require the same conditions to, uh, survive?"

Miranda squinted at me at that last word choice. I realized too late I should have said something like 'to be properly preserved.'

A spark ignited in Timothy's eyes. "Yes, yes, you're right.

It would need a great deal of humidity and heat to...remain intact."

He did a better job talking around the whole god stuff than me. Then again, he had thousands of years of experience with that. I'd only been at this a couple of weeks. I deserved a gold star for how well I was playing it. A gigantic one, to put on my leather jacket so everyone would know what a special girl I was. I was just about to ask Timothy for a sticker, when I saw his eyes slide yet again to the coffee counter.

"Need your caffeine fix that bad, huh?"

With a startled jerk, Timothy looked at me again. "What? Oh yes, the party was...draining. If you'll excuse me, I could use a pick-me-up."

Then Miranda and I watched him cross over to Aaron.

"What's with him?" Miranda asked.

"Oh, I think the better question is, what's up with *them*?" I crossed my arms and leaned back. The new vantage allowed me to see both Aaron's and Timothy's faces.

The two men greeted each other in low, soft voices.

"Hello Aaron, how are you today?"

"Right as rain. T-the usual?"

"Better make it a triple."

"L-l-l-long night?" Aaron gazed at Timothy with hooded eyes while Timothy couldn't bring himself to meet it. The assertive, buttoned-up god was actually flustered. I tried to suppress a smile as I watched.

Miranda leaned in, a mischievous smile at the corner of her lips. "No, seriously? Those two, you think?"

When Timothy went to pull out his credit card, I saw how Aaron watched his face, as if he were intent to memorize the lines. Once Aaron stepped away to make Timothy's drink, Timothy surreptitiously dropped a hundred-dollar bill in the tip jar. As the California bro went about the motions of making Timothy's drink, Grim's aide pretended to look at his tablet, but his dark eyes were fixed on Aaron.

Miranda and I sat watching with open curiosity. Coffee *and a* show. I should sell tickets.

Handing over the hot latte, Aaron awarded Timothy with a big, lopsided smile that would have made even my heart pound a little faster, had it been able. Timothy gulped, then tilted his head and gave thanks. When he turned around to see both of us staring at him with unabashed curiosity, Timothy looked ready to run for cover.

However, before we could ask what that was all about, Timothy checked his phone. "Duty calls." Then he shot out of there like a bat from hell.

While Miranda chuckled at his hasty retreat, my energy ebbed. All the excitement finally got to me. Exhaustion settled around me like a weighted blanket.

"It's time for my beauty sleep," I declared, getting up from the table. "But I'd say check around for humidifiers or heat lamps. Wherever this croc has gone, it's going to need a lot of hot moisture."

Miranda set her jaw and gave me a nod. She'd complete the mission. That's what badasses did.

Making my way back to my room to catch some zzz's, I realized I'd be hungry again when I woke up later. And there was no more avoiding Grim and our 'dinner' plans. As I crossed the lobby, I admitted to myself it was nice not to be a frozen block of starving pain.

This time I wouldn't fight going to Grim to drink his blood.

No, I just had to fight every other urge that would boil up.

12

After absorbing the souls from my reapers, I fell into a deep sleep. Nightmares plagued me.

Seth wrapping his fingers around Vivien's neck, crunching her bones.

Vivien lifting her head from Idris's shoulder, fangs and lips dripping with his red blood as something shattered inside of me.

Vivien as a small girl, staring at a smoking wreckage. She turns her sea-green eyes up to mine, and they're glassy with tears.

Qwynn's fingers slide over my shoulders and down my chest while whispering into my ear. Her words slide into my ears, tiny snakes. A blindfold wraps around my eyes. Then the cold, biting metal of shackles clack shut around my wrists.

Vivien screams for me to help her, but I can do nothing, still under my ex-wife's spell.

Drowsiness hung on my eyes and body like a mountain of wet towels as the tension of my dreams slid away from my body. I blinked until the figure at the door of my bedroom came into focus. Vivien walked in. Her glow stretched out toward me, calling me to her.

A streak of possessiveness ripped through me. The sekhor was mine and no one else's. I wanted to grab her and pull her into my black satin sheets. Kiss, lick, and mark her all over the bed.

Despite my active imagination, I hadn't yet moved.

"Knock, knock," she said softly as she approached.

I ran a hand through my hair as I sat up, the silk pooling around my waist. Vivien's eyes followed their descent to my bare hips. I was naked underneath the sheets. Those near-translucent green eyes were hesitant yet unable to hide a flicker of desire.

"I thought you didn't sleep much?" Vivien asked, walking into the room with a forced casualness.

"Normally, I don't." My voice was rough. An hour or two typically sufficed. Gods didn't need to sleep like humans. A god's energy center ran like a nuclear reactor compared to a mortal's. But it felt like I'd consumed a vat of ambrosia. Pain pounded through me like a live wire. Yet focusing on Vivien's presence gave me a modicum of relief. I wasn't sure if that was because of our blood bond or because of the powerful feelings she evoked. I suspected it was a little of both.

"Why are you looking at me like that?" she asked.

"Like what?"

With a nervous half-smile, she said, "I came here for dinner, but you're looking at me like I'm the meal."

Vivien was now standing by the bed. Her baggy slacks sat low on her hips, and she wore a crop top that showed off her taut stomach. Over that, she wore a leather jacket covered in metal spikes. If she thought the spikes would deter me, she underestimated her allure and my ability to handle dangerous creatures.

Before I could think it through, I reached out and placed a hand on her hip. My fingers played with the bare skin. Vivien's pupils dilated as her mouth parted, but she didn't stop me.

The mere touch of her skin sent desire pounding through my body, drowning the pain. Under the sheets, my cock stiffened. Her skin pebbled into goosebumps, and I wondered if her nipples had done the same.

One of her hands rose, pausing a moment before she slid it through my hair. Nails scratching against my scalp, I was close to losing it right there.

"Are you hungry?" I asked, my voice low. My thumb slipped under the band of her pants. Her skin was cool to the touch.

Vivien shivered.

My sense returned to me. "You're cold, you need to eat."

As I dropped my hand, Vivien let out a soft mewl of disappointment.

Maybe she was hungry for more than blood, after all.

Vivien wetted her lips, then opened her mouth as if to say something, but no words came out.

Perhaps it was wishful thinking, but I felt she was on the edge of asking. On the verge of inviting me to kiss her senseless.

In fact, if she kept looking at me like that, I might break my word.

Perhaps there were ways around my promise. I said she'd have to beg me to kiss her again, but there were plenty of other things I could do to her that didn't involve kissing. My eyes travelled down to the v between her legs, imagining the variety of ways I could fill her. Her usual scent of leather and sugar intensified, now accompanied by her arousal.

My mouth watered, and my resolve snapped. In the blink of an eye, I had her on her back under me.

Though she didn't need to breathe, Vivien caught her breath in surprise.

I trapped her wrists over her head as I ran my nose up along the delicate skin of her neck, inhaling. She'd wrapped that piece of leather around her neck again, somewhat obscuring the scar of the master vampire's bite. I pressed my tongue to her flesh between the strands.

The spikes of her jacket bit into my flesh, but it only intensified my arousal, so I pressed harder against her.

The sheets had twisted when I threw her on the bed, acting as a barrier between us, though there was no way she'd miss my hardness pressing into her. Feeling her under me drove me to near madness with desire.

"Was there something you wanted to ask me?" I murmured against the shell of her ear with a nibble.

Her full body shiver made my cock twitch in response.

It was there. At the base of her throat, working its way up. She was going to ask. On a moan, a whimper, or a rasp, I wasn't sure. But she was going to beg me to kiss her, take her. I dropped one hand and ran it up along her bare torso, sliding up under her shirt. My fingers traced her bare ribs. Vivien groaned and wriggled under me, her arousal thickening the air, mixing with my own.

I was a millisecond away from cracking and having my way with her when Vivien stiffened under me. Like a rubber band snapping, an unspoken tension rang out in the air. Whatever thought had crossed her mind, it had killed the fire in her belly, and she was now stock-still underneath me.

With a sigh, I collected myself, pulling back from the

sexual edge I'd been skating along. With a sharp roll, I further twisted the sheets between us until I was on my back and Vivien was sitting on me, knees on either side.

Unable to stop touching her, my thumbs continued to massage her bare hips. A mixture of arousal and blatant terror shone in her eyes. Locking with her gaze, I silently communicated my patience. I would not push her. If there was one thing I was capable of, it was control.

It was enough I got to be in her presence. Vivien may be undead, but she was more alive than most people I'd known. Her mix of unpredictability, humor, and caring cut through the centuries of monotony I'd white-knuckled my way through.

Bit by bit, Vivien relaxed, her shoulders dropping an inch, until she realized she would set the pace. Her fangs had already elongated. Then I turned my head against the bed, baring my neck to her.

Vivien's hand dropped to my chest as she bent over, her breath fanning against my collarbone. I shut my eyes, reminding myself, yet again, that I was the epitome of restraint.

When her fangs sunk into my neck, I reflexively tightened my hands on her hips, grinding her hips against mine. A deep growl vibrated from my throat, while Vivien whimpered in pleasure.

Gods, I loved her like this. When she drank from me, it was with utter abandon and evident pleasure. The pressure of her suckling made me dizzy. The spikes of her jacket pressed into my chest again, intensifying all the sensations. Then I felt it, the invisible tether between us as the world receded, until there was only Vivien and me. The world seemed to darken and fall away, and I wondered if she felt it too.

Her cold skin warmed against mine as my life force flowed into her. But she gave as much as she took. As she drank from me, it felt like Vivien had crawled inside me. I'd never known such an intimate closeness. Vivien became a part of me, more than a limb, another vital organ I could not exist without. Her nails raked down my chest and arms as she squirmed against me.

Of all the gods, I'd been the only one to hold back bonding with a sekhor in the ancient times. Now I understood why the heat of the war had been a blaze, not a candle flame. She was as bright as the sun. I'd do anything for her, I would die for her.

No, I would live for her.

Vivien went limp after less than a couple minutes. I knew how powerful a god's blood could be, especially in the beginning. Vivien pulled back, lapping at the skin of my neck now, her body relaxed. I couldn't help my arms from going around her and holding her to me. When she'd fed yesterday, she seemed to lose awareness of her surroundings.

I rolled her off me, then propped up on my arm to hover over her. Eyelids fluttering, and cheeks flushed, Vivien still seemed to be somewhere else. Perhaps another plane of existence. But I'd stay here and protect her on this plane until she was ready to return.

Pushing the hair back from her face, I let the silken copper strands slide between my fingers. An aching tenderness came over me, robbing me of my breath.

When Vivien opened her eyes, returning to her senses, I continued to smooth back her hair.

"I need to get ready," I said. "We are going out tonight."

Normally, she would have been mouthing off and demanding to know where I was dragging her off to this time, but Vivien seemed too lost in her own thoughts to respond. Voluminous hair fanned around her head like a fiery halo. Vivien studied me with intense concentration, as if in some internal debate.

With great reluctance, I rose, the sheet wrapped around my waist. I left her for the bathroom, debating the merits of taking my unmet pleasure into my own hands. Instead, I decided to do what I always did. Lock those needs into a box, just like I'd done to the souls I harbored inside me.

IN LESS THAN TWENTY MINUTES, I was dressed, showered, and ready to depart. I found Vivien standing in the living room. She held a bottle of sprinkles and kept shaking them into her hand before tossing them back in her mouth. Just as I was about to ask where she'd gotten the sparkly rainbow sprinkles, my reapers Nahgem and Simetra appeared. Their eyes glowing. Then four more appeared. The reapers needed to be relieved, again. A growl of frustration escaped me. Nothing was going my way today.

"That was fast," Vivien said, a line forming between her eyes. Still, she reached down and began petting the eager heads of my jackals as six more stepped forward, crowding my kitchen. Nibor yipped when he didn't get Vivien's attention right away. I shot him a warning glance to behave. The reaper's butt dropped to the floor, obedient and patient now.

"Yes, faster than I expected." I wanted to make haste to our destination, but duty came first.

Straightening, I lifted a hand and called the souls to me again. The reapers came to attention, their eyes glowing more intensely. An acrid, copper taste flooded my mouth as

I drew the souls to me. Pressure ballooned inside me as the ball of essence squirmed and roiled.

I finished on a pained gasp as my being threatened to tear itself apart. I stumbled, grabbing the back of a nearby chair. Vivien appeared at my side, steadying me. "That cannot be healthy for you." Genuine concern laced her voice.

I couldn't respond for several long moments, pressure and darkness swirling inside me. I tasted the violence, the fear, the broken parts of the souls. How many would go straight to Amit, and how many would still be judged worthy of the afterlife?

"I need a moment." My words came out hoarse.

I retreated to my bathroom and leaned over the sink to spit. Black ichor splashed against the white porcelain.

Hands braced against the edges of the sink, I tried not to think about what would happen if this kept up.

"How could you do it, Grim?"

Pushing myself up, I saw my ex-wife through the mirror. "Are you really here?"

I hadn't counted on the hallucinations plaguing me until I'd absorbed far more souls into my body, but I couldn't rule anything out.

"I'm here," Qwynn said with a sigh, resting her arm against the door jamb. The deep purple dress complemented her bronzed skin. Her luxurious black hair fell in waves far past her bottom, and her sultry eyes and pouty lips seemed real enough. But last I'd seen her, Osiris had locked her up in a hell dimension to teach her a lesson for attempting to unseat the balance of power.

"I'm here, and I need to know why," she said.

Turning around, feeling the cold ceramic against my back, I studied her. I'd known Qwynn for almost as long as time itself. As much as she tried to pretend she was an impenetrable sex goddess and trickster, it was all a smoke show covering up the bottomless pit of a hungry god who would never know the meaning of 'enough.'

She sashayed toward me, her hips swiveling with her usual brazen sexual invitation. But something was different about her. Osiris had trapped the goddess in a hell dimension. It could have felt like minutes, or it could have felt like hundreds of years. The haunted look in her eyes told me it was likely the latter. The woman before me was pretending to be the goddess she was before.

"Why what, Qwynn?"

"After all those years, all this time, why would you make a blood bond? Why would you take a sekhor now?"

"Do you mean why would I take one now? Or are you asking me why her?"

Something dripped from my nose. I pressed the back of my wrist to my face, and my hand came away smeared with black blood again.

Qwynn didn't answer. She merely gave me that look she had perfected so well over the years. With any other man, or woman, they would feel as if they were drowning in an ocean of pleasure and exultation. Most would do and say anything to make sure that feeling never stopped. Even I, at one time, would have done anything she wished of me, just so I could fall into her.

Turning back around, I grabbed a tissue and cleared my nose before dropping it in the garbage, then spit once more into the sink.

I'd once been her plaything, and life was a game to her. But I'd since gained immunity against what I now recognized as her selfish vanity. And I didn't play games anymore.

When she realized I wasn't going to answer her, Qwynn melted back into the shadows from where she appeared.

It surprised me she didn't press more. Either she didn't want to know the answer, or she already knew what made Vivien special.

Did I know why Vivien was special? Did I know how I could have gotten into this situation? No, it had all happened in a whirlwind, and there was no logical reason why I had done it. I always used my judgement and logic to control things, but with Vivien, something else was driving things. A force I couldn't stop even if I tried.

Osiris had looked into my mind and proclaimed he saw and understood. But I didn't. Cryptic bastard.

Vivien appeared at the open doorway. Worry tightened her face when she saw me.

"I'm alright," I assured her.

"Are you sure you should leave the penthouse?" Vivien asked, gesturing to the mirror. I turned around. Black veins stuck out on my face once again, my death mask flickering more chaotically than last time.

I spit one last time, forcing my body to absorb and settle. "Yes, I'm sure." We were going out tonight, to Wolf Town. There was no question we needed to be seen as if all was right, now more than ever.

My gaze settled back on Vivien through the mirror.

Why her?

I couldn't answer the question, but staring into her eyes, I knew it had to be her.

Perhaps I wasn't meant to walk this earthly plane alone, as I'd long thought. But how I could be worthy of such a gift, I'd no idea.

13

After splashing some cold water on my face, I got control of my powers and we headed out. The entire way, Vivien didn't mind sharing how skeptical she was of my ability to keep it together.

She continued to harangue me, even as we walked by the velvet ropes of the mile-long line to get into my club, Wolf Town. It was that way every night at Sinopolis.

My club was well-renowned for the best DJs, drinks, and VIP treatment. The bouncers held the line, and the swell of people who began taking photos of us on their phones. It was going to be one of those nights. Perfect. It was what I'd hoped for. I slowed our gait, giving everyone a good look at us.

Last night's debacle proved more than ever that I needed to make my presence felt. If any of the gods were in doubt that things were amiss or that my power was compromised, the evidence that would sweep social media would help dispel any such theories. They'd see Vivien and I were a united front, completely in control of things.

We'd almost reached the entrance when two party-goers broke from the line.

A short and curvy young woman headed straight for us with single-minded focus. She wore a silk jade-green dress that was striking with her dark hair. Her much taller friend wore a faux fur jacket, leather skirt, and lots of gold jewelry. Long mahogany-colored hair, and soft dark eyes that couldn't hide her enthusiasm.

"Oh my god, it's really you," the taller girl breathed. "Grim Scarapelli." She was so awestruck, I feared she'd forget to breathe and pass out.

Freckles peppered the shorter girl's face and bare arms. Her pert nose made her appear equal parts adorable and mischievous. She smiled seductively. "I'm Dawn and this is my friend Makarena. We're big fans."

Vivien scanned the taller girl up and down. "Girl, you are working that leather mini skirt and fur jacket."

"It's faux, of course," Makarena said, beaming from the compliment.

One of my bouncers crossed the distance to us, ready to intervene if need be. It wasn't unusual for a mob to form. "Everything okay, sir?"

"Everything is fine, thank you, Tom."

He stepped back, but didn't go far, in case I needed him.

Vivien gasped. "Oh my god, is that what I think it is on your shirt?" She pushed aside the orange fur jacket to reveal Makarena's white shirt with a black-and-white picture of my face on it. I don't recall when the picture was taken, but I wore a serious, brooding expression.

Makarena laughed nervously, her eyes darting to me. "Yeah, I got it from a fan page online, Grim's Groupies."

I smiled back at the girl and nodded. It would be rude

not to accept the compliment. Her spine straightened with pride.

"Fan page?" Vivien repeated, gobsmacked.

Dawn sidled up to me. "Can I get your autograph?"

Removing my hands from my pockets, I pulled out a soft-tip pen from the inside of my jacket. "Do you have something for me to sign?"

Dawn bit her lip in a worried move.

"So are you two dating?" I overheard Makarena ask Vivien.

"Dating?" Vivien squeaked. I kept an ear out for her answer.

Dawn's lips peeled up in a positively wicked smile. Dawn fingered the top hem of her dress, drawing attention to her more voluptuous assets.

Uh oh. I recognize that look.

"How about here," Dawn said, pointing at the swell of her bosom.

Vivien shot me a glance out of the corner of her eye as she stumbled for something to say. "Um, we are more like co-workers."

Co-workers? Less than an hour ago, I had Vivien in my bed keening and moaning for more than blood. I bristled.

Co-workers, my left buttock.

Unleashing the full extent of my charm, I smiled first at Dawn, then Makarena, who instantly forgot all about Vivien.

"Why, it'd be my pleasure." I uncapped the pen, then asked, "Do you mind if I steady you against me so I may better write." My words came out a purr as my predatory side kicked in.

Dawn nodded, her eyes the size of saucer plates now, while Makarena sighed. "What a gentleman."

I wrapped an arm around Dawn to draw her against my body. The felt tip slid against her skin.

Dawn bit back a moan and her eyes widened, and in them I saw what I saw in every human who worshipped me.

"I speed all the time," she confessed. "Sometimes at night with the lights turned off."

There it was. The reason I'd never taken a sekhor before. The reason I never engaged in an actual relationship with any human. Every human possessed a death wish.

No mortal ever truly saw me. As I was the god of death, they only saw a reflection of their own death wish. And it often made for a lonely existence among them.

I didn't believe she was even aware she'd said anything. Sometimes mortals confessed such things to me without even realizing it. Though usually the confession was along the lines of using drugs or wanting to be choked during sex. As if sharing their most dangerous vices would bring them closer to me. I could bring them closer to heaven, or hell, and humans were drawn to the unknown of that end despite themselves. There was a bravery in that curiosity. While I appreciated humanity's bold sense of expansion, I often viewed myself as no different from the bouncers of my club.

"Can you sign my shirt?" Makarena asked, rushing forward. She broke the spell Dawn was under. While Dawn blinked and remembered to breathe as I stepped away from her, Makarena tripped, falling face-first toward the floor. I grabbed her just before she hit, holding her in a low dip. Makarena's mouth parted in a "o" as she gazed up at me in open awe. Then before I could right her to a standing position, she confessed, "I eat way too many French fries." Then she grabbed my face and laid a kiss right on me.

Before I could gently extract myself, Makarena was pulled out of my arms.

"Okay, there ya go," Vivien said, her words now clipped. She'd yanked Makarena back and was now straightening the girl's clothes and jewelry. "We need to get inside, and I'm sure you ladies have somewhere to be."

I hid a smile as I wiped my mouth with the back of my hand. Vivien's arm snaked through mine as she led us into the club. Behind us, high-pitched squeals of delight rang through the air.

"What the hell was that?" she demanded once we were inside.

"What was what?" I said, feigning innocence.

"You were all over those girls."

"Does that bother you?" I asked, keeping my tone light. "Why would it? After all, we are just co-workers."

Vivien screeched to a halt, turning toward me. Her mouth opened and closed like a guppy's.

Yes, I heard. Yes, I did it on purpose to make you jealous.

I stepped in close, invading her space. I breathed in her scent, leather and sugar. "Is there something you want to ask me now?"

Vivien's jaw snapped shut. Then she turned and walked ahead of me.

She was determined to remain stubborn.

I chuckled. After seeing Vivien with Idris, I couldn't help but feel a little mollified at giving her a taste of what she'd done to me. As much as I wanted her to break down and beg me to kiss her, a part of me enjoyed stoking her jealousy.

Now I understood why she so enjoyed stirring me up. Perhaps our role reversal would be permanent. I followed her, not bothering to hide a wicked smile.

~

In my private VIP booth, we overlooked the dance floor.

Aerial dancers, adorned in fluorescent black-light paint, twisted and danced midair. The smell of adrenaline, sex, and sin permeated the night club. The heady pheromones mixed with the pulsating music.

Below, off toward the terrace, the well-lit indoor pool was a popular scene tonight. All the round, red plush chairs surrounding the water were occupied, until some of the party-goers stripped to their underwear and stepped into the water, dancing and laughing.

The slanted pyramid wall, consisting of dark windows, reflected all the bright lights pulsating from the DJ booth.

"Why are we here?" Vivien asked. "You said this was important, but I don't see how partying is going to help us find Amit. Miranda is still looking for heat lamps and humidifiers, not to mention the truck, but I could be out there, hunting the thieves down."

"You were right. Someone is trying to upset the balance. And by being out tonight, I am proving that nothing is wrong. We are showing a strong front."

"Saving face and all that?"

"Yes."

She made a rude noise. "That's dumb."

"What is?"

"Gods and people putting on airs. Why are people so afraid of messy?" Then, giving me a doubtful look, she said, "You also look like you could use more time in bed."

I couldn't help myself. "Are you offering to put me to bed?"

She bit the inside of her lip and glared at me.

Before bringing the sweaty glass of scotch to my lips, I said, "That wasn't a no."

Vivien shook her head and rolled her eyes, but I could tell she was suppressing a smile like I was. I couldn't help the playful part of me that came out when we were together. Though, in this instance, I was the one who started it.

Before my thoughts could go any further, I said, "You disdain the importance of appearances, but you played everyone at that ball as if you'd been born and bred into such airs. While I'm an excellent dancer, I could not take responsibility for your elegant moves across the floor."

Vivien ran a hand along the metal railing as she looked away. Her expression sobered and for a moment, I didn't think she would answer. Then she said, "I was, or close to it. When my parents died, I went to live with my aunt and uncle. They had never planned on having kids, but they kept me because it was good for their image." Staring down into the crowd, as if she could find an escape in there, she said, "They were rich, well-respected, and did all the right things. Which meant *I* had to do all the right things. I had to get perfect grades, attend all the benefits, and they required that I be a deb."

I couldn't have hidden the shock if I tried. "You. You were a debutante."

Shock and surprise warred for dominance. Timothy had discovered Vivien's rich roots when we uncovered her identity, but I hadn't asked about her upbringing. I knew that when she turned eighteen, she moved across the country and seemed to cut all ties with her aunt and uncle. It roused my curiosity, but I knew better than to push people about their pasts.

Vivien's smile bordered on a grimace, as if it pained her to admit it. "Oh, I know all the dances, what cutlery to use at dinner, and the proper way a young lady should groom herself. And of course, the best way to cut someone down with a few well-placed words, all while wearing a sweet ladylike smile." Then in a lower voice, she added, "That world was all about saving face, no matter the cost."

"I take it you didn't care for your aunt and uncle."

Vivien snorted, but there was no humor in it. She leaned back, threading fingers through her hair, agitated. More than I'd ever seen her before. When she was upset with me about having bound her to me, she was openly hostile, but whatever this was, she actively sought to push it away. When I'd interrupted her dance with Seth, she seemed to be in the same state of distress.

"They spent their whole lives trying to convince everybody they were good people. They were perfect, they had everything and therefore everyone should look up to them and believe whatever bullshit they spouted." Vivien's head snapped to the side, to meet my gaze with a sudden anger. "But they weren't. They weren't what everyone thought they were. They were like ducks on a pond. Appearing to glide along the surface, but underneath, they were always flapping away, working so hard, every second without a moment's rest. It was fucking exhausting."

Uneasiness churned in my stomach, so I set down my scotch on the table behind me. "And they expected the same from you."

Vivien's eyes flattened as she ran her tongue along her teeth, then nodded. "Even more so. When I was six, I used the wrong fork at dinner. I didn't get to eat for two days as punishment."

I straightened as the uneasiness flared into full-on alarm. "You were a child." It was a statement and question in one.

Vivien shrugged. "That didn't matter. If I was going to

eat like an uncivilized animal, they would treat me like one." She was paraphrasing, if not quoting something said to her. "If my smile wasn't bright enough for my uncle's boss, if my curtsy wasn't graceful enough, if I ever did anything to embarrass them. Talking too much, not talking enough... they would *correct* me."

A knot formed in my stomach, and not because of the souls I harbored there. "Did they hurt you, physically?"

She sucked in her cheeks as if thinking about what to tell me. "Did they smack me around? Occasionally, but I preferred that to being locked in my room and going without food. And I preferred he touch me in anger rather than..." She reached around me, grabbing my drink and tossing the last of it back. Then she plastered on a smile that made me positively ill. "What's the name of this song again? I forget."

"Vivien," I pressed. We stood on the edge of something together, and I wasn't sure if she would fall over with me. I should have backed away, content not to know, but I desperately wanted to take the plunge with her.

Vivien set the glass back down, then straightened and rolled back her shoulders. She was stalling.

I sidled closer, but was careful not to touch her. "Vivien," I pleaded, barely above a whisper this time. If I wasn't careful, she would run away. To avoid scaring her off, I averted my gaze to over her shoulder as I waited for her answer.

"It's in the past, Grim. He was a shitty uncle who took advantage of a young girl. I knew it and split as soon as I got my shot. I left that all behind me long before the master turned me into a sekhor."

Pain constricted around my chest, forcing me to close my eyes. The way Vivien white-washed over her pain...so much more of her made sense to me. While Vivien was impossibly rebellious, stubborn, and downright childish at times, I now understood why. She'd endured a childhood wrapped in invisible chains, careful to control her every action and word. The soul should never be kept under such tight confines, especially in such a loveless environment.

Many a soul broke under such conditions, a number of them currently roiling around in my body. But it wasn't my job to save everyone. I couldn't even if I tried.

The treatment she described had born many a violent, vengeful being. Vivien could have folded into wrath, pain, and hurt, then paid it forward.

Instead, she struck out on her own, and built a life on her terms. Until a master vampire destroyed that life, and I bound her to me. No wonder she refused to give in to me, to us. She craved freedom, but that would never be so.

"You didn't deserve that." My power whipped out around me with a ferocity that shook the room. The pounding music and writhing dancers covered up the tremor.

"I know that, now," she said. Then Vivien looked up at my face. Vulnerability was not something I often saw on her face, and now confronted with the rawness of her past, it was almost too much to meet with the naked eye. She pulled her jacket closer around her, retreating into the spiky vestment.

You, who have confronted all the torments, desires, tragedies, deaths, and endings of all beings. You can't stand to look into this sekhor's face without wanting to fall on your knees before her, apologizing for the injustices she's faced.

Was this what it truly meant to have a blood bond? To be so connected, I struggled to know where she began, and I ended. The price of not being alone. I'd gladly pay it.

In one quick motion, Vivien slid her jacket off, throwing it over the lounge couch. Then she grabbed my hand, flashing me a brilliant smile. "Want to show them everything really is dandy? Come dance with me."

Before I could protest, she dragged me down the stairs to the main floor, where the bass thumped so hard the ground shook beneath my feet. Vivien swayed her hips and threw her hands in the air. The floor was so packed, she had to brush against me as she danced circles around me. Stopping to dance in front of me, she burrowed her fingers through my hair. Then with a mischievous smile, she dragged them down, down, down my neck, my chest, my thighs as she swept her ass close to the floor. She looked up at me through hooded eyes that sparkled with wicked promise.

The music receded from my focus. There was only Vivien, practically on her knees before me. Vivien openly teased me. I was never sure if this thing between us was a game to her. My frustration demanded I yank her up, throw her over the bar, and take her roughly. Thrust into her repeatedly until she could think of no one and nothing else except me filling her.

God, I was a selfish bastard.

Why her? Why, after all this time?

When she slid back up my body in a smooth movement, her hands fell to my hips, pushing and pulling, signaling she wanted me to move.

I shouldn't. This dance was far more dangerous than it appeared, and I couldn't afford to lose. Still, my hands closed around her sides, and I fell in time with her swaying body. Our rhythm synced with a silent click that resounded through my being. I twirled her around, pulling her back flush against my chest. Then another twirl and I dipped her back before sweeping her up against me.

We both stood facing each other. Sweat slickened our

skin from the dance and the pressing heat of the writhing bodies around us. I swallowed.

One dance with Vivien and I was ready to break my oath to her. I stared at her lips, letting her know full well what I intended to do next.

And then it happened.

A knife slid into my gut.

14

Grim's eyes first widened, then his brows dipped as if he were in pain. I thought he'd been about to kiss me, but now he sneered.

Then I smelled it. The ambrosia that was his blood hit the air like a shot. I stepped back to find the handle of a knife sticking out of Grim's side.

Grim took a deep breath, sliding his hand around the hilt and then pulling it out of his gut with a jerk. Whoever had done it, must have walked right by us. I searched my memory and recalled the scent right before someone stuck Grim. Money, lime, and steel.

Looking around, I traced the scent to a man. Bald, under six feet, wearing sunglasses and a suit. Then I noticed there were six more like him that stuck out like a bunch of sore thumbs.

Well, that was a bit cliché. Maybe wearing a sign that said in big red letters, *I'm an antagonistic thug*, was too showy for them.

"We need to get everyone out of here before—" Grim started.

The thugs pulled out guns in tandem. Ratatattat. They went off in explosive pops.

The crowd burst into screaming hysteria. People dodged out of the way, trampling each other, some of them falling. Grim jerked under the onslaught of bullets. He threw out his arms, his supernatural force sending the people closest to him flying out of range of the gunfire.

Time slowed around me, as I reached down and touched my stomach. My fingers came away bloody.

The fuckers shot me. They actually shot me.

I turned to share my disbelief with Grim, when the guns went off again, rapid-fire. Sizzling hot steel tore through my flesh, sending pain screaming through my body.

Oh wait, *I* was screaming. It didn't matter that I didn't need to breathe, I gasped, wanting the pain to stop.

The cascade of bullets finally ceased as our attackers reloaded. When had I fallen on my knees? My blood-soaked hands were shaking.

That's when I saw Grim. He lay prone on the floor, curled in on himself. Blood streamed out of him, pooling onto the lit fuchsia square of the dance floor.

Fear and anger crashed over the initial shock and pain as adrenaline hit me like a shot. They'd awoken something primal. Pure vampiric wrath pulsated through me.

I blurred over to one gunman, pushing his gun up before tearing out his jugular in a vicious feral move. Bullets tapped my back. Someone had reloaded.

Twisting around, I hissed at him in pure animal fury. In the blink of an eye, I snapped the neck of a second gunman.

The club had all but emptied, leaving five gunmen standing. A faint green glow surrounded them. They were human, but they seemed charged by some supernatural power. The rain of gunfire kept me at bay, but soon they'd need to reload and then I'd rip them to pieces.

One gunman dropped his gun, mouth going slack, eyes wide in terror. I followed his stare.

A nightmare come to life, Grim hovered inches above the floor. His eyes turned to black sucking darkness, as inky veins stuck out along his face. Even knowing who and what he was, I took a step back. Fear rattled my bones like a xylophone.

Grim looked like this after absorbing souls, but this time it was different. It was as if any trace of his humanity had vanished, and a true and powerful, monstrous god remained.

Before I could say or do anything else, Grim lifted his arms and with the motion, power surged through the room. It pressed against me with lethal force. The men around me all went stock still as if he had them in his grasp. Then Grim closed his hands and jerked them toward him in one motion.

Their souls cracked from their bodies and went to him —spirit slaves called to their master. The bodies of the men all dropped to the floor, dead.

I'd seen Grim do this once before. He'd taken a man's soul, cracking it from his body and pulling it out. Ice shot through my veins as my stomach somersaulted. By comparison, the deaths I'd dealt the first two were a mercy. Watching him rip out their souls was so unnatural, violent, and terrifying, that it shook me to my core.

"Grim," I yelled, stumbling over the bodies to get to him. Black veins still pronounced, his eyes were unseeing voids. It scared me to look into them, afraid I'd find my end there too. He was out of it.

I pressed a hand against his face. "Grim, come on now. Come back to me. You're freaking me out."

He said nothing. Power continued to ripple the air around him. Then he spoke in what sounded like tongues. His voice was low, sonorous, and layered like a demon's.

"I don't understand you." Panic crawled up my throat. Was I losing him? I thought gods couldn't die. They were immortal, but something wasn't right.

It was dangerous enough for Grim to absorb the souls from the reapers, but this was piling on the problem. By taking those men's souls, he'd thrown gas on the already almost-out-of-control fire.

He continued to speak in tongues.

"Get away from him, Viv."

Miranda stood off to the side, her gun raised at Grim. She'd only just joined the party. More of the security team would arrive soon.

Stepping in front of Grim, I held out my hands. "No, don't hurt him."

Grim's arms jerked out for the second time, and the power nearly peeled my skin off. Miranda stiffened, the gun falling from her fingers as her eyes widened with fear.

"Grim, no," I cried, but it fell on deaf ears. He seemed locked in some kind of trance.

Oh god, he was going to reap Miranda's soul if I did nothing.

The little men with hard hats rushed around my head, searching for a solution. Only one came to mind.

It was dumb. It would never work. But I had to try.

"Grim." I turned around and reached my arms up around his neck.

With a bracing swallow, I looked deep into those fathomless pits where his eyes should have been. It felt like falling, careening into space. A void of death. I'd entered some kind of alternate dimension.

Though I wanted to turn and run, I dug my fingers into him, as I drew his head down. "I'm right here with you," I said. Every part of me demanded I shut my eyes, but I stayed with him. If I felt scared and adrift, he must be too. "I'm here," I repeated. "And I'm begging you now. Please. Kiss me."

This time the free-falling sensation wasn't because of what I saw in the death vortex of his eyes. It was the last vestiges of my pride and self-preservation sifted away through my fingers like sand. It left me bare and vulnerable. Asking him to kiss me wasn't about a kiss at all. And while part of it was meant to save Miranda, I knew it was a confession. I couldn't lie to myself anymore. I needed him, I wanted him. I would bleed for him.

My lips brushed his and electric zings shot through me, pressure building in my chest until I thought I'd burst.

Please let this work. I can't lose Miranda. I can't lose Grim.

I didn't want to be aligned with another god or be with anyone else. I wanted the god of the dead.

I kissed him again, framing his face with my hands. At first, he was unresponsive, as I continued to freefall by myself. Just when I'd thought he was lost, strong arms encircled me. His feet were back on the floor. Grim matched the pressure of my lips, coaxing back until I opened my mouth, so he could deepen the kiss. The depths of oblivion dissipated until I was staring into his eyes again. Drowned in gold, they glowed with power and desire.

I let my own lids drift shut as the kiss continued to intensify. His hand wove into my hair, while the other held me fast against his hard chest, as if worried I'd try to get away. I clung to him, unsure if I was dying or coming to life. Everything about this was right. Meant to be. As if all of time and space had gone through its dance to bring us to this moment. My submission wasn't a point of weakness, I was strong enough to open myself up to him and let him inside.

The nagging feeling of a forgotten promise tugged at me again. But my desire and need to feel Grim drowned it out.

He kissed me until my knees turned to Jell-O and my body pulsated with need and heat. The more I tried to satiate myself, the hungrier I got. Licking, sucking, nibbling.

Remembering we weren't alone, I pulled back on a sigh of either frustration or relief. My rioting emotions made it hard to tell which.

Grim blinked a couple times until his golden eyes returned to his more human warm whiskey color. He was back. I hadn't lost him.

Twisting to look over my shoulder, I realized I hadn't lost Miranda either. She'd recovered her weapon and backed up. She met my gaze with a hard stare of her own. Miranda had known Grim wasn't human, but I couldn't guess what she was thinking now. Would she try to shoot us? Force Grim back into a soul-sucking state?

Her eyes went from me, to Grim, to the bodies on the floor with guns strewn about them, then back to me, calculating. Then her jaw hardened, and she gave me a curt nod.

My shoulders sagged in relief. She'd picked her side and it was still on ours.

Jesus, when did I start thinking of it as 'our' side? The second I submitted and kissed him?

Before I could think much more on that I turned back and smacked Grim's chest. "What are you, an idiot? We don't have enough problems?"

That's right, Vivien, let's blow right past all the vulnerable mushy feelings. Pretend you didn't give up the little ground you had.

Confusion clouded Grim's expression. Obliged to enlighten him, I said, "You are already carrying souls beyond capacity. You decided it was a good idea to pile on? Absorb a couple more souls because this is so fun for you?"

His brows dipped and he released me from his hold. The loss of his touch made me feel empty.

"I lost control," he said. Holding out his hands, he stared at them as if he could call back the souls he just reaped. Grim seemed deeply disturbed. The god of death was a control freak for good reason. No one wanted that powerhouse off the rails.

"Who were those guys and why would they try to kill us?"

Grim shook his head, still staring at his hands. "They weren't here to kill us."

The holes in my body said otherwise. "Then why riddle us with bullets?" I challenged.

"To get exactly this reaction. Someone wanted to push and see if I'd lose control. Confirm the god of the dead is vulnerable." He dropped his hands and closed his eyes tight, adding a few more curses. "Whoever is trying to upset the balance wants the others to see I am losing control. That the tides are changing because I am fallible. A public display of weakness on my part could cause all hell to break loose."

"And the longer Amit is gone, the more unstable you become," I finished.

The invisible clock we were up against, sped up.

We didn't have time for stupid games of saving face of presenting a strong front to the other gods. Someone was fucking with us, and it was time it stopped.

Jaw tightening, I took a step back. "Alright, that's it. We need to get Amit, and we need him back now."

Expression clearing, Grim suddenly reminded me of a lost boy. "What did you have in mind?"

"Let's get cleaned up first," I said, gesturing to our bloodied clothes. "Then I plan to call on an old friend."

It had been a long time since I was a debutante, but I was pretty sure the etiquette handbook said it was rude to call on people, asking for a favor, while still riddled with bullet holes, bleeding on their floors.

"Ouch," I yelled.

"It wouldn't hurt so much if you stayed still," Grim said, followed by the *tink* of a bullet dropping in a metal bowl.

I wrapped my hands tighter around the chair I was sitting backward in.

After the shooting, Timothy showed up, in a whirlwind of damage control. He had ushered us out, for which I was actually grateful. Grim insisted I come up to his penthouse, and since I was woozy from blood loss, I didn't fight him. Now I was sitting at his kitchen bar while he played *Operation* with me. I even yelped like in the kid's game when he dug around too much.

My body had pushed most of the bullets out again before the skin knitted closed. Cool vampire trick. But there were a few that hadn't quite made their way out and were now trapped just under the freshly healed skin. They itched like hell. I'd had to take off my shirt and face away from Grim so he could extract the last couple slugs.

Grim ran a finger under my bra strap. His tone was hesitant. "There is another here, but it will be difficult to get out with this still over it." I felt the bullet as he pressed against it.

I swallowed. The pain receded as a fire started in my belly. Five minutes ago, peeling off my shirt and getting cut up seemed medically sound. But now, an ache thrummed between my legs, while a sense of vulnerability skated across my skin at the prospect of being even more exposed.

Why should I feel more exposed now? I'd already broken down and begged him to kiss me. Not to mention I shared my deepest darkest secrets about my past with Grim. I wasn't sure why I'd told him, either. It wasn't in my nature to conceal things, but I didn't walk around volunteering that personal shit.

It was dark, heavy, and I kept it locked in a steel box, wrapped in chains, put it inside a metal chest, and then threw it in the ocean that was the recesses of my mind.

The very second after I'd shared with him, I wanted to bite back the words.

Grim had studied me so intently, I could feel the heat of his possessive fury. I knew in that moment he was a hair away from hunting down my uncle and killing him, igniting both my fear and desire.

Fear because I didn't want to stir up things from the past. And desire because no one had wanted to take care of me the way Grim seemed to always want to do.

Grim was slow to unhook my bra, giving me ample time to change my mind. I bit my lip as the last band of flesh was revealed to him. The straps hung useless at my sides.

The tip of his knife dug into my skin, but this time, the pain was second to the erotic thoughts now tumbling through my mind.

Tink.

He ran his fingers on either side of the wound. "There,

it's already healing." His voice was husky, reminding me of when he first woke up earlier. It had taken everything in me not to strip down and jump him in his bed. The sheets had puddled around those hip indents that make girls stupid.

We'd come so dangerously close to crossing that line. Did I really want to hand over my heart when he'd already bound my soul?

I couldn't even pretend we could casually bang things out and then walk away.

No, if I gave in, I would be entirely his. The thought had turned me to ice underneath him in his bed earlier. Like a light switch, my brain flipped over to my vow to never give in to him.

My aunt and uncle had done a swell job of fucking me up.

As Grim's expert fingers continued to move along my skin, leaving trails of fire in their wake, I wondered if that wasn't enough? Maybe it wouldn't be so bad? So far, he had done nothing to betray my trust.

Not to mention my feelings had always been my primary guidance system. They usually steered me clear of any real relationship, or clear commitment, but now those guided missiles were locked straight on the god of death who was currently sending sparks of pleasure shooting through me.

"Grim?" My voice shook.

"Yes?" His voice rumbled.

Goosebumps rose on my skin under his touch.

My feelings screamed at me. *Give in again. Do it. Pride is for losers.*

"Can you hand me my shirt?"

I'd stuck a sharp needle in my ballooning feelings, and they exploded in an overly dramatic display of confetti and frustration.

"Of course." His words were laden with disappointment.

The little men in my brain ran around.

What is she doing, sir? We locked on a target. She was supposed to fling her bra across the room, turn around, and try out her new vampire abilities with a literal god in the sack.

Jenkins, she's gone off the rails. There must be a kink in the system.

A kink, sir? Wouldn't that mean she'd be tying him up already?

Not that kind, you idiot. She's broken, so she doesn't always run smoothly.

That's sad, sir.

Yes, Jenkins, but the real tragedy is, who here is going to deliver the message to her cha cha?

I didn't want to put my bra back on until the cut healed more, so I slipped my bra off the rest of the way and took my shirt from Grim, who dutifully remained behind me with eyes averted.

That's when I caught sight of a box in a corner of the kitchen, one I hadn't noticed before. "What's that?" I asked, shirt still pressed against my bare breasts.

Grim followed my gaze. "Oh, it's uh..." He shifted his weight onto the other foot. "It's baking ingredients."

I could see that. The box had no top on it, and I could see a bag of flour, sugar, and...was that a bottle of sprinkles?

"Why do you have baking ingredients? From what I've gathered, you never baked."

"I don't, but I remember how intent you were on wanting to be a pastry chef."

It was true. Amnesia had stripped away my identity, and the one I'd chosen for myself was a well-loved baker who could make sugary confections. Cake and donuts made everyone happy, right? But it turned out I only lived above a bakery. In reality, I was a bounty hunter who lived in a hovel by herself with no one to share a life with.

Grim continued. "So, I thought we could bake together."

I couldn't have been more stunned than if Big Bird walked in the room and slapped me across the face with a massive yellow wing. "You know how to bake?" I asked.

His voice seemed far away as my mind spun. "Well, no, but I thought maybe we could learn together. Maybe ask a pastry chef from one of my restaurants to teach us if we didn't do well on our own."

Then I noticed the two fire hydrants on the floor in the same corner of the box. I'd be offended if I weren't so stunned by what he was saying, and the truth that we'd probably need a third.

"Thank you," I said, glancing over my shoulder.

Big mistake. Grim's hair was a messy tousle, and he'd taken off his coat, leaving only the tatters of his near-destroyed shirt. The god was barefoot in slacks, some of his own blood smeared over his shoulders and chest. Unlike me, his body didn't reject the bullets. Scarily enough, his body absorbed the lead left inside and healed over.

But what held me captive was his expression. Instead of the imperious steel I usually saw in his face, he radiated naked pain and longing. Not only was he bashful about the insanely thoughtful gesture that pretty much blew my tiny mind, he was still shaken from what happened at Wolf Town.

It was as if he didn't quite know what to do. He'd lost control and I could tell he was questioning everything about himself. Would he do it again? How could he stop it? If he didn't have control, what did he have?

Me.

Before I could think things through, I tossed my shirt to

the side and jumped onto Grim. He caught me as I wrapped my legs around his hips.

My mouth crashed over Grim's, and he met my onslaught head on.

I was like a girl who had broken her strict diet for an irresistible freshly baked cookie. And now that the diet was smashed, I would destroy it with a metric fuck-ton of pizzas, cakes, and burgers.

Time to change my middle name to *extreme*.

Our lips, teeth, and tongues fought for dominance. The taste of him was as heady as it was addictive. He surrounded me, enfolding me in exotic lilies mixed in with the powerful masculine scent that was uniquely his.

I was careening into the god of the dead at a million miles per hour, and he kept pace with me. Large, strong hands palmed my ass, allowing me to leverage my hips the way I wanted. The hardness I felt growing under me spurred me on to grind against him.

I kissed him until we were both gasping, logic and sense left in the dust. My naked breasts smashed against the tattered shirt he wore that resembled swiss cheese from the blitz in the club. Desperate to get closer, my nipples pebbled, straining for more.

More, was all I could think.

My feet hit the floor and I ripped Grim's shirt the rest of the way off. It floated to the floor, but not before I undid his slacks in record time and shoved them down just enough to reach a hand in and grab his hard length.

The pure animalistic growl that emerged from Grim's throat made my bones shiver and the glassware tinkle against each other in the kitchen.

Something deep inside me purred in satisfaction. *My monster.*

If I had half a mind, I would have stopped to ask if I could accidently push him over the edge into his god-likeness of a jackal. It would be most inconvenient for him to go big and furry on me right now. But minds were dumb. Thoughts were stupid.

Touching, tasting, and feeling were everything. Sucking on his neck, I reveled in the salt of his skin while I stroked his hardness. I should have pushed his pants down all the way. I'd put us both in a bit of an awkward position that trapped my hand, which only afforded limited movement. But there was fun in that too.

When I pulled back to watch him endure my deliberate torture, his molten gold eyes flashed with a need that bordered on violence. A tremor of fear wove along my desire, twisting it even tighter. I'd always liked to live on the edge.

Grim's hand morphed into razor sharp claws. Before I could react, he grabbed me with his human hand and threw me up against the wall. My body smacked against it, exciting me more. I'd always enjoyed sex and liked it on the rougher side and now that I was a vampire...well, there was a very real danger my kinky side could get out of hand.

GRIM HAD CHANGED our positions so fast, I barely registered the switch even as his hand closed around my neck. His claw sliced through my pants until they fell away from my body. Cool air brushed against my bared hips and legs. He left me wearing only a pair of panties, and the leather strap I kept wrapped around my neck.

The need sizzled and intensified between us. It had been there since the beginning. According to everyone it was because vampires and gods had this innate attraction to each other, but I knew it was more than that.

From the time Grim stalked toward me with all his terrifying power on display, it was almost as if I recognized him from a long-forgotten memory.

His presence tugged at my gut and my heart in ways no one else ever inspired. Whether I wanted to admit it or not, this man, this god, was slowly but surely weaving a chain of trust between us. And trust was a luxury I hadn't been able to afford since my parents were alive.

He dragged a finger between my legs at my sensitive center, causing me to jerk. My hips bucked, wanting more. The teasing touch was driving me to madness with want. With anyone else, I would have been the one pinning them down and melting their mind. I always liked to be in control, but letting Grim dominate me like this was positively addictive.

When he pulled out his cock from his pants, I bit back a gasp. The dizziness that overcame me was either from his tight hold around my neck, or the impressive size of his member. My inner muscles clenched, anticipating that long, hard girth sliding inside.

He grabbed himself at the base and ran his grip down to the tip in a long, hard stroke. Someone groaned but I wasn't sure who. My mouth watered at the erotic display as he did it a second time.

I needed the panties gone. I needed Grim inside me, now. I needed him filling me until I couldn't think. The ache inside me was unbearable. He wasn't close enough and some part of me screamed I would be safe once he was inside. And I needed Grim to lose himself in me. I may have been the one restrained, but not for a second did I doubt the control I had over him.

"Mine," Grim snarled. My hips jerked as Grim ripped off my panties.

He kissed me again, hot and deep. I felt the word and his kiss reach the depths of my immovable soul.

Our tongues met in a dance only we knew the steps to. His fingers danced along my slit, until incoherent pleas streamed out of my mouth.

He watched me carefully, reading me like a book. Slipping a finger in to the first knuckle with an experimental dip. Then a second and third time before he reached further in. "You like the way I torture you?" he rasped. "I could do this all day for months on end and never tire of giving you what you want. I'll give you anything you want."

I believed him. He was beginning to know me better than I knew myself.

No one ever matched me in passion or strength before, not even when I'd been human. I was always "too much" for everyone, whether it was friends or boyfriends that seemed to come and go overnight. I was too independent, too wild, too weird, but I'd spent too much of my life squishing down who I was to please other people. I promised myself I'd never do it again.

And the more Grim got to know me, the more he embraced who I was. He wanted to bake with me because he knew it would make me happy, even if I burned down his kitchen in the process. When Seth publicly insulted me, Grim went berserk.

My own family suppressed, abused, and starved me physically as well as emotionally. Grim nearly beat down my door when I didn't drink from him, he cared about my well-being, whether I'd eaten or not.

If I was being honest, it scared the ever-loving shit out of me. I felt exposed, and not just because I was naked and pinned to the wall.

That sinful finger slipped all the way inside me, stroking in a 'come here' motion, hitting a spot that coaxed live fire.

It was too much. The feelings pulling and expanding in my chest, and the tight heat at my center both threatened to explode and turn me to ash.

I pushed his hand away, and his finger slid out. Part of me screamed and cried in protest, but I needed to get out of my head, out of my feelings. Get back in control and make him squirm under my touch.

Submitting to the shift in power, Grim stepped back to push his pants off the rest of the way, and I saw my chance. He'd barely stripped before I fell to my knees and swallowed him whole. Grim's cry reverberated through the penthouse. The windows shook and his power crackled in the air like a live wire.

I hummed around the sinfully salty taste of him. My tongue reveled in the feel of his satin skin pulled over impossible hardness.

Taking him all the way to the back of my throat, I rolled my tongue against his cock. The god of the dead panted, desperate for more, and I gave it to him. Digging my nails into his sculpted ass, I took him down my throat again and again.

Without the need to breathe, I could shove him down my throat ten ways from Sunday as I never could before I was a vampire. The exploration was half-meant for science, half-meant to be torture. Maybe I'd write a paper and publish it after this. Though I'd need to do far more research before putting pen to paper...

Grim gripped my hair so roughly, I almost couldn't move, I knew I had him on the edge. With one last slam down the back of my throat, I dropped back on my heels, sucking him off before covering him with my mouth as quickly as I'd released him.

Grim's cry turned into a roar as he came. I swallowed every last bit, looking up at him under my eyelashes and sending him a silent message.

I may be on my knees, but we both know I'm the one in control here.

Witnessing his control snap was the most gloriously beautiful thing, and I wanted to find all the ways I could break it. Over and over, forever.

Eternity didn't seem like such a bad deal if you had an enjoyable hobby to pass the time.

I finally released his cock with a satisfied smirk.

In the blink of an eye, Grim hoisted me up, maneuvering me so my legs were thrown over either of his shoulders. He stood up, taking me with him, hands supporting my ass again. Grim pushed my back against the wall as he buried his face in my already drenched, aching sex.

The first touch of his tongue had me reeling through time and space, like when I drank his blood. He knew exactly where I wanted that talented tongue from moment to moment, until I began to wonder if he weren't a mind reader. The rough scratch of his stubble against my inner thighs and most sensitive parts set me on fire.

As the pressure increased and his tongue delved deeper, my need for friction only increased. He met my demands, going harder, faster, until all I could do was grab onto his hair and ride his talented fucking face. Then his lips latched onto my sensitive bud as he worked a hand up between us to slip two fingers into my throbbing, wet heat, filling me.

As Grim sucked my clit and pumped his fingers into me with relentless vigor, the bright, hot, coil of fire inside me tightened to the breaking point. There was no mercy as he pleasured me, pushing me toward the edge of my orgasm.

When the coil of tension shattered, I didn't even try to control my screams as my orgasm rocked me from fang to toe.

Grim didn't stop. He sucked, licked, and moaned into me like a starving man. Before the first orgasm could settle, a second one ripped through my body. The intensity clouded my vision, as I shook uncontrollably. I thought I might die.

No, never mind, I'd died once already.

No, never mind, it was the Grim Reaper himself murdering me with his tongue.

As senses returned to me, I found myself slumped against the wall that Grim had propped me against. "You taste like sugar, ambrosia, and sin," he said against me.

He was still lapping at me, like he was reverently cleaning me up. A shiver of aftershock jerked me.

After a bit of squirming, Grim let me down. Thankfully, he still kept me in his arms, otherwise I would have flopped to the floor. All feeling had left my legs.

I stilled as his golden orbs caught me, like a fish in a net. Such unbidden, ferocious feeling radiated out of them I feared I'd melt under his gaze.

Oh god, I wanted to run to his bedroom and pretend nothing else existed. He was hard again, and I still ached for him.

But then I noticed the black veins crawling up his neck. I swallowed over a hard lump in my throat.

As much as I would have loved to play *how many times can a vampire come*, duty called.

"What have you done to me?" he rasped. "Why you?"

I couldn't bring myself to answer. Anxiety slipped into the cracks, filling me up. About losing myself to him? I didn't know. I didn't know why me. The god of the dead had met a gazillion people, not to mention he had many gods to choose from. But he wanted me. And it still scared me to death.

Pun intended.

"We need to go meet my contact." My voice was scratchy, my throat choked with intense emotion. I wanted to make a joke. Insert some kind of levity, but nothing came to me.

Grim didn't seem to hear me at first. Simply stared at me with abject amazement. His hand threaded through the hair at the base of my skull. Sex and power still surrounded us as he seemed to consider dragging me off to his bed.

Then with a curt nod, he released me and was gone, cold air remaining where his warmth had been. Grim disappeared to his bedroom and I was left alone.

Tenderness was not my strong suit. As soon as I finished getting my jollies off, I'd be out of a dude's apartment like a shot. But I'd wanted Grim's arms around me as we lay in bed for hours, telling secrets and making jokes, until we eventually worked back up to another round of lovemaking.

Still shaking, I dragged my hands over my face, trying to get a grip. Looking out at the city lights of the Strip, I realized the serious shit I was in. I'd avoided it for my entire life but there was no denying it.

I didn't just need Grim, I wanted him.

Which meant I just handed over the power to destroy me. I might have preferred a wooden stake to the heart.

15

"Can you tell me where we are going? It is, after all, my car." Annoyance creeped in my voice as Vivien navigated the near-deserted streets.

Like my apartment, I'd had the windows of all our vehicles treated with a UV protection so if we needed to drive about during the daylight, Vivien would be alright. It was still risky, but there were a couple of hours until dawn.

Vivien pulled a small metal USB drive out of her pocket. "I had Miranda give me a copy of the security footage, and I have an idea on how we can locate that moving truck."

Vivien had insisted on driving us to an undisclosed location to meet her "contact." Since this person was particular about their privacy, Vivien tried to make me wear a blindfold for the drive.

I told her there was only one circumstance in which I would allow myself to be blindfolded, and that would require we be in my bed chambers. The tone of my voice must have communicated I wasn't joking, so she backed off. Though not before I saw a spark of excitement and curiosity in her eye.

I'd had her. In my arms, on my cock, gods help me, in my mouth. The taste of her still lingered on my lips and it was all I could do not to force her to pull the car over and bring her to orgasm with my tongue at least five times more.

Souls pressed insistently against my insides, straining to get out. A hot wave of nausea rolled through me, chasing away my amorous thoughts. At least I was comfortable in a bullet-free suit. Leaning back, I braced myself against the unpleasant pressure. Vivien was right to get us back on Amit's trail. Timothy was doing his best to find Amit, and I'd even brought Bianca into the loop, and she had retreated into deep meditation in order to receive any helpful visions about Amit's whereabouts.

None of my hotel guests were injured. If Timothy weren't so adept at damage control, I might have been worried about there not being one, but two massacres at my club in the last week. But he had been cleaning up after godly messes for thousands of years. I needed to remind myself to send him a thank you gift.

But I could verily feel the eyes of the other gods as they sharpened their swords, waiting for me to falter. After the club shooting, it was only a matter of time now before someone took their shot. And I'd proven to be unstable under pressure.

"What is this plan of yours again?" Vivien had changed into a pair of shiny black pants and a bright blue faux fur coat, which she referred to as Cookie Monster. I realized her temperature must be dropping again after losing so much blood in the shootout. Cursing myself, I should have noticed earlier and insisted she drink from me.

"I've got a guy," Vivien said.

"You've got a guy?" I repeated.

"Sure do," she nodded. "The best hacker on this side of the country."

"And they are awake at this ungodly hour?"

"I'd say this hour is rather godly. You're a god and you are awake," she shot back with a smirk.

The things I wanted to do to that smart mouth of hers. "You didn't answer my question."

"This is Vegas," she said, turning the wheel. We'd left the lights of the Strip fifteen minutes ago. "The city that never sleeps."

"That's New York."

She shrugged, unbothered. "Same diff."

I couldn't be sure if it was the dark souls roiling around in my gut or the situation, but my nerves were back to being on edge. It wouldn't be long before my reapers appeared again, needing to be relieved of their cargo.

Coming back to the present, I said, "I don't think it is wise to involve any more people in this affair. It's my problem."

Vivien rolled her eyes. "Someone pushed your buttons, forcing you to go loco and reap the souls of everyone around you. I would say this will become everyone's problem if we don't find Amit soon. My hacker could track down a coffee bean in a mountain of gravel. Trust me, I used her all the time when I was a bounty hunter."

I didn't bother to ask why a coffee bean in gravel, knowing to forge on. "I thought you said it was a man."

She shrugged. "No, I said I got a guy. It's a saying. Ya know?" She shot finger guns and exaggerated the words this time, "I got a guy."

It didn't matter if this person was a man, woman, or mouse. I simply wanted to keep up with Vivien. My first mistake.

Vivien added, "And believe me, she's the best."

"And what does the best cost?"

"You can afford it." Vivien took another turn, pulling into a lot surrounded by industrial buildings. "Plus, I have the equivalent of a coupon code for her services." Vivien parked the car. Then she pulled out a small backpack from behind my seat and patted it with a knowing smile.

Before we left Sinopolis, she'd insisted she needed to grab some things, though I was too busy spitting up more black blood to know what she'd packed.

I followed Vivien to a nondescript metal building and punched in a code to open the door. The place smelled like cardboard and machine oil. My first guess was it was some kind of fulfillment center since it was well-stocked with boxes and packaging supplies. Vivien waltzed right past it all to a caged lift at the corner of the building. Not unlike my hotel, there was more to this place than met the eye. We travelled down three floors before it stopped.

When the lift stopped, Vivien yanked the cage back with a near ear-splitting squeak. Before I could take a step out into the long, dark hallway, Vivien threw an arm out, holding me back.

"Echo," she called.

Automated guns dropped from the ceiling with a mechanical hum. All four swiveled until they pointed straight at us. I froze. While I was immortal, I wasn't in a hurry to receive over a dozen bullets straight to the face. Again. I'd been shot enough for one day.

Vivien tapped her foot with obvious impatience. "Come on, Echo, don't be like that. It's me, Jane."

I'd almost forgotten Jane was Vivien's given name. Her vampire name suited her so well, it was almost jarring to hear her introduce herself like that.

A crotchety voice crackled over an electronic speaker. "What do you want?"

"What I always want. Information. I'm willing to pay the entry fee." Vivien slid the bag around and patted it.

The guns disappeared. Cold florescent lights lit up the hallway with loud, echoing *ker-chunks.*

A slim Asian girl about eighteen years old stepped into the hallway at the other end. Bright turquoise hair in pigtails matched her boarding school uniform, complete with plaid skirt. Though no school I was aware of would allow such garish fluorescent colors or punk rock accessories like the chains she'd attached to her outfit.

The girl's eyes raked me up and down with overt flirtatiousness. Her small nose and chin gave her an impish look, but her eyes burned with a perceptiveness that made me doubt she was a teenager. The violet contacts were a bright contrast against the copper tan of her skin.

The girl popped the sucker of out of her mouth. "Hiya Jane."

"Hey Aioki." Vivien waved back.

Then, with a flick of her wrist, Aioki had us follow her.

Down the metal hallway was a large vault door, with a classic spinning wheel mechanism. Aioki punched some numbers into a keypad and the vault wheel spun. When it stopped, the door opened with a gasp.

Aioki waved us in. As I passed her, the scent of cotton candy filled my senses. Aioki gave her lollipop an extra loud smack and winked at me. As she followed me in, I was almost positive I could feel her eyes on my rear. Not that I was unused to such attentions, but she seemed a bit too young for the confidence she was bandying about.

With the high ceiling and concrete walls of a warehouse, the inside of the vault revealed a strange mashup of a tech fortress and vintage furniture. On one side was a floral couch and table set for tea. On the other end there was a mass of screens flickering different channels. Some aired soap operas, several were anime and news channels, but more than a few played live feeds of the city.

A hot pink gaming chair swiveled around from in front of the wall of screens, revealing Echo, presumably.

"Who's this?" She gestured to me, sounding even more crotchety without the crackling speaker. I was not easily surprised, but Vivien continuously found ways to do so.

Frizzy white hair puffed around the older woman's head like dandelion fluff. Her face was set in a permanent frown under a flat nose. Echo was likely Samoan and wore a floral mumu. Her dark eyes were hard and suspicious.

This was one of the best hackers?

"A friend," Vivien responded to Echo's question.

"You don't have friends," Echo shot back.

Vivien rolled her eyes. "With friends like you, who needs more?"

Echo studied me before recognition flashed in her eyes. She knew who I was, but I couldn't be sure if I saw a flicker of admiration, hate, or fear.

There was something off about the woman. The energy around her vibrated at a higher frequency that suggested she was more than human. The same vibration emanated off her daughter, but their energy wasn't godly. I'd recognized my brethren, even the younger gods.

Eyes locked, Echo and I both refused to break contact first. A mutual understanding passed between us. We knew there was far more to the other, but chose not to out the other.

Vivien set down her backpack, breaking our silent

standoff. I wondered if Vivien was aware of Echo's abnormality.

"Payment first. I remember," Vivien said. Then she made chittering and clicking sounds with her tongue. Vivien pulled a banana out of her backpack.

A tiny soft nose peeked out from under the couch. Then a little bunny slinky-ed out and hopped toward Vivien, sniffing the air. Tiny ears stuck straight up, and aside from the black circles around its dark eyes, the rest of its fur was snow white. It was one of the smallest rabbits I'd ever seen. I daresay it would fit snuggly in my cupped palms.

"You look different," Echo said to Vivien with accusation in her tone.

Meanwhile, Aioki leaned against the massive computer desk, still looking at me while suggestively licking her lollipop.

"I am different," Vivien answered, still clicking to the bunny. "Got my name changed and everything."

Realizing it was safe, the bunny ate the tip of the banana with vigor. The rabbit's butt twitched in pleasure and made surprisingly loud smacking sounds.

Vivien sent a questioning glance around the room. "Where is Lulu?"

As if on cue, a rabbit five times the size of the tiny one appeared. This one was brown and gray with a long face and massive floppy ears. The rabbit stumbled over its own ears in its haste to join the little bunny in chowing down on the banana. This one was practically the size of a dog and the sight of both rabbits next to each other was as endearing as it was comical.

The two rabbits wolfed down almost half the banana before Vivien took it away, delicately wrapping it up in the peel again and setting it on the coffee table.

The little one backed up and stamped his back foot.

"Don't sass me, Darth Vader," Vivien said to the little bunny.

He stomped twice in quick succession and grunted. The bigger one looked back and forth between his tiny companion and Vivien.

Vivien threw her hands in the air in pretend exasperation. "Fine, I suppose I brought another treat too." As she reached into her bag again, the two rabbits ran in circles around her feet. Darth Vader leapt in the air, his butt shaking, while the bigger one looped around, much slower. Aioki giggled as she watched, while Echo pretended to do something on the keyboard, though she was watching Vivien.

The rabbits became frenetic when they heard the crinkle of a bag. Vivien pulled out a small bag of Cooler Ranch Doritos. After opening it, she bent over and gave each rabbit a chip. The little one darted off with his treat as if afraid someone would try to take it from him, while the big one stayed to crunch at Vivien's feet.

"Okay Echo, let's get to business," Vivien said, after petting the large rabbit a few times. "I need you to find a truck. More accurately, I need to find the cargo on that truck."

Echo squinted one eye and held a finger out. "What makes you think I'm going to help you?"

The little rabbit made his way back over to Vivien, standing up, begging for another chip. And lord help me, I wanted her to give it to him.

What was Vivien doing to me? The god of death wasn't a softie for rabbits.

"Because Lulu and Darth Vader here think I'm the bomb," Vivien said, pointing first at the big one, then the little one.

As if on cue, both bunnies stood up, their little noses twitching. There was something off about them.

"The rabbits, they are...different..." I said.

"Genetically engineered," Aioki supplied.

Echo grabbed a cane that was propped up nearby and smacked the younger girl with it. Aioki cried out in protest, though she was far from seriously hurt. Echo and Aioki's interaction led me to believe they were mother and daughter, though they had only vague physical similarities.

"We do not tell strangers our business," said Echo. Then, leaning back in her chair, the older woman surveyed me with open skepticism. "Especially billionaire hotel owners who have far too many secrets of their own."

The rabbits turned their attention toward me as if waiting to see my response.

Aioki shrugged. "What? You want him to think it's okay to feed rabbits Doritos?"

"Never feed a domesticated rabbit Doritos or chocolate," Echo announced as if scolding the entire room. Then in a more miffed tone, "And should you make the mistake of ever doing so, be prepared dole out the treats regularly or they will destroy your family's heirloom rocking chair."

She glared at the little one, Darth Vader. The rabbit flicked his paws and then licked them so he could clean his face.

"Yeah, pretend you don't know what you've done," Echo groused.

Seeing as I'd been made, I stepped forward and bowed. "Grim Scarapelli, and indeed, I am the owner of the Sinopolis Hotel. It would mean a great deal to me if you could help us."

Aioki let out a soft sigh and dropped a shoulder, relaxing into a more seductive pose.

"Aioki, stop swooning," Vivien snapped. "He isn't going to come over there and catch you if you faint away."

All Aioki did was devilishly grin around the lollipop.

"We would be grateful for your help," I appealed to Echo.

She harrumphed, but her defensiveness softened ever so slightly.

Vivien pulled the thumb drive out of her pocket. "We need this, uh...statue of a crocodile back. A crew came and stole it from Sinopolis. It means a great deal to Grim, and it's important we get it back fast."

To her credit, Echo didn't ask why we needed it quickly recovered, though curiosity sparked in her eyes. "Where was it?" Echo asked, squinting.

"Stored in an impenetrable location deep underneath the hotel," said Vivien.

"Cool," Aioki breathed.

Echo snorted. "Not so impenetrable if someone stole it out from under you."

Tapping her foot, Vivien continued to hold out the drive. "Can you help us or not?"

Echo looked at Vivien, to me, to the rabbits, then back to Vivien, as if calculating something. "Fine. But only on one condition." She shot up one chubby finger. "Instead of the usual fee, Mr. Scarapelli will owe me a favor at my discretion and time of choosing."

I was not sure if I was getting in over my head with this woman who had access to genetically engineered rabbits, a beat on the city enough to track Amit, and a bit of a temper. But I assured myself she was nothing I couldn't handle. I glanced at Vivien, who gave me a shrug as if to say, 'it's your call.'

"Of course, madame," I said. "At your time of choosing,

you may call upon me for a favor." I pulled my personal card out of my pocket. Aioki flounced over to collect both the drive and the card, casting yet another look of promise and sexual interest my way.

Then Echo broke into a satisfied smile as she pocketed the card Aioki handed her. "Well, Jane, it appears you've come into better company."

Just then, a door opened off to the right and a little, old, balding Japanese man walked in with a tray set with a tea pot and two cups. He wore a knit vest, khaki slacks, and bunny slippers. He stopped, surprised by our presence, but quickly recovered and bestowed a friendly smile. "Two more for tea, my love?" He directed the question at Echo. Her husband, judging by their matching wedding rings. His resemblance to Aioki was far more noticeable.

Echo snorted, already turning back around to her computer lab. She'd dismissed us.

Vivien smiled back at the man, her affinity for the old man apparent. "Thanks, Ryuki, but we have to get going. Some other time." Then to Echo, she said, "My new contact info is on the drive for when you have something." She linked her arm through mine, grabbed her bag, then led me back out the way we came.

The rabbits jumped up onto the couch next to Ryuki as he sat down, while Aioki waved her fingers at me in farewell.

"And Echo"—Vivien paused at the door—"don't call me Jane anymore. Call me Vivien."

These were the people who were going to help us find Amit? I hoped Vivien could trust them because if we couldn't, she must realize I'd have to kill them.

16

We got back to Sinopolis just before the sun rose. It was not even 6:00 AM, but we found Miranda in the hotel's security office.

It was a hell of an upgrade from her digs in the castle hotel next door. First off, it wasn't a broom closet. With a full wall of sleek monitors, the long desk in front of them could have sat ten to fifteen people. Miranda was the first one in. Surprise, surprise.

Miranda pushed away from the desk, her chair rolling out so she could face us. Alarm was evident on her face. Last she'd seen us, Grim had been a massive scary monster about to rip her soul from her body.

Jamal popped up from a leather recliner in the back corner by the fridge and water cooler. He dropped his phone on the seat and joined us.

Miranda sent a panicked look at Jamal. She wanted answers, and she was likely scared for Jamal. When she met my eyes, I gave her a slight shake of my head, silently promising I would give her answers as soon as I could. I also hoped she would receive my reassurance that Jamal was safe around Grim. For now, anyway...

Oblivious to the silent communication between his mom and me, Jamal breezed by her. We high-fived in greeting while he nodded hello to Grim. Though the kid would never say it out loud, I could tell he was somewhere in awe and fear of Grim. He was only ten years old. By fifteen, he'd be fearless, which was either really good or mega bad.

"What are you doing here, little man?" I asked.

He frowned at me. "I'm not little."

"Uh, sorry, what are you doing here, man who is perfectly sized for his age?"

Jamal rolled his eyes, then said, "Mom won't let me hang out at home and play video games even though it's summer vacation."

With a quick glance at Miranda's stony face, I knew it still scared her to leave him on his own. Not after learning the supernatural existed, and after Jamal almost dying. Not to mention she'd seen Doctor Death here in action. I could see the questions in her eyes, but with Jamal present, it wasn't the time.

She was still here, though, which meant she still trusted us somewhat. Or me. Or maybe Grim paid her enough not to care.

As soon as I thought it, I dismissed it. Miranda was not the kind of gal who could be bought. She was only here because she thought she was working for the right team. Or likely, she was sticking around until she could learn more, then do what she thought was right. It was hard-wired in her system. I respected that.

Miranda said to Grim, "He sits quietly in the corner, and he goes to basketball camp in a couple hours where he stays most of the day." It wasn't an apology or excuse for bringing her son to work. She was dutifully explaining his presence, but the underlying meaning came through. She'd do her work, but her son came first.

Grim nodded, his stern boss-face on. "It's fine. But if Jamal is going to be hanging around, I'll have Timothy set him up on one of the monitors"—he gestured to a massive one at the end of the room—"with some gaming systems." Then he turned to Jamal. "What do you play? Xbox? PlayStation?"

Whoa, how did Grim know about either of those? There certainly weren't any games at his place. Was he a secret gamer?

Fireworks of love and admiration were exploding for Grim in Jamal's eyes. "Uh, yeah, either is fine."

Grim's eyebrow dipped. "Both, then. I'll have Timothy supply you with games to go with them."

"You don't need to do that," Miranda said with a frown.

"Nonsense, Jamal should be made comfortable, so you can also better focus on your work."

The urge to take a step back was strong. I wasn't sure if she was against him buying her or her son off, or if she had something against video games, but she seemed reluctant to take any handouts. It was like watching two alphas go head-to-head. Grim may be the god of death, but Miranda was a force to contend with. To be honest, I wasn't sure who I'd put my money on.

Before they started growling at each other, I interrupted. "Have you found anything?"

"I've definitely got something," Miranda said, snapping back into work mode. "You said the statue would likely need humidifiers and heat lamps to be preserved, and I found there were only three locations that rent those out. So, I called and found out two of the places rented out that equipment recently. I got the store manager to chatting, which wasn't hard. The first renters claimed it was for an outdoor 50th wedding anniversary party up in the mountains, while the second didn't specify why they needed the lamps."

"So it's probably the second guy," Jamal said, swiveling around in another chair.

"Not necessarily, boy wonder," I said. "The anniversary people could have been lying."

"That's why I had Javier check it out." Miranda sighed. "And indeed, the Rodriguezes have been married fifty years."

The door creaked behind us as Javier walked in on cue. He said in a Spanish accent, "They claim the recipe for a happy marriage lies in frequent, reciprocal back rubs and good green chili."

"Makes sense," I nodded.

The stone-faced Hispanic man served with Miranda in the Army and had also worked as security for Castlegate. Miranda had put in a good word for Javier, citing that they worked as a highly effective team, and apparently Grim hadn't wasted any time giving him a job.

My un-beating heart still fluttered. It wasn't only the way a man treated a woman, it was how he treated her friends that mattered. God, I was in such big trouble.

"Have you checked out the second renter?" Grim asked as Javier pulled out a chair next to Miranda's and took a seat. Jamal returned to the leather recliner in the corner, his attention already back on the game on his phone.

Miranda and Javier shared a look before Miranda spoke. "It would be helpful if we had a name or address, but we can't barge in there and demand his records. We aren't cops."

Grim waved a hand as if magically washing over the problem she presented. "Give the information to Timothy, and he will acquire a name and address for you."

The corners of Javier's lips turned down, while Miranda drummed her fingers along the desk. I wondered if Grim had known what he was in for when he'd hired these two. Knowing him, he probably had, and hoped to use that to his advantage.

My brain babbled about who else he could use to his advantage. Especially now that I'd kissed him. Would he think he could do whatever he wanted with me?

Nope, not going there right now.

So what if I'd bared the broken shards of my past to him? I had dirt on him, too.

Miranda spoke for both of them. "As much as we understand you want your property back, we don't care to break any laws in order to do it."

Grim was silent for a moment, while I bounced on my heels. Was he also thinking about spilling the beans? Did he desperately want to tell Miranda and maybe Javier what was going on? Gods, giant soul-eating crocodiles, and conspiracies?

Oh right, no. That was just me.

"I don't expect you to break any laws," Grim said. "I appreciate both of your hard work. Let Timothy take things from here."

A reaper trotted in the room. Though I knew Miranda, Javier, and Jamal couldn't see the reaper dogs, I still had to glance at them to see if they'd react.

The dog made a beeline for me, rubbing his head against my thigh, asking me to pet him. It would be weird if

I started petting empty air, so I ran my knuckles back and forth along his skull.

Then two, three more reapers trotted in, staring up at Grim with expectant, gold, glowing eyes.

Grim's jawbone shifted, already bracing himself.

It was great the worthy souls were still ferried directly to Osiris in the afterlife, but on top of internalizing all the souls that Grim needed to judge, the ones that were supposed to go straight to Amit were stretching Grim's body to the max. And good gravy, no wonder Timothy always ragged on Grim for being a workaholic. How many shitty souls did he have to feed to Amit a day? The answer was definitely not zero.

How long could he keep this up? I trusted Echo and Miranda to find something to lead us to Amit. But it had been twenty-four hours since Amit had gone missing, and I still couldn't wait around until Grim exploded or sucked everyone's souls by accident.

It was time to do some legwork of my own.

GRIM DISAPPEARED to absorb the souls, but not before trying to insist I drink from him again. I shot him a grin and insisted I was still full from the last time before making a hasty exit saying I needed to sleep since the sun was up now.

Sure, I was wearing Cookie Monster because my hunger chills made themselves known, but I didn't want to risk triggering Grim into another reaping episode. I'd also claimed I needed to return to my suite, and said I'd see him for dinner again unless we heard something from Echo or Miranda.

It wasn't a total lie. No, never mind, I had my own

mission to follow. Daylight be damned. I went back to my room, but only to grab a hair tie to throw my hair up in a ponytail. Counted enough for me.

Strangely enough, I wasn't exhausted like I usually was once the sun rose. Even inside the windowless hotel, I felt the sun sap my powers like Superman's kryptonite. But after drinking from Grim, I turned into Popeye loading up on a can of spinach. Which meant I had enough energy to follow my lead. Maybe if I drank even a little more from him next time, I would stay up all day and night.

Since Seth was so active on social media, he wasn't hard to track down. He was happy to post his controversial political opinions and take the time to troll his followers back with great vigor. And he'd do it all while poolside, with a priceless bottle of cognac nearby.

And one thing I'd learned after some social media stalking was his favorite breakfast spot. Ombos was a restaurant hotspot on the strip, at Seth's hotel, the Menaggio. The ceiling of colorful, glass-blown flowers was the main draw.

Seth was our guy. I just knew it. It was dangerous for me to go out in daylight, but it was worth the risk. I'd kept the keys to the car with UV treated windows and Grim hadn't noticed. After parking in the shady parking garage of the Menaggio, I was pleased to have made it inside to see Seth seated at his private table.

Twenty years ago, the blown glass installation was in the lobby, but when the hotel came under new management some years ago, they had moved it into one of the Menaggio's restaurants. It pissed off a lot of people that they couldn't just walk into the hotel and get a gander. Now they had to pay for an outrageously priced meal if they wanted a glimpse. Having met Seth, I knew the elitist dick move was intentional.

I requested to sit at the far side of the restaurant.

Thank the gods, *literally*, that the place was as windowless as the hotel lobby. With all the oohing and ahhing of a tourist, I pretended to examine the glass-blown flowers that decorated the ceiling.

Seth made it easy to watch him as he sat on the second level of the restaurant, as if he was doing everyone a favor, allowing them to watch him take breakfast. With any luck, I'd be able to watch and follow Seth until he would either lead me to Amit, or drop some clue about where the croc god was.

A server approached me. "The owner requests your presence."

Well, blood bags. So much for being discreet. Maybe I should have left Cookie Monster in the car. Perhaps the bright blue was a little conspicuous.

Following the server with every bit of swagger I could muster, I dropped into the seat across from Seth. Then I threw my boots up onto the edge of the white-clothed table. The god paused, digging into a bread roll with a healthy slathering of butter.

The server gave Seth a concerned look, but Seth waved him off. "It's fine, can you bring the woman a—"

"Juice box," I interrupted, not knowing what possessed me, but going with my mad impulse.

Both men paused, but then Seth nodded for the server to do as requested. Once he was out of earshot, Seth repeated, "Juice box?" No longer dressed in the extravagant, fashion-forward robes, the god wore a cream-colored suit and an eggshell blue shirt left open at the collar. He wore several strands of gold chains, several rings, and the most expensive watch I'd ever seen. Between his dress and smug expression, he seemed ready to jump on his private plane or party on some mega yacht with hoochie mamas and expensive champagne.

I shrugged. "It's not like I can order blood." Then dropping my feet and leaning in to whisper while looking around conspiratorially, "Or is it?"

"Does Grim appreciate your childish games?"

I shot him a grin. "The real question is, do you?"

"So I am meeting the real Vivien, at last. I can't deny I'm surprised. The pristine princess sekhor act seemed a tight fit over your bones." He dabbed at the corner of his mouth with his napkin.

What an asshat. I could be a princess if I wanted to be. Ninja princess. *I will karate chop you without losing my tiara, captain douche.*

Instead of voicing my thoughts, I said, "You missed a spot." Then I enjoyed watching Seth take extra care to wipe away the imaginary butter.

The server returned with a juice box. I took my sweet time unwrapping the straw.

"Why are you following me, Miss..."

"Just Vivien is fine," I said, poking my tongue out the side of my mouth as I carefully lined up the sharp end of the straw to the target hole.

Instead of answering, I took my time slicing through the juice box and sticking the straw inside. Then I bent it to the perfect degree before sipping.

Seth continued to stare at me as we played our silent battle of wills of who could piss the farthest. I drank the juice until it was empty, which was all too soon. Then I spent a full minute and a half slurping up any last errant drop. Diners nearby stopped and stared, while Seth continued with his best impression of a statue.

"Why are you following me?" His tone snapped like a rubber band.

Statues all crack and crumble, eventually.

Setting the empty juice box down, I asked, "The real question is, what is your problem with me? Or is it Grim you hate so much?"

A condescending smirk played at his lips. "Why don't you ask Grim?"

"Grim is too tight-lipped, plays things close to the chest, and says cryptic bullshit about how I wouldn't understand. But you, I figure you can level with me. It's clear you have no problem expressing yourself." Even if it threw a whole damn party into violent chaos.

Seth took great care to fold the napkin in his lap. "Like I said, we have a long history that is difficult to synopsize."

I interlaced my fingers and set my hands on my stomach as I leaned back. "But you're an articulate guy. I bet you could sum it up nice and tidy."

A darkness flashed in his eye. Maybe I pushed him too hard. But I'd also leaned on his vanity a couple times just now, and I'd placed a silent bet he melted under that a little each time I did it.

Seth rearranged the napkin in his lap and explained as if I were a simple child. "Grim is the god of the dead and wields the most powerful raw energy there is. That of a soul."

"Right, and you gods need to be near that source of power."

"Indeed, we feel the warmth and power, as if it were our own. But that is not all we can do with the power of souls. Grim, by decree of Osiris, keeps them under lock and key. We are here to serve humankind with our powers, but we could be so much more, do so much more if we had access to those souls."

I didn't think he realized he'd set an elbow on the table and grasped his hand into a fist. A hunger shone from his eyes. A look I'd seen a handful of times, but only in the eyes of madmen.

"You want to rule the world." It wasn't a question.

He dropped his arm and shrugged. "Not necessarily. We want to take our rightful place. At the top of the chain instead of spending our days in secret, catering to these"—he opened his hands to the people milling about us—"animals."

At that, a small snake slithered out of his sleeve. Icy fear clenched my insides. I hated snakes. He was trying to make me lose my cool.

Well, forget it, bucko. I pointedly ignored the teeny serpent and the larger one that followed it. Though my stomach did sickening flip-flops.

I grabbed one the rolls off his plate. "Must be frustrating." Then I took a big bite, doing my best to look enrapt in his description. Oh yeah, if he wasn't behind the theft of Amit and the whole conspiracy to upset the power among gods, I'd cut off my left boob.

Not the right one, though, never righty.

"Indeed," he continued, his tone more careful, "and now Grim has control over a sekhor, which makes me wonder..."

Oh goody, now it was my turn in the spotlight.

Seth folded his hands and looked over them at me. His expression sharpened as he surveyed me.

"Why does Osiris permit your blood bond? What is he having you do?"

The smaller snake wrapped around the large one, both raising their heads to look at me. Their forked tongues darted in and out. It took everything in me not to pull my arms back off the table, to recoil from them.

I debated between lying and giving him a smartass answer.

"Turns out, some scumbag is trying pull some shady shit and upset the balance. I'm here to help Grim make sure that doesn't happen."

A grinch-like smile curled Seth's lips up. "And you think you will be a key component in bringing down the conspiracy."

Ha! I never said conspiracy, but he did. Seth was definitely our guy. He basically confessed to it. But how it helped me, I struggled to see right now. He wasn't likely to tell me where Amit was. Maybe I could tell Grim to beat him up...again?

Seth leaned in. "You think you are out here operating of your own accord, playing Nancy Drew, but you don't know what I, Osiris, and Grim already know. You are just a pawn. You aren't the brains of this little operation. You are the junkyard dog, and when Grim tells you to jump, you'll jump. When he tells you to bite, you'll bite."

I tried to keep a straight face, but my stomach soured.

Tilting his head with a knowing smile, Seth added, "You think he won't do it, do you? Grim has promised never to hurt you, never to abuse your will. But you are the first sekhor he has taken and let me tell you, no one can resist that power. At first, the connection between god and sekhor is almost heavenly as it is earth-shattering. Not to mention, sexual." He smirked. "But over time it is easy for a god to come to terms with the only reason the link exists."

The larger snake moved up Seth's arm, and over his shoulder until it wrapped around him like a necklace. The little one edged toward me, watching me with those black eyes.

This time I moved back, taking my arms off the table. "To have a lifelong buddy for taco Tuesday?"

"To wield more power. One must use the link to their sekhor, to give their slave purpose."

I couldn't hide the sneer. "I'm no one's slave, and no one needs to give me purpose. I find plenty to do all on my lonesome."

He remained unaffected by my menace, tearing off another a piece of the roll, deliberate as he buttered the chunk of bread. Apparently, I bored him now. "Grim was the one responsible for eradicating all sekhors all those centuries ago, and he won't hesitate to do whatever he thinks is necessary if he believes it is the moral, correct thing to do. Especially if it pleases Osiris. You think he cares for you. But the honeymoon phase will end, and your appeal will wane until you are nothing but a tool to him." Then he popped the bite-size piece in his mouth, chewing at me like he'd just won some war.

"You don't scare me, Seth. You talk a big game, but the truth is you are a whiny brat who is jealous of Grim's toys."

As I leaned in, I keyed in on the distinct smell of lime that wafted off him. It was the same scent in the elevator, and then again on those gunmen from the club. Seth was at the center of this. All I needed to do was shake him down for Amit. Then we could all go home.

The snakes jerked their heads up as if they'd heard something. Then quick as lightning, they slithered back up Seth's sleeve.

He swallowed before speaking. "You're right. You've heard me speak a lot, but action is what makes history..." His face blurred and shifted until it rearranged into my uncle's face for the second time. Thick mustache, dark, hungry eyes, and salt-and-pepper hair. His body had once been strong from being a Navy captain, but it had softened as he aged. "...and history is inescapable."

A screeching sound brought me to my senses, and I realized I had violently slid the chair back against the tile floor and was now standing, drawing attention to myself.

Smiling with sick satisfaction, Seth said all too familiar words in my uncle's voice, "You see, Vivien, the way the world works, is some people are winners and the rest are sheep."

I was out of there like a shot. A mixture of my uncle's and Seth's laughter followed me. Panic tightened my chest, and an acrid taste took over my mouth. I couldn't see straight until a pair of strong arms caught me.

Looking up into the ice-blue eyes of Idris, I'd barely had time to recognize him before a needle plunged into the side of my neck.

"There, there, I won't let the bad man get you," the god cooed.

Oppressive, heavy darkness swept over me, and I was lost to the world.

17

The splitting headache woke me.

Idris. That sonofabitch drugged me. Between Idris and Seth's shitty shenanigans, I was getting real sick of bad men thinking they could do that whenever they damned well felt like it.

"You're awake. I'm glad. It was getting boring." Idris ran a finger along the steel table I was strapped to. The white tiled room smelled sterile, and the cold of the metal cuffs bit into my wrists and ankles. What I would have given to drink from Grim at that moment. Not only because I needed something to warm my blood, but so I'd be supercharged enough to pound Idris into a bloody pulp. I couldn't take on a whole ballroom of gods, but I bet after a healthy meal I could take on just the one.

"What did you give me?" My voice cracked.

"Don't worry your pretty little head about that."

"What the hell do you want, Idris?" I growled.

"Isn't it obvious?" He shrugged with a boyish smile. "You." His near-bleached blond hair was now a messy coif compared to the slicked-back style of the ball. He'd traded out the suit for casual wear, but he was still in all white. It seemed to be his signature as much as Grim's was black.

"Didn't your mother teach you no means no?"

His eyes darkened. "My mother taught me the only thing that matters in this world is power."

I was officially done with this game. If I could have smacked this god upside the head, I would have. "And what do I have to do with you getting power?"

Admittedly, the man was attractive as he smiled down at me. He was lean, young, and something about his face promised wild, carefree sex. I'd argue it would have been sexier if I weren't strapped to a table.

"You don't even know what you are capable of." Idris laughed in disbelief. "Grim won't show you because he is such a control freak, but you..." He shook a finger at me as he circled the table. "He could command you to take out these egotistic bastards and you'd do it. Just like that." He snapped his fingers.

"You mean the other gods? That's a load of bullshit. We both know they would kill me in a second."

Stopping at my feet, Idris put his hands on either side of my feet and leaned in. "Not if you were made powerful enough. Think about it. You and me, cutting our way through these outdated assholes and going straight to the top."

"Wow, have you talked to Seth? You guys should start a club."

"Fuck Seth," Idris said with sudden ferocity, his good humor vanishing. "You saw how demeaning he was to you. What if I gave you the power to kill him?"

"It's impossible to kill a god," I shot back.

A blond eyebrow rose and that wicked mirth returned to his expression. "Oh, I can't, but you can."

I shook my head in denial.

Rounding the table, Idris neared. "Grim wouldn't tell you, of course. It's forbidden. It's why the sekhors were exterminated. Vampires haven't been allowed to exist ever since they learned how to wield the power."

"What are you talking about, crazy pants?" While he went on like a lunatic, I tested my restraints. Metal shackles. Dammit.

He ran a long arm up by my head, leaning into me. "If you drink enough blood from a god, you will eventually become more powerful than you can imagine. Powerful enough to slay gods." With his other hand, he swept a finger down my cheek.

I wanted to jerk away but something in his eye stopped me. There was a deep pain buried there. For a moment, I found his pain as personal and dark as my own, though I couldn't explain why. Since I met Idris, I felt a kinship with him. Not just because he was young and irreverent compared the rest of the stuffy, scary gods. There was something deeper to him, and Idris used smoke and mirrors to cover up his pain. But he couldn't hide it from me. As I blinked, I realized he saw it in me too. There was recognition on his part. I couldn't hide my pain from him either.

"I don't want to kill gods," I said, staring up at him.

His finger traced down my neck, over my shoulder. Expression now deadly serious, he said, "Give it time. You will."

Then he walked out of view, behind me.

"I'm not going to bite you or drink your blood," I said to his retreating form.

Bending my neck at unnatural angle, I could see he walked over to a laptop that sat on a table. "I know. I saw the way you looked at Grim."

"What does that mean?"

Instead of answering, he typed a few things on his laptop.

"Hey, what does that mean, you saw how I looked at him?" I demanded. No one ignored Vivien the vampire. Rawr.

Even my bravado couldn't cover up the nerves in my belly that were insisting with each passing minute that I really needed to get the hell out of here.

Idris looked up at me from under his messy blond hair. "Like you'd follow him to hell and back, just to stay near him. Like you are in love."

Everything inside me stilled. Those weren't words dropping, they were bombs. The truth of what he said blasted through me with a vibrational violence. Now that I'd returned to Grim's side, it was painful to leave it. Need him? Sure. Want him? We'd broken that barrier. But love him? I would never admit it to myself. Not even on my dying day, but Idris threw up a mirror and showed me what I'd been hiding from myself.

Those near translucent blue eyes remained fixed on me. "I really am sorry for this."

"Sorry for wh—"

He tapped one last key and what felt like a hundred spikes cut through my body from the table underneath me. My cry of pain came out as a gurgle as blood filled my throat.

Then Idris was by me again, smoothing the hair back from my forehead as if it did anything to ease the pain lancing through me like a thousand knives.

"I know you won't betray Grim, but you have what I need. If I can't have you, I'll find a way to make someone like you."

Every second slowed into what felt like an hour as my life force ebbed out from me. Blood pooled from my body, trickling out to the side troughs, collecting the red liquid. The god's long, cool fingers disappeared.

Though my vision blurred through the intense pain, I could see him take a few steps back before disappearing into the next room, closing the steel door behind him.

Panic rose in my throat. I couldn't fight the restraints, and there wasn't any way I could slow the bloodletting. A croak came out from my throat as I tried to yell for help. Swallowing back the copper blood and bile, I tried again. This time my cry came out audible. Again, I yelled for help.

Was there any chance Idris had strapped me down to a torture table in earshot of anyone who could help? It wasn't likely.

Grim had warned me to stay away from Seth, he told me not to trust the other gods. But I'd been so thrown by my uncle's face a second time, I'd walked straight into the arms of the enemy.

Taking quick stock of my surroundings, I thought, yep, I might not get another chance to hold my own. Blinking, I realized I must have blacked out. For how long, I didn't know. I was so weak.

Did it make me weaker that I wanted Grim to bust down the doors and save me like he had in the past? Tears leaked out of my eyes, leaving hot trails down the sides of my face. I'd always been so careful to make sure I didn't need anyone, but right now I could use some saving.

The door creaked open, and I jerked. I must have blacked out again. A little part of me jumped for joy. It had to be Grim. He'd somehow known I'd gotten myself into trouble and he'd come. He had a sixth sense about when I was in danger.

Marcella stepped through the door, assessing me with a critical eye and pouty lip.

Oh shit, I really was going to die. The black goddess made me feel like the fungus under her toenails and must have been in with Idris to kill me.

A mewl of pain and surrender emerged from my throat.

Marcella walked over, her frown deepening, making her lips appear even fuller. "The idiot is going to accidently kill you."

I wanted to shoot back a witty retort but my mind was full of cotton and my tongue wouldn't obey me. A grunt came out instead.

Marcella walked over to sit in front of the laptop, likely to add some secondary form of torture to my current state. After tapping with impatience on the keyboard, Marcella stood and walked over to the table. "I was never any good with computers." She reached underneath the table and her arm jerked. There was an electric whine along with a sparking sound as if she'd yanked some wiring out. The spikes in my body dropped back into the table and I grunted in relief. Still, I could not get up, all my energy and power gone with my blood that disappeared into the troughs at my side.

Maybe if I rolled over and lapped at my own blood, I could get strong enough to stand? The thought was repulsive, but my will to survive was stronger.

An arm slipped under my shoulders, sitting me up. When I got a better look at the troughs, I realized they emptied into some kind of funnel that carried my blood in tubes down into the floor and away from me. More tears leaked out of my eyes, this time in frustration.

"We need to get you out of here," Marcella said, getting me to stand on useless noodle legs. My bright blue jacket had been tossed on the desk chair, so she threw it over my shoulders, but it did little to warm me. I was a frozen vamp-sicle. My fingers and eyelids were stiff from the relentless inner chill.

Marcella carried most of my weight. The goddess was strong, but the problem was I was quite a bit taller than her, which made it awkward for her to support me.

"Why?" I slurred.

"Because Idris will be back any minute."

With my arm over her shoulder, Marcella helped me stagger forward. She pushed the door open and we emerged into a refrigerated stock room full of liquor bottles. I was already so cold from the blood loss, but I didn't have the energy to shiver.

Licking my dry lips, I tried to speak again. "I won't bite you." If she thought Idris had made me weak enough to betray Grim, she had another thing coming.

Marcella's head snapped up to look at me with irritated impatience. "Of course not."

I must have blacked out again because the next time I came to, I was seated on what felt like a block of ice. With a bit of focus, I realized it *was* a block of ice. We were in some kind of ice bar. No one was around, though.

Marcella was texting someone and shooting furtive glances around.

With my last vestige of strength, I asked, "Why are you helping Grim?"

The goddess seemed to become even more offended as her face twisted in a sour scowl. "I'm not helping Grim. I'm helping you. Because I'm one of the only ones who didn't want to see the sekhors die." Unshed tears made her eyes glossy. Whatever agony she'd endured, it was as fresh to her as if it'd happened yesterday.

My surprise could only register at the back of my mind. I thought she'd hated me because I was a sekhor. I could not have been more wrong.

"We need to move," she said, getting me back on my feet. "We aren't far from Sinopolis."

My head was too heavy for my neck and I no longer had the energy to tell her, we would probably be too late.

18

The moment my eyes set on Vivien, a fury so overwhelming nearly had me burst into my godlikeness on the spot. Vivien's skin was so pale it was translucent, and her lips were blue. Her eyes were open, unseeing.

Marcella's appearance with Vivien also evoked gratitude and a deep pinching guilt. But I would pay my thanks to her later. She seemed to understand, because she hurried back out, along with Timothy, as soon as Vivien was situated on her side, on my couch. I'd removed her coat and shirt, leaving her clad in a bra. Puncture wounds lined her arms and legs, and her back was a bloody mess.

My hands shifted into long black talons and the penthouse shook from the power of my wrath as it vibrated off me. I wanted to turn fully animal, rage, and rip this world apart.

But Vivien wasn't dead yet. The glow of her soul's light was still visible, though dullened and flickering. Her condition was delicate and required me to keep it together. I shut my eyes and concentrated on shoving the swelling mount of my fury.

A god could get swept away in all that tumultuous emotion, and I couldn't afford that. Vivien couldn't afford it, time was running out. Bit by bit, my talons shifted back into fingers.

I dropped to my knees next to her, smoothing back her hair before cradling her head up, bringing her lips to my neck. "Vivien, you need to drink."

She didn't respond. Idris had almost bled her dry.

"Vivien," I scolded, as if she were a disobedient child, "Drink."

She remained nestled into the space between by neck and shoulder. Her lips moved, her words barely audible. "I'm not thirsty."

"Gods help me if you punish me for this later," I murmured.

I sunk power into the tether that bonded us together. My words came out sonorous with compelling force. "Vivien, drink." I'd promised never to wield her will. She might never forgive me, but I couldn't let her die. I refused to let her die.

Her teeth cut into my neck, finding the vein. The pain was brief, but I'd welcome a tsunami of blades if it meant she would drink from me. The first few sips were slow, laborious. Then soon enough she was clutching to me like a lost child, drinking deeply. My hand brushed against the back of her arms and felt the skin rapidly knitting back together where there had been gaping flesh wounds. She was recovering.

As she drank harder, faster, her fingers dug into my back. I couldn't help the arousal she incited. She moaned and writhed against me. I wanted to give it to her. All of it. I would turn myself inside out if I could produce the very last bit of blood, so she would live.

Fear wound around me, squeezing with lethal pressure. I swore I wouldn't lose control of my emotions like this again. I couldn't afford it. The world couldn't afford it. But it didn't make it any less true that I would have given anything to revive the vampire in my arms.

Our positions shifted as she drank more, until Vivien was on top of me, legs on either side of my hips. She'd consumed enough of my blood to heal all of her wounds, but I couldn't let her go just yet. A growl broke from my throat as she ground her hot center down onto my hardness. She moaned in ecstasy. I had to stop her. If she drank too much, she would become too powerful and the others would kill her. Osiris would end her in a moment.

"Vivien," I rasped, as she continued to grind and suck. My hands grabbed her hips, halting them. The sharp movement broke her concentration and Vivien sat back, some of my blood trickling down the side of her mouth. Fangs extended, and her sea-green eyes were glossy with bloodlust. There was an innate elegance and violence to all vampires, but on Vivien, she was a force that could move the speed of the earth. She took my breath away.

"Did I do that?" she asked quietly. The top buttons of my black shirt had been ripped off when she tried to get closer. Blood trickled down my exposed collarbone, but I could feel my skin healing already.

Vivien's skin was hot and flushed—she'd be fine. Thoughts of wanting to rip myself apart to save her echoed back to me. Not even for Qwynn had I been so willing to give up everything. It was the very thing Qwynn wanted of me, but I couldn't give it to her. But for Vivien...I was scared of what I might do. The god of death couldn't allow this sekhor to die.

"Why you?"

I didn't realize I'd said the words out loud until she said, "Why me, what?" Her words were slurred.

I didn't answer. Instead, I pulled her down, kissing her with all the fear and desperation I'd felt at having almost lost her. Vivien didn't hesitate to reciprocate. She allowed me to plunge my tongue into her mouth, needing to be inside her in any way possible. Vivien's nails dragged through my hair, sending electric shocks straight to my already hard length.

I stood and carried Vivien to my bedroom, massaging her perfect ass along the way. Her glow surrounded both of us, and it was like being kissed by the sun.

My bed chambers were of the gothic persuasion, complete with deep plum tufting and dark, paneled walls. I dropped Vivien onto the oversized bed of silk sheets. Leaning back on her elbows, she looked up at me.

This was the moment. She would jump up and scream at me for breaking her trust. For forcing her hand, making her feed. She didn't want me. I'd trapped her against her will.

Still, I pulled my shirt off over my shoulders.

"Tell me to stop," I said, unable to do it myself. I needed to hear her say it. I needed her to go off on how she loathed me in colorful epitaphs and creative curses, and I would back off.

With a barely perceptible shake of the head, she remained silent.

My knees hit the edge of the bed. I undid my belt, slowly, deliberately. The need to make her mine, make her scream with pleasure until she could think of no one and nothing else, rose into an almost unstoppable wave. But it was still cresting. Once I released it, there would be no stopping.

"Vivien, tell me to stop, or I won't until I've made you come more times than you have in your mortal life."

The zipper to my pants slid down with a sharp hiss and still she said nothing.

"Vivien," I growled in warning. Leaning over, I put my hands down on the bed on either side of her legs. Taking my time, I crawled up, hovering over her body. The haze of bloodlust cleared from her eyes, but Vivien's pupils dilated as she looked up at me like she needed a second meal.

"I won't hold back."

Challenge flickered in her eyes. "Promise?"

With that simple word, she broke the chain holding my beast back. I ripped her clothes off in mere seconds, then rid myself of pants.

I pushed her up the bed and covered her body with mine. Taking my hard cock in my hand, I positioned myself at her entrance. It was already slick, hot, and inviting. I rubbed the tip against her opening, reveling in her readiness for me. A choked groan came out of her throat. The challenge in her eyes dared me to go faster.

Instead, I leaned over to capture her lips in another kiss, this time with aching tenderness. She wasn't just another woman in my bed. This wasn't about relieving pent-up desire...or it was, but also so much more than that. The hurry to join with her fell away as I kissed her with all the reverence I could muster. I may be a god, but it was my turn to worship another.

Vivien's hands cupped my face as she matched my rhythm, teasing my tongue and moaning her approval. Then her hands moved down to press against my backside as her kiss became more urgent.

I obeyed, sliding into her in one long stroke. We both cried out as I filled her. All logic fled, as my senses honed in on how fucking hot and tight Vivien was. She clenched around me with possessive friction. There was nothing but her heat, her skin, her eyes. Vivien sunk her nails into my ass as I began to thrust into her. My release pounded against the door, in a battle with my willpower. In all my years on earth, never had I wanted to give in so quickly, or make something last forever.

Then we rolled and she hovered over me, riding me hard, sinking her nails into my chest. My hands found her hips, guiding her, while my eyes were fastened to her expression of pleasure. That alone was enough to push me to my limits. The way her fangs elongated before she bit her bottom lip.

She was sensual, wild, and fucked me with utter abandon. There was censorship to her responses, and it's what made her pleasure so easy to find. I slipped a hand between us and played with her tight bud.

Sea-glass-colored eyes snapped open as she gasped. For a moment she was frozen, looking at me as if shocked I stopped time itself for her. Then she broke into shudders, arching her beautiful breasts into the air as she succumbed. I wanted to take those pink peaks into my mouth, but I wouldn't interrupt her riding the waves of her orgasm for anything.

Unbidden flashes of her near-lifeless face as she lay on my couch went through my mind.

As Vivien came down from her high, I rolled us, so I covered her once again. I ran a hand over her soft hair and forced her to meet my eyes. I needed to know she was here with me, that I wasn't alone. Never before had I been compelled to feel so utterly connected with a woman.

Usually, the pursuit of orgasm with my partner resembled a challenge or a race. This was something else entirely.

The dark souls inside took advantage of the moment, pushing, straining to get out. This time I groaned in pain as I felt them stretch me to my limits.

Vivien's hand slid up the side of my face, drawing my attention back to her. She gave me a look so tender and fragile, as if she was afraid of what was happening inside her. I knew what she felt.

The light of her glow flowed up into me while the darkness of my power mingled with hers. We were becoming inextricably entwined in a way I'd never thought possible. I felt it at the root of my core. Vivien had become as essential to me as the sun was to the earth. I would perish without her.

My need for Vivien slammed the rioting souls inside me with a force I didn't know I possessed. Then it was only her and me again.

The deliciously sinful sounds coming from her throat as she squirmed under me got me moving again.

Our moans of pleasure wove around each other as I sped up. Time disappeared as I rocked into her, trying to elicit the loudest, most drawn-out moans and screams of pleasure. I dipped down, capturing a pert nipple, rolling it between my teeth. She jerked and arched under my ministrations.

The friction drove me to near madness, as I gritted my teeth, holding my release at bay. I was on the edge, and I needed her there with me.

"Do you want to come?" I asked.

She squeezed her eyes shut and shook her head. Stubborn to the end. She didn't want to finish, though I could tell she was close. Based on my earlier research, I recognized the signs and sounds she made as she neared the edge.

"You are going to come," I informed her.

Those green eyes pinned me with white-hot fire. "You are so bossy," she managed to get out.

"You think I'm a control freak?" Then I lowered my mouth, so it was even with her ear. "You have no idea."

With that, I pulled out of her. Vivien cried out in dismay, but I flipped her and pulled her back onto her knees, my hand around her throat as I thrust into her from behind. Our bodies were now glistening, slick with sweat. We both gasped as I reached new depths inside her. From this angle, I fucked her faster, harder, deeper than before.

The sight of her perfect, round ass and long elegant span of her back was shockingly erotic. The urge to sink my teeth into her buttock passed through me, but I wasn't willing to give up my current position.

Vivien's fingers repeatedly clutched and released the sheets. I tightened my grip around her throat and her guttural groan vibrated against my palm.

My lips curved up.

The sounds she made were like a map. When I followed the pitch and volume, they led me to the angle and speed that had her gasping and crying out, near sobbing with pleasure. She bucked against me, uncontrollably.

Pressing my mouth against her ear, I used my other hand to reach down between her legs to find the center of her pleasure. "You are going to come for me." I rubbed her clit, and she cried out. Shudders wracked her inside and out as she succumbed.

She was mine, and I felt it in every atom of our joined bodies. Vivien drove me to distraction in a way I'd never known. I never wanted to live without her.

My blood pounded as my arousal built to an almost unbearable pressure.

I slammed into her harder from behind and continued rubbing between her legs until she came a second time. I joined her then, the intensity of my orgasm turning my vision black around the edges. The room shook until a mirror fell off the far wall, smashing into sharp splinters in a beautiful cacophony.

Falling back on the sheets, I panted, trying to recover. Vivien landed next to me. On her side, she stared at me in wonder, while also trying to catch her breath. It was one of the small things I loved about her. She often forgot she didn't need to breathe and simulated it, anyway. I hoped she never stopped.

"I should kick your ass," she finally said, though there was no real heat behind her words.

I raised an eyebrow in question, but not before wrapping an arm around her and pulling her close. She rested her head on my shoulder but positioned herself so she could look up at me.

I expected she'd rail at me for breaking my promise, for bending her will to mine. And she could berate me all she wanted, but she'd have to do it naked while allowing me to touch her.

"You are absolutely the bossiest, even in the bedroom. I mean, I knew you were a control freak, but I bet you have chains, cuffs, or ropes around here somewhere." She feigned looking around the room for them.

Lowering my voice, I said, "What if I told you I had all three?"

Lust ignited in her eyes again as she licked her lips. "I'd say that as your sekhor, I have to perform an audit to verify your claims. But I'll be wielding my own whip." She grinned.

My cock twitched against her leg.

"Oh, someone likey," she taunted with glee.

Reaching over, I pushed the hair back that stuck to her damp, glistening face. My thumb ran back and forth along her jawline. "You're alright?"

The question was loaded with meaning. Not only had I taken her will, forcing her to feed from me, we'd crossed a new threshold of intimacy. She hadn't stopped me, but now in the aftermath, I questioned myself. Was I too rough, too demanding, truly too controlling? I believed she enjoyed herself and with any other woman I wouldn't have worried, but she was my sekhor and I hadn't held back. I couldn't remember the last time I acted on pure pleasurable instinct like that. And I couldn't ever remember feeling so unsure of myself in the aftermath.

Her smile faltered as she met my searching gaze, as if taking the time to seriously consider my ask.

Then in a lower voice I added, "I don't want to control you."

A hesitant smile played at her lips, but it didn't reach her eyes. "Well, I guess the only way to even the odds is next time I get to chain you up and have my way with you. In the spirit of fairness, of course."

I couldn't help the grin that sprang to my face. "Of course." Then I kissed her. It was slower, searching, more tender but no less passionate than the previous kisses. The desire to wring more pleasure from her body began to make itself known again. I hadn't forgotten my promise to make her come more times than she'd ever in her mortal life.

Something rolled in my stomach with a weighty lurch. When I pulled back, Vivien's hooded gaze sharpened.

"Grim..." she said in warning, her hand coming up to stroke my face. Sitting up, I could see myself in the remaining mirror on the wall. Dark, near-purplish veins covered my face, traveling down my neck, chest, and shoulders. My eyes were black as coal. Another internal lurch had me pressing a hand against my stomach in a futile attempt to calm the internal cacophony.

Vivien was out of the bed like a shot. "Okay, fun time is over. We need to go track down Seth and smack him around until he tells us where Amit is."

Panic rose up my throat. She disappeared into my closet, emerging in one of my button-down shirts and was cinching it in the middle with one of my belts. I was considerably taller than her, so it came down to her mid-thigh, giving the appearance of a dress.

I rounded the bed, still undressed, to stand in front of her. "You are not leaving this penthouse again."

Irritation warred with indignation on her face. "Grim, we are running out of time. Seth all but admitted to stealing Amit. I can smell it on him. We need to shake him down, now."

"You almost died."

"And you might be dying right now," she said angrily.

I didn't contradict her. I'd told her gods couldn't die, but I knew I was being torn apart from the inside out. No one knew the scent of death better, and I reeked of it.

Her lips tightened. "Unlike you, I can't sit around and do nothing."

"Well, that's exactly what you are going to do. You are not to go near Seth again, do you understand me? He is dangerous and would delight in toying with us, wasting time. Going after Seth would achieve nothing. We are best to continue searching for Amit, and by we, I mean me and

Timothy. You've helped enough by contacting Echo and soliciting her help, and Miranda is also on the case." I strode into my closet, and she followed, not done arguing.

"You need all the help you can get," she said as I quickly dressed.

"You're right, I do." I grabbed my cellphone to shoot off a couple messages in quick succession.

Anger welled up inside me, fueled by the darkness I held at my center. Vivien was right. I had forgone my duties, more concerned with her. I cared about Vivien's safety more than doing what must be done.

And the moment I lost myself to Vivien, I lost sight of what was important.

I needed to find Amit, protect the souls of this realm. The simplest way to do that meant removing Vivien from the equation, whether she liked it or not. Then I could do what must be done without distraction, while keeping her safe at the same time.

Infusing my words with steel, I gripped her arms to make sure I had her attention. "I will deal with Seth and Idris, while you will stay in the penthouse until I get back."

Eyes narrowing, Vivien met my warning glare. "Back to being a controlling asshole, are we?"

Her words felt like a splash of ice water. Any trace of our intimacy vanished.

A series of sickening jerks inside my torso sent a sour taste into my mouth. "I guess so."

The elevator pinged as it opened. Timothy and Fallon stepped into the room. I grabbed my jacket and said to them, "We are going hunting."

Fallon shifted back and forth from foot to foot, while Timothy's lips tightened with worry. They must have sensed the tension in the room.

I started to join them, and Vivien followed. I whirled around.

"If you insist on following, I will have to either tie you up, or make you obey." My threat rang in the air. The moment I said it, I wished I could take it back. Not because I didn't mean it, but because of the pain and betrayal that flashed in her eyes. Even as she glared at me, she took one step back.

I joined Timothy and Fallon in the elevator. As the doors shut, I expected her to yell insults, hurl an object at me, or some last demonstration of defiance. But she remained silent to the last. It was worse somehow. I would have preferred she scream how much she hated me. But I wasn't sure she could hate me more than I despised myself in that moment.

19

After Grim left, I jumped into the guest room shower. I'd give them a couple minutes head start before I struck out on my own.

At first, I thought to take advantage of Grim's personal shower with the waterfall showerhead and multiple jets. But I didn't want to smell his soap. In fact, I worked hard to scrub his delicious yet infuriating scent off me.

How could I hand over every part of myself to that imperious alpha-hole? Wasn't it enough he controlled my will, I had to hand over my body and heart to the insufferable bastard? Scrubbing my skin until it turned red, I berated myself for making such a massive mistake.

It wouldn't happen again, though. And Grim should have tied me down when he had the chance, because there was no way in Egyptian hell I was going to stay here and do nothing.

Stalking out of the bathroom, keyed up, it surprised me to find some of my own clothes laid out on the guest bed. I hadn't heard or sensed anyone. But I'd been so caught up in my head, fantasizing beating Grim with a sock filled with cold butter, I wasn't surprised I missed it.

Throwing on the black leggings and a crop top with a gap slit between the breasts, I grabbed my boots and walked out into the main area. I stopped short when I discovered I wasn't alone.

Galina was gracefully positioned on the couch with a book. Her long legs stretched out as perfectly as if she were at a photoshoot. There was a cool, supermodel, I-don't-give-a-fuck vibe about her that I found both calming and intimidating.

"What are you doing here?" I asked, sitting down in a leather chair across from her to pull on my boots.

Dropping the book, she gave me a wry smile. "I believe I'm on what you would call bodyguard duty."

Fucking Grim. I was going to kill him.

"Does he always get everything his way?" I ground out, yanking on my second boot with unnecessary violence.

The side of her mouth quirked up in a secret smile. "Usually."

"Can I ask you a question?"

"Anything," she said airily. An orange tabby slunk around the edge of the couch and leapt onto Galina. She stroked its back while it stared at me from her lap. Right, Galina was Bast. The cat goddess.

"What is the difference between a god and a demigod?"

"Power," she answered without hesitating. "A demigod is often young and yet to come into the full force of their power. Some never graduate to full godhood because they squander their powers."

Grateful to finally be getting some straight answers, I asked, "How can you squander power?"

Galina scratched between the tabby's ears and the cat's

eyes turned to slits of pleasure as it purred. "One way is by not using them enough, or correctly. A god's power is like a muscle. Like a muscle, powers can atrophy if they aren't used. Or if they are overextended, they can be injured, like pulling a muscle. Some demigods bandy about their powers like human teenagers, and thusly weaken themselves. There's something to be said about working smarter, not harder."

"So in the way a human can pull a hammie, you and Grim can stunt your power?" I had a feeling Galina was dumbing things way down for me, but I didn't mind.

Her laugh was light and charming. "Grim and I are not in danger of such a thing. We are too old to make such amateur mistakes. We know our limits. Well, Grim knew his limits..." She trailed off.

Did she mean because of me? Or was she aware that he was stretching himself far beyond his abilities, subsuming all those souls? Grim acted like he could handle anything, but he needed help.

She went on. "There is also the power of souls. When gods are worshipped, they are fed by the souls of their followers so they can become even more powerful."

"So every time someone goes to church and prays, a god can get more powerful?"

"Not anymore." Galina's long lashes swept down as she regarded the cat while she scratched under its chin. Another black cat padded in from the kitchen and hopped up to the chair across from me. "No one prays to the old gods, or at least, very few still do."

"You guys are pretty big on social media. I feel like that would count as worship." Seth wasn't the only one with a staggering amount of followers proclaiming their love for him.

She nodded. “True, but our ancient names must be evoked in prayer to pledge power, but Osiris has forbidden us from taking on followers for several thousand years. Gods fought for followers, souls, and power and ended up warring more often than not. It is why we do not use our true names among humans.”

“And the souls that Grim protects...”

Galina looked up at me now. She didn’t hide that she was impressed with my series of questions. I may be new to the game, but I was a quick study. “He keeps them under lock and key from the rest of us. Osiris trusts Grim above all else to never use his power for his own gain. Osiris believes this world belongs to humanity and we are the guardians. Anyone who becomes too powerful, he considers a danger to this realm. And Grim is the duty-bound son who helps keep the order of such things.”

“Yeah, Seth all but said he resented Grim for being the good son.”

Galina sighed. “There are ages of history there, all involving Seth’s jealousy. He once slayed Osiris, but Grim resurrected him.”

“Seth killed Osiris for power?”

Leaning in with a devilish spark in her eye, Galina said, “Seth killed him because his wife lay with Osiris, his own brother.”

Wow. Galina was the go-to gal for spilling all the tea. Seth and Osiris were brothers, and Seth’s wife banged the big O?

“Not only that, Seth’s wife and Osiris’s union bore a child.” She shot me a pointed look.

Oh snap. “Grim?”

She nodded slowly. “Grim is a constant reminder of the infidelity. No, never mind Seth has slept with about a million concubines." She waved her hand in dismissive disgust. "Her betrayal is still an affront to his power and ego, feeding the spark of his anger and resentment. So as you can see, Seth despises Grim and Osiris, and believes he should act as head of the gods."

No wonder Seth stole Amit. Destroy Grim, grab all the souls and power he can, and let gods reign over the earth again.

"So you see why Grim doesn't want you going near Seth," she said gently.

"Because Seth is a jealous evil dickweed, got it."

She laughed in that airy way again. "Seth isn't evil, but he is the god of chaos. He wishes to change the shape of things and can, of course, change his own shape as well." Her tone became serious. "Chaos is an acquired taste, as it has violent effects. Few can handle that. Yet some of the most chaotic moments in history have brought about the necessary change humanity needs to grow."

As much as I hated to concede her point, without a few protests, riots, and wars, evil would have continued its reign unchecked. But I was no philosopher, and I was far from thinking about global events from the macro perspective of a god. So, I put those considerations in a box to ponder another day. Preferably with a six pack of beer and Miranda around, who always seemed to add good insight to situations.

"What about Idris? That asshole drained me dry of my blood because he wants a vampy plaything of his own. Is he also looking to take over the world?"

Galina's eyebrows shot up in surprise, but she recovered quickly enough. "Ah yes, that brings us to another class of demigods. Some will never achieve the status of full godhood because mortal blood runs in their veins. But if

Idris possessed a sekhor, or perhaps a group of them, he could wield them as a weapon to gain power even if he can't achieve full godhood."

"What does Idris want all that power for?"

She shook her head. "I couldn't say. I've not conversed with the demigod enough to take notice of his agenda."

I had one more god left on my list to figure out. "Marcella?"

A somber expression of near pity came over Galina's face. The tabby leaned his head back and meowed at Galina as if to say, 'it's okay, mama, I'm here.'

"Oh yes, poor Marcella. When she saw Grim waltz into the ballroom with you on his arm, she verily shattered on the spot. She'd attempted to come to terms with Grim slaying her soulmate all those years ago, but everyone knows she has never recovered. Grim had no choice but to exact Osiris's will, exterminating an entire race. Though he did add his own zeal of prejudice and violence to his duties. But then to walk into that room with you, as his bonded sekhor..."

No wonder Marcella looked like she would blow a gasket. To her, Grim must have appeared to be the most hypocritical son of a bitch of all time. Still, she helped me. I needed to thank her for that.

Absorbing the windfall of information, I rubbed my temples.

"Now that I've answered your questions, I have one for you," Galina said, sliding on the couch and bringing her legs around to set her feet on the rug. The tabby jumped off her lap with a discontented meow.

It was only fair. She'd all but handed over physical dossiers, complete with favorite colors and social security numbers. "Shoot."

"I'm surprised you are so adamant to...help, Grim."

"What do you mean?"

Galina seemed to search for words, as if she could put it more delicately. "From what I understand, I'm here to keep you from gallivanting off to pick a fight with Seth, so you could discover the whereabouts of Amit."

I refrained mentioning the missing crocodile god, but Grim must have confided in her.

She went on. "But you seem to resent the control Grim has over you. Did he somehow force you into this blood bond against your will?"

The words were on the tip of my tongue, how I'd asked Grim to save Jamal's life, how Grim explained a price must be paid in exchange. Since I couldn't bargain with my soul, he took my will in a blood bond. So the answer was yes and no. But something told me to hold back from divulging all the details. It seemed too...intimate to share.

"Let's say I didn't know what I was getting myself into."

"Meaning, you resent how he uses you?"

"I'm not Grim's bitch," I said, referring to Seth's tasteless gift. "He doesn't use me like a tool. Grim knows I'd kick his ass if he tried."

The way her eyes darted away, I knew she thought my sense of control in the situation was deluded.

"But you don't want the blood bond dissolved?" she asked.

I didn't answer right away. Of course, I didn't want Grim controlling me, and I was mad as a bag of shaken hamsters right now, but I got the sense she was alluding to something specific.

Galina filled the void with those specifics. "Because, if Grim doesn't find Amit soon, and he takes a turn for the worse..." She wasn't crass enough to say he would die out loud. “Then you would be freed from your bond. A free agent once again. Granted, a number of gods would seek you out for their own purposes, but I’ve no doubt you could hold your own.”

While I appreciated her vote of confidence, I was still chewing on the new bit of information. If Grim went nuclear, the blood bond would be broken. It hadn’t occurred to me before that there was a way I could ever get out from under Death’s thumb again. My heart squeezed with warring desires.

“But gods can’t die.”

A curious expression flitted over her face.

“And this world needs a Grim Reaper, right? That wouldn’t even be possible.”

Galina’s voice softened. “It is very difficult to kill a god, but not impossible. And if Grim does not survive, another will be appointed god of the dead.”

As angry as I was at him trying to house arrest me, and boss me around per usual, the idea of Grim dying made my stomach lurch with nausea and dread. And a new god of the dead? My mind couldn’t even wrap around that one.

“I don’t want him dead.”

Galina rushed to speak. “Of course not. I wasn’t saying you wanted him to die. I was just wondering. Don’t mind me. I’m nosy and it was an impolite question.”

I shook my head, dismissing her apology. Despite all her answers, more questions swirled around my head. Did I want to be free of Grim that badly?

“Well,” I slapped my legs as I stood, “I’m jonesing for caffeine and some sugar. I’m going to jog down to Perkatory and see about fixing that. Can I get you anything?”

A sly, feline smile slid across Galina’s face. We both knew I wasn’t allowed to leave the penthouse and that Grim would tear both her and me to shreds if she let me out of her sight.

Then Galina reached over and picked up her book, resuming her elegant repose. “Pick me up a milk steamer with vanilla, whole milk,” she said, as her eyes scanned the pages.

The cat goddess was a rebel. I liked her.

To be fair, I wasn’t totally lying. I did stop by Perkatory.

Much to my delight, Aaron was behind the counter again. The devilishly attractive surfer boy grinned when he saw me. “I-I-I was beginning to think you were mad at me.”

“Why would I be mad at you?” I asked, confounded.

“Maybe I didn’t put enough s-sprinkles on your drink, so you weren’t coming back?”

“Well, Aaron.” I leaned an elbow on the counter. “I forgot to count them the last time, so load me up with another, and extra sprinkles because I *will* be counting this time.” He laughed as I shot him finger guns. “I will also need one of those cream puffs.” The need to press my nose against the glass to get closer to the confection was strong. The fact that my sensitive vampire taste buds allowed me to taste all the better was something I would not waste.

At least, Grim couldn’t say I was getting in trouble. I was just shot-gunning sugar, preparing for the trouble I was gearing to get into.

The smell of gardenias and gunpowder cut through the sugary aromas, and I knew Miranda was behind me before I turned around. “There you are,” she said.

“Hello, friend,” I said, turning.

“Friend my ass, we need to talk.” Miranda grabbed my

arm and dragged me over to the other end of the cafe, where a bunch of tall tropical bushes gave us the illusion of privacy.

"What the hell is he?"

I didn't even pretend I didn't know what she was talking about. Our talk was well overdue.

"I can't tell you."

"I saw Mr. Scarapelli, my boss, turn into a scary-ass monster that made me feel like the world was about to end."

For her, it almost had.

"Then you stopped him doing whatever gut-wrenchingly awful thing I knew was about to hit, by kissing him until he turned back to normal. *Then* Timothy swept through like a hurricane, sweeping up the mess, convincing everyone it was nothing. Does he have mind control powers, by the way? I can't believe people still come back to this hotel with all the shit that goes down."

Huh, I actually didn't know how Timothy swept violent incidents away so that patrons and party-goers kept returning to Sinopolis. I'd bet my left boob it was a supernatural thing, though.

Miranda poked a finger in my chest. "Answers, now."

Raising my hands in the air, I said, "Seriously, I can't tell you. I wish I could, it's just one of those *things*." I stressed the last word, hoping she'd get my meaning.

"One of those things, meaning some crazy supernatural shit keeping you from telling me, though you can't tell me why?"

I held out my arms. "Lethal, hot, *and* smart. This is why I love you."

"Verbally blow me later. I plan to figure this out." She chewed on her lip for a second. "What if you don't tell me? What if I guess it?"

How long would it take for Miranda to guess Grim was Anubis, god of the dead? Probably a while.

She must have caught my skeptical expression. She said, "Or maybe you could help me by acting it out since you can't say the words. Yeah, would something like that work?"

I brightened at her ingenuity. "Like Charades? Maybe. I haven't tried that."

Aaron showed up with my frozen coffee dessert and cream puff in a baggie. "What are we doing hiding back here? S-s-secret meeting?" There was a mixture of mirth and confusion in his sparkling blue eyes. Good god, they even reminded me of Hawaiian ocean waters. No wonder Timothy was crushing hard.

Miranda snatched the goodies from Aaron before he could hand them over. "We are playing a game of charades." Then, to me, she waggled the drink and bag at me. "You can have these after."

"Rude," I pouted. I considered snatching them from her, but Aaron would likely get suspicious of my vampiric reflexes if I used them against Miranda.

Instead of leaving us to play in the bushes by ourselves, Aaron remained where he was, wanting to be part of it. Miranda didn't send him away, so I guess this was going to be a group effort.

Okay, Vivien, let's think. How can we mime god of the dead?

My first instinct was to flail wildly, throwing my hands toward the heavens as if god were looking down on me, but that would likely come off a bit psychotic and not very helpful.

Flap my hands like wings until they guessed angel and then hope they guessed heaven or god from that? Blood bags. This was going to be a lot harder than I thought.

"You do know how to play Charades, right?" Miranda asked.

Aaron's stutter worsened. "If it—if it—if it's more than one word, you have to s-s-signal."

This probably wasn't the best game for him, but he seemed adament to play even if it was frustrating to get words out.

I would have been offended by their bossiness if a lightbulb hadn't lit up over my head. I knew what to do now.

I tapped my arm with four fingers.

"Four s-s-syllables," Aaron said.

Gah, I didn't know Charades as well as I thought. I shook my head and held up four fingers.

"Four words," Miranda said. I nodded.

I held up one finger.

"F-first word," Aaron said.

Cupping my hand to my ear.

"Hearing, listening," Miranda started shooting off.

I stopped and rolled my eyes.

"N-n-no," Aaron turned to her. "In Charades, that means 's-sounds like.'"

As I nodded he was correct, Miranda sipped on my drink.

"Hey," I said in a whiny voice.

"No talking in Charades," Miranda shut me down, using her mom voice.

Cupping my ear again, I then held up my hands, wrists turned down, as I stuck my tongue out like I was panting.

"T-t-thirsty," Aaron guessed, breaking off a piece of my cream puff and popping it into his mouth.

A sound of protest and disappointment came out of me.

"Hey, focus on the game," Miranda snapped at me,

pausing from sipping off my drink again. "Aaron will get you another when you are done."

The blond barista nodded as he tore off another chunk of pastry and ate it.

Why did I only hang out with bossy people? Was I naturally drawn to them? Or did I look like I enjoyed being told what to do?

Tyrants.

Back to the game. I continued to pretend to pant while holding my hands up. For added effect, I wiggled my butt.

"Dog," Aaron said, getting it right the second time. I snapped my fingers in approval and he launched into guessing what sounded like a dog. "B-bog, grog, fog."

I groaned. This was going so well.

Miranda sipped on *my* drink, a deep line of concentration between her drawn eyebrows. I could practically smell the burning of her brain as it worked overtime.

"God." She was so quiet, I almost missed it. I snapped my fingers in approval.

"G-god?" Aaron said. "I would have picked a d-different word than dog to rhyme with, but okay." Almost half my cream puff and drink were gone. This game needed to pick up.

I held up four fingers to indicate the fourth word. Then I pantomimed a noose over my neck and pulled it up, allowing my tongue to loll out of my mouth again.

"Hung?" Aaron guessed, then laughed.

This time, I crossed my arms over my chest and leaned back, closing my eyes.

"D-dead," Aaron guessed correctly. He was good at this game.

"God, dead, four words," Miranda said, thinking out loud.

Aw crap, how did one pantomime 'of the'? But I didn't have to.

"God of the dead?" Aaron said off the cuff with a doubtful laugh. Before I could confirm he was right, Aaron's attention was drawn back to the café cart where a couple of people were waiting to order.

"D-duty calls," he said, handing me the last quarter of my cream puff and jogging over to help the customers. I popped the last piece into my mouth. I'd earned it, dammit.

"That's it, isn't it?" Miranda said in a low voice. "Grim Scarapelli is the god of the dead." She stared at the plants behind me with a haunted look on her face.

When I went to confirm she was right, this time I couldn't. My limbs and tongue froze like it usually did, keeping me from sharing. But Miranda already got it. She was smart to have us play Charades. I was more focused on the game, so it bypassed whatever mental block Grim had created.

Then, meeting my gaze, Miranda reached back to find a chair and lowered herself into it. I yanked my coffee from her and began sucking on it.

Her voice was barely above a whisper. "I knew he was embroiled in some kind of supernatural bullshit, what with fighting vampires and all, but a god?"

Miranda needed time to process, so I continued to drain my cup, slurping up the last bits of whipped cream.

"Is-is he evil?" She almost seemed afraid to ask the question. That made sense considering how much she'd let Jamal around him, and now worked for him. Little did she know it was technically Grim who saved Jamal from dying.

"No." I sat down in a seat next to her and played with my straw. "Controlling and powerful, but not evil. Believe it or not, he's one of the good ones." And he was. Grim cared about protecting this earth and the souls. He cared about me.

"One of the good ones," Miranda repeated slowly. "Because there is more than one god."

"You said it, not me," I said, breezing past her realization. "Next time there is a game night, I want you and Aaron on my team."

My cell phone vibrated against my thigh. I pulled it from my pocket and saw Bianca's face flashing on the caller ID. There was a tightness in my stomach, as if my body sensed something was wrong. I answered the call.

"Bianca?"

"Oh god, Vivien, something terrible has happened." Bianca's voice was unsteady with fear and emotion. I couldn't see her, but I sensed the goddess had tears welling in her eyes.

I shot up to my feet. "What's happened?" Icy shock curled around me before I even knew what was wrong. Mirandas stilled, her attention now sharp as a blade as she listened to my side of the conversation.

"I-I had a vision." Bianca rushed to get the words out, but was still overwrought. "There was blood, so much blood."

"Where? Is it Grim's?" Maybe it was nothing. Maybe she saw me feeding on him and got so freaked out she had to call.

Bianca's voice turned faint and thready, as if she were in a dream. "In Syria. War and chaos have broken out and there is so much blood..." Her voice dropped to a husky whisper. "So much death."

I kept waiting for the shoe to drop. For her to say more. But then I understood.

"Grim," I said as an answer and a question.

If one of the most war-torn countries endured a large-scale massacre, that meant a lot of deaths, which meant a lot of souls would need to be reaped. Grim was already at capacity. Who knew what would happen if he absorbed a few more, much less a war's worth of souls. Maybe there was time to stop Grim from throwing himself on the sword.

Bianca's whisper turned ragged. "Find him."

Whirling around, as if I could find him right there, panic flooded every cell in my body. I ended the call.

Miranda was now standing next to me, her body rigid, preparing for the worst. "What is it?"

"Grim is in trouble," was all I could get out. I half-jogged out of Perkatory with Aaron waving after us, a confused look on his face.

Phone still in hand, I called Grim as I walked toward the lobby. I didn't even know what direction to go in. I just needed to move. Once I found out where he was, I'd waste no time. Grim's phone went straight to voicemail.

Miranda was on my heels, not knowing the extent of the danger, but ready to help.

I called Timothy next, but it rang twice before Miranda pointed to the front doors. Timothy and Fallon had each of Grim's arms looped around their neck as they dragged him inside.

Shit, shit, shit. I was too late. The beginnings of black veins were creeping up from the collar of Grim's suit, and his face was ashen. His eyes were closed, but if they were to open, I'd bet I'd find dark oblivion in them.

The staff appeared agitated, like they wanted to do something or call someone, but Timothy was there and they took their orders from him, so they held position.

Shoving the phone in my pocket, I ran over to meet them. Miranda was glued to my heels.

"What the fuck happened?" I asked, though I already knew. They paused, so I could cup Grim's face, his dark scruff scratching against my fingers.

"The reapers came," Fallon groused. "All of them, then as soon as Grim absorbed the souls, they came again, already filled to the brim."

"It's Seth," I growled. After my rundown from Galina, I knew this was Seth's fault somehow. War was chaos, and that was his specialty.

Fallon and Timothy exchanged a wary look with each other.

"You don't know that." The raspy words came from Grim.

My unbeating heart leapt. He was still responsive. "Of course I do, you big dummy. I'm the smartest vampire you know."

"You're the only vampire I know." His eyes fluttered open, and I could see him battling for control against the sucking darkness. Black clouds swirled in his golden eyes. The idiot was doubling down on his internal fight. Some of the strength returned to his posture, so Grim didn't need to lean so heavily on Timothy and Fallon.

Miranda interrupted our wholesome banter. "Not that this isn't fun, but maybe we should talk about this somewhere more private?" She cast an eye about the lobby. We were getting some looks. But Timothy had cleaned up far messier situations, so I wasn't worried about making a scene. But she was right.

"We need to get him to the antechamber," Timothy agreed. "He needs to rest."

A slimy, cold prickling sensation ran up my spine. I turned around. Seth was at the other end of the lobby. He nodded his head in my direction, a smug smile on his dumb face.

Had he come here for a fight? Because I was ready to punch his face in. Whatever Idris' beef with Seth was, suddenly I understood the demigod's desire to kill a god.

Then Seth's gaze fixated on something over my shoulder. Despite myself, I followed it.

Everything in me froze, and it was like the blood had been drained from me all over again.

"What is it? What's wrong?" Grim asked, pushing off Timothy and Fallon.

My mouth wouldn't move for a moment as I watched the mustached man wearing a polo shirt roll his suitcase into the lobby.

Was this some kind of trick? I looked back at Seth. He lifted a martini in my direction. No, it wasn't him putting on another magic show for me.

When I turned back around, my aunt entered the hotel next, with a girl in tow. About fourteen years old, her hair was dark, pushed back by a headband. Her outfit was stylish and too elegant for a kid. Like a miniature Jackie O.

But what made my heart clench in a vice grip was her expression. Her face far too stony, too serious. She wasn't a child, she was a mannequin pretending to be a child. In her mind, she was on some faraway fantasy world, while she used only a little of her consciousness to puppeteer her movements so no one would suspect. I knew that look all too well, because it was the same one I'd seen in the mirror for years.

My uncle finished checking in, turned around and stopped cold when he met my eye. First surprise, then confusion, and finally a sparkle of delight entered his eye.

A shiver of revulsion went through me.

You could rip his throat out, splash the onyx floor with his blood and not lose a night's sleep over this.

Still, I didn't move. I'd worked so hard to leave my past behind and, as my aunt turned to see what my uncle was looking at, I found myself staring at it head on. Like looking down the barrel of a .45.

No amount of Botox could erase the lemon-sucking, pinched expression my Aunt Delilah always exuded. She was not pleased to see me. I knew what she thought of me. Ungrateful.

There had been a few blowups before I slipped away in the night. She demanded I show her respect and gratitude for all they had done for me, taking care of me after my parents died. I'd yelled back through a torrent of heart-broken tears that they didn't care about me.

She locked me away, controlled what I ate. Forced me to enter pageants and run charities so she could look good. And for a while I had tried. I really did. I thought if I did what they asked, they would finally love me. But my absolute best had only gotten me ignored. When I asked why she didn't praise me, she drily laughed and asked why she should congratulate me for doing what was expected of me. It was then that I knew no amount of trying on her terms would make her love me. I was a pawn to her and her ladies' social club.

Aunt Delilah grabbed the young girl's hand and marched to the elevators with their luggage, where they disappeared.

Everything had passed in only a few seconds, but decades' worth of torment rolled through my body, riding a rollercoaster of trauma.

I looked one more time in Seth's direction, but he'd vanished. No doubt in a puff of smoke, like the damn villain he was. I knew to my core he was responsible for this.

My uncle continued to stand there, taking me in with appreciation. The lewd sparkle in his eye was just as I remembered it, and I wanted to upchuck right there in the middle of the lobby.

Uncle Phillip took his time returning his credit card to his wallet. It always amazed me how he seemed to own the world with his unhurried movements. There was a certain amount of control he wielded whenever he was in a room. It took me years to realize the calculating snake knew exactly how to play to his environment. Get the most respect from his bosses, and peers. How to make me squirm and obey.

"Vivien," Grim said. His hand squeezed my arm to get my attention, bringing me out of my inner hell. His pupils nearly swallowed his irises, but he'd somehow managed to gain control over himself.

"It's my family," I breathed. Following my gaze to my uncle, Grim's grip on my arm tightened. Had I been a human, my arm would have bruised under the force.

His power thickened the air, his ferocity turning palpable. "That's the man?" his words came out a growl.

Then before I could confirm, he strode past me, his deathly power sweeping out in a dark mantle. The very atoms in the air shook with an unstable violence. The pressure in the room built the same way it had right before he'd torn the souls out of those gunmen.

The god of the dead had gone off the rails.

20

Vivien grabbed my arm, in a futile attempt to slow me. "Grim, stop. Don't."

The souls inside me roiled around, shaking my core with furious energy. The violence this man inspired in me excited them.

The need to end him tipped me over the edge. The dark souls took over. Clouds of power and death swirled around me, and I felt the darkness flood my veins, contracting the muscles in my shoulders, arms, and up my neck.

I honed in on Vivien's uncle, able to taste his tainted soul. My tongue awash in a syrupy, acrid copper. His soul rotted inside his body like a fetid fruit. Even if I waited to reap him, I knew he would not pass judgement to enter the gates of the afterlife.

My stomach dropped as the floor seemed to fall out from under me. Adrift in dark oblivion, I reached out for the surrounding souls to anchor me back to the world.

Vivien stepped in front of me, her hands on my face, trying to get my attention, but she felt so far away. The glowing light of her soul gave me pause. She'd followed me into the void, and I knew it hurt her to do so.

When she spoke, her words were muffled, as if she were underwater. "Grim, don't do this."

"He deserves to die. The abuse he inflicted on you is unconscionable. I must cleanse the world of his rotted soul."

"If you do this, you might die. You've taken on too many souls."

The words seemed to take forever to penetrate as I drifted on another plane of dark expanse.

"He hurt you. No one will ever hurt you again," I ground out. My power doubled as I thought of her uncle, Idris, Seth...all those who wished to harm Vivien. I would extinguish them all. Turn myself inside out if that's what it took.

Her eyes searched mine with desperation while a sadness travelled through the tether of our souls until I felt it as my own.

"If you do this, *you* will be the one hurting me."

The glow around Vivien intensified until it matched my level of power. She was my light, my everything.

Then from my otherworldly plane, I sensed the warmth of her thumbs brushing back and forth along my cheeks.

"Please don't hurt me. Let them go." Then Vivien's lips pressed against mine. The kiss was sweet yet pleading. It beckoned me to follow her light. Feeling and need travelled through our blood bond. Slowly, but surely, she reeled me back in. The other souls I'd anchored myself to, the rotted soul of her uncle I'd grasped tight, were nothing compared to her. Letting their souls slip through my fingers, I grounded myself in Vivien, who drew me in like the most powerful magnet in existence.

Why her?

I batted the thought away along with Qwynn's voice, as I

sunk into Vivien's embrace. Never had I given my power over so completely, but Vivien felt safe. As if she were perfectly meant for me and no one else.

Fatigue hit me like the blow of a hammer. The delicious intimacy of Vivien's kiss broke as I slumped against her. She managed to keep me up. I shut my eyes against the harsh lights of the lobby as the current reality slapped me.

"I've got you," Vivien said in my ear.

"Holy fuck," I heard Miranda say on a shaky exhale from somewhere behind me.

A powerful hand gripped my shoulder and righted me. It was Fallon, his face as grave as it was fearful. "What the hell was that?" he demanded. His words were harsh, almost angry, but behind his displeasure was fear.

"You went to find Amit. What happened?" Vivien asked Fallon, still not releasing her hold on me, her arm wrapped around mine.

Fallon shook his head.

"I found something," Miranda said, muscling in next to Fallon.

I noticed my aide was absent. Timothy had already kicked into high gear, gathering staff and those nearby. I'd about lost control again and he was cleaning up my mess, as he always did.

Pressure so insistent at my stomach, I felt close to splitting. I pressed a hand against the souls, trying to keep them at bay.

"Spill," Vivien told Miranda.

"I located the second guy who rented heat lamps and humidifiers, thanks to Timothy's help. Javier has been following him, and he drove to a warehouse on the outskirts of town. He acted nervous, checked to see if he was being followed. When Javier went to investigate the warehouse, the man confronted him. Javier just called to ask what he should do next."

She already had her phone poised.

"We'll take it from here," Fallon said.

Managing to straighten, I nodded. "Tell Javier to return here, but text me the address. Fallon is right, we need to handle this." If Seth had Amit stored in a warehouse, I couldn't rule out there being more danger.

Vivien tugged at me. "You should stay here. Fallon and I will go check it out."

"If it is Seth, who knows what danger there may be. It could be a trap," I pointed out.

"Yeah, that fucker loves to push us over the edge," Vivien said with a grimace, then looked over my shoulder as if searching for someone. "Which means you shouldn't go."

"And why aren't we going straight for Seth again and make him tell us where Amit is?" Miranda asked.

I answered. "Because Seth plays games. He uses smoke and mirrors and will needle us without revealing anything. He is hoping to distract us by any means necessary."

"I'll say," Vivien muttered.

She confirmed what I already began to suspect. Vivien's family being present was no mere coincidence. But she was right. We would deal with that in due time, though it vexed me to put it off for even a minute longer. The monstrous things I felt from her uncle...

"Grim," Vivien said in a warning tone.

My hands were clenched into fists. Again, Seth managed to sidetrack me.

I shot Miranda a sharp look, making sure she took me seriously. "Seth is more dangerous than you could possibly imagine. Under no circumstances are you to pursue him. It is as dangerous for you as it would be Jamal." Then facing

Vivien, I said in a firm, low tone, "The sooner we find Amit, the quicker I'll be able to feed him the souls of the damned. Which means the sooner I will have my power under control."

Vivien looked at Fallon for help, but he shrugged. He knew I was right.

"I'll get the car," Miranda said in a clipped voice. Then she disappeared before anyone could stop her.

I'd forgotten Miranda was there. Speaking of godly business in front of a human was forbidden, but by her prompt, unsurprised response, I realized she already knew more than she was supposed to. When I searched Vivien's face for confirmation, she gave a sheepish smile. Confound it, how did she manage to subvert my one and only command?

Vivien's smile disappeared, her eyes widening in alarm. "Let's go get Amit."

Staring down at my open palms, I saw the skin began to crack and seep black mist. Vivien followed my gaze before meeting my eye. There wasn't much time left, and we both knew it.

VIVIEN KICKED in the doors and they exploded into the windowless warehouse. I was right behind her. Miranda and Fallon entered from the opposite side of the building.

The two teenagers inside scrambled to get out of the way as we stormed the place.

"Freeze," Miranda shouted as she pointed her gun at the nearest one. The first teen stopped in a half crouch, eyes bulging out in fear.

Vivien blurred over to the other. In a moment, he was on

the floor, her boot digging into his back as he loudly protested in pain.

Fallon and I surveyed the contents of the warehouse. Heat lamps were running hot, along with several humidifiers. It was a crude setup, but it seemed to do wonders for the rows of plants in the warehouse. The teens were growing a tremendous amount of marijuana. But that didn't mean it wasn't a cover.

Reaching out with my senses, I searched for Amit, while Fallon did a physical sweep of the place.

Despite the plant life teeming in the warehouse, I couldn't detect the god's presence. Fallon rejoined my side with a quick shake of his head. His eye could see beyond any magical traps or secret walls with his glowing blue eye. Which left one conclusion.

"He's not here," I said for Vivien and Miranda's benefit.

"You've got to be fucking kidding me," Vivien breathed. Then she barked at the kid below. "How old are you?"

"Twenty-one."

She dug into his back a little harder with her boot.

His voice turned squeaky with pain. "Seventeen."

"So what? You couldn't wait to become an entrepreneur for a couple more years?"

"Don't say anything, Jimmy," the other one shouted out, then with a firm tone, he told Miranda, "I want a lawyer."

Miranda dropped her gun, while Vivien let the kid below her stand up. While the teenagers bickered about whose fault it was, Vivien walked over to me. Her eyes brimmed with unspoken fear and worry. She reached up and set her cool hand against my cheek. At first, I thought she was growing cold and needed to eat again. But then I realized it was my skin that was burning up.

"We need to get Grim to his antechamber," Fallon said,

coming to stand next to me. Vivien never took her eyes off my face. "The city will be safest with him there."

Vivien and I sat in the back of the car, our knees touching. Vivien covered my hand with hers and continued to hold it for the entire ride back to Sinopolis. She kept saying we would find where Amit was. That everything would be okay. But my vision darkened at the edges until I could only see Vivien's glow.

The cacophony of bloodthirsty, twisted, dark souls of war raged through my entire being. I could taste their hate, fear, and the dark deeds they'd committed. The torture and pain they inflicted on others. How they reveled in destroying the innocence and love of others to remake the world in their own hateful image. These souls carried a hate so severe, they could only spread it, like a cancer. Souls like that could not be contained, though I tried in that moment.

I felt more than saw Vivien shiver.

"Are you hungry?"

"No, I'm positively stuffed. Couldn't drink another drop."

One side of my lips curved up. *Liar.* In truth, I could not spare a drop of my power. The amniotic sac I'd created to contain the souls inside my being was thinning near the breaking point. Once it broke and they flooded my system…I couldn't say what the consequence would bring other than it would be dire and potentially nuclear. Fallon was right to hurry me back to the antechamber.

"Vivien, maybe it's time you think of bonding with another."

"What are you talking about?" Her voice was low.

"I'm afraid I won't be able to protect you for much longer."

She didn't respond. Perhaps she was considering who

her next choice in the godly line was, or more likely, she'd try to strike out on her own.

Squeezing her hand that covered mine, I said, "Should I not make it…I fear the rest of the gods will come after you in force."

"You think I can't take care of myself?" she asked wryly, though her tone lacked the usual irreverent mirth.

I rubbed my thumb along the back of her hand, grounding myself in the feel of her soft skin. "Of course, you are ready to fight a war on your own." I was right. She wanted to strike out on her own. Perhaps she even looked forward to my demise so she could be free again. I wouldn't blame her. "Even should your bargain with Osiris remain and you agree to find the conspirators amongst the gods responsible for killing me—"

She cut me off. "Don't say that. You aren't going to die, drama queen."

I continued anyway. "You will still need an ally amongst the gods. I'm sure you know Timothy will protect you, but Fallon may be a more strategic ally. Many of the gods fear his power, though he is not overt in using it. They would think twice before coming after you. Though if you revert to drinking human blood versus a god's, I think you know that your power and strength will somewhat decrease."

"You think I should form a blood bond with Fallon?" she asked, her voice flat.

The thought of her drinking from Fallon turned my mouth sour, but I swallowed it. "It might be the best thing to do. I want to make sure you are prepared, that you know all your options."

"It wasn't long ago you wanted me dead," she said with a dry laugh. "And now you are trying to make sure I inherit a god in your last will and testament?"

My heart constricted. She was right. I had lived thousands of years and in a mere matter of days, Vivien had become one of the most important influences in all my existence. It didn't make sense. The only thing I knew was that she opened up my feelings in a way I'd never known. I'd always been feared, admired, and coveted by those with a death wish or a desire for my power.

But Vivien didn't care about any of that. She seemed to see me for who I really was, and never let me forget it, even when I sometimes wished she would. And instead of punishing me like Qwynn had, she coaxed me open with her jokes, surprised me with her boldness.

Tugging her over, I moved to pull her onto the seat next to me, needing her close. Her hand stroked my cheek again as her face came into focus when I brought her closer.

"Your eyes..." She trailed off.

I tangled a hand in her hair. "Vivien, you need to know, before I cannot speak it...for as many dark, tainted souls I have encountered, I have also seen the very best of humanity. I've been amazed by humanity's strength, kindness and capacity for love. Something my brethren do not always appreciate. And I must confess, I'd lost sight of the good. I enslaved myself to my duty and lost my sense of wonder. But you, you've awakened something inside of me. When I'm near you, it's like I've awakened from a long arduous dream and realize there is more to existence than judgement and service. This may not make sense to you, but I think Osiris somehow understood. You were my gift."

"I...I don't know what to say."

"It's a miracle."

Vivien smacked my chest, but I used her motion to draw her up to me and kissed her softly. I tried to convey the reverence, appreciation, and deep passion I felt for her in that kiss, and she responded in kind.

At last, I understood how Marcella must feel. A justified, and well overdue, irony. How she must have loathed me all these years for destroying a part of her. I was the only god who had never taken a sekhor, which made me the perfect candidate to lead the war against them when they tried to take over the earthly realm. I'd believed them all bloodthirsty, power hungry, and a blight on the earth.

But now I wondered if Marcella's sekhor was her fated match.

While the vampire had yet to make a move against the gods, I believed it was only a matter of time before he joined their ranks. But I could no more see Vivien turn power hungry, as Marcella had pleaded with me for her sekhor's case. Had she treated her sekhor differently than the rest of the gods?

Marcella said I would pay the ultimate price because of Vivien. A broken heart that would never heal. Marcella was doomed to continue an eternal existence with no relief from her pain. It was a rare case, but to the rest of us, we knew how she suffered. And with her love gone, there was nothing to be done.

And I was the one responsible.

The heaviness of my past weighed me down. It was long overdue I judge my own actions, and I wondered if I shouldn't be fed to Amit once we found him.

When our kiss broke, Vivien rested her forehead against mine. "You will not die. Gods can't die. You've beaten me over the head with that factoid. And you so love being right. Besides, you need to stick around to punish me."

"Oh?"

"Miranda knows who, or rather what, you are now," she confessed with false guilt.

I groaned. "How did you manage to subvert my one command?"

"Let's just say it involved a high-stakes game of Charades."

My chuckle turned into a wheezing cough as the souls sharply twisted inside me. I couldn't say I was surprised. Part of me was relieved Miranda knew. She'd been privy to so much, it only made sense she would discover the rest for herself in some manner. She was as much an ally to me as she was to Vivien.

"See? I deserve a spanking, and you can't go anywhere until I've been punished." She put an emphasis on the last word, indicating she wouldn't actually hate me punishing her.

Of course she neatly side-stepped responding to the feelings I laid bare. Perhaps she did resent me at her core for binding her to me. But right now, I needed Vivien to understand how she'd affected me. Before it was too late.

The sac separating the souls from my being broke. I cried out as the darkness flooded my system.

There was no going back now.

21

I didn't want to leave Grim. His eyes turned black, like a demon's, and his skin cracked. Black mist seeped from the fissures and the skin at the cracks grayed and flaked. With a long, near-animalistic groan, Grim writhed in the back of the car. I called to him but he didn't respond. God, could he even hear me? My hands hovered over him, not sure if I should be holding him fast, or giving him space. I felt so helpless as he let out another keening growl of pain.

When we got to the back entrance of the hotel, Fallon and Timothy opened the door, hustling Grim out.

"We need to contain his power," Timothy said.

"What's going to happen?" I asked, fear making me feel like a small child.

Timothy shook his head. "I don't know. He could explode, destroying half the city, unleash all the dark souls onto this plane where they could terrorize mortals and taint other souls. Or he could become a black hole and implode in on himself, taking them with him. Anything is possible, but destruction is inevitable."

With that, Timothy pressed a hand to Grim's forehead.

Chains of glowing glyphs wrapped around Grim's head as Timothy's eyes glazed over and glowed as he continued to surround Grim with what looked like protective energies.

My phone buzzed with a text from Echo. Aioki would meet me at Perkatory with some information. "It's my contact. She may have something for me on Amit's whereabouts." Hope sprung up inside me.

"Just go," Fallon said. "Timothy and I need to stay here with Grim. If he goes nuclear, we'll do the best we can to keep him from falling apart."

"We need to make sure if he expires, we do our best to contain the fallout," Timothy explained.

They had their mission, and I had mine. I made my way to the elevator, and the gods didn't follow.

Even if I had to confront Seth and shake him until his teeth fell out, I would find Amit. But I hoped Aioki would have something for me first.

It was time to call in my own backup. The doors of the elevator opened and Miranda was there, waiting. She matched my pace as I strode out into the lobby with purpose.

I'd texted her a synopsis of what was happening. Scary end-of-the-world shit would go down if we didn't help Grim. Still, I asked her, "You sure you're ready for this?"

"Does the pope shit in the woods?"

I twisted around to look at her. "Wha-what? I don't know."

She shot me a scary grin. "Exactly. But I'm with you no matter how it plays out."

I shook a finger at her. "You. I like you."

Her smile only intensified.

When we got to Perkatory, Aioki was standing at the café stand with a frozen coffee chatting up Aaron. The two seemed to be fast friends, deep in the midst of discussion about the best Miyazaki film.

Aioki said, "*Howl's Moving Castle* is my absolute favorite."

"But *Spirited Away*? Come on. That piece is golden. So much subtext you can watch it a million times and still get more from it," Aaron said with minimal stuttering.

"Aioki," I said, getting her attention as Miranda and I crashed the party. Catching our serious business demeanor, Aioki's smile faltered. She wore her typical punk school-girl uniform, which drew attention from the guests passing by. And I thought I stuck out here.

"My mom sent me to give you the latest. We tracked the truck for quite a ways but they drove off-grid, or so they thought." Aioki shot me a triumphant smile. "But no one can hide the echo of their presence. They switched the cargo over to a different truck driver. Her name's Clarissa and she's fabulous. You think my hair colors are bright, that lavender-colored hair against her chocolate brown skin is epic."

"Aioki," I snapped. I was all about the chitchat, but there was no time.

"Right," Aioki said. "Mom got hold of her and Clarissa said she was paid big bucks to transport the cargo."

"What did she transport?" Miranda asked for me.

Aioki shrugged. "She doesn't know. Someone paid her a hefty price, but she was told they would be loading and unloading the truck. The contents were undisclosed."

"And she didn't think that was weird?" Miranda asked, her voice becoming icy.

"When we spoke to her, she went off, claiming how she knew the money was too good. She worried it was drugs or some other illegal contents, but they had assured her it was nothing illegal and the money was too good for her to pass up. Truck drivers can make a pretty penny, but do you even know how much it takes to keep those massive vehicles serviceable?"

I imagined this Clarissa shared exactly how much. "Aioki, where did she drop the cargo?"

"Oh, that's what I'm here to tell you. She dropped it off at the Fuji Sushi and Hibachi. It's a new restaurant at the Menaggio Hotel."

"That's Seth's hotel," I said to Miranda.

"Oh, that's the one with the c-c-crazy display with the crocodile," Aaron said, not even pretending to not eavesdrop.

Everything inside me froze. "What?"

He went on. "Y-yeah, this new restaurant opens today, and it's all the rage because they have a g-g-glass container featuring this massive crocodile. L-l-looks like something out of a museum. They have it lit up with all these hot lights and exotic foliage. The statue looks so r-r-real, some people think it is a taxidermized dinosaur."

I leaned over the counter, grabbed Aaron's face and landed a big wet kiss on his forehead. "You are a lifesaver." Aaron blushed ten ways from Sunday.

Miranda and I were already on the move.

"Hey, I deserve a kiss too," Aioki yelled after us.

"Later," I shouted over my shoulder. "And tell your mom I'll keep the buns flush in treats for the next month."

WE MADE excellent time to the Menaggio.

"Should we call Grim or Timothy?" Miranda asked. "If we are going to steal this crocodile thing from a god, we might need some heavy hitters with us."

My tongue had been loosened from whatever restraint Grim had put on me. That was either because Miranda already knew about the gods or because Grim was near death. "The crocodile is also a god." I quickly explained how it ate the dark souls that Grim was holding in his body. She'd been patient as hell, and I was grateful I could share the details with her finally. I finished with, "I don't know if we should pull them away from Grim. They need to keep him and the city safe."

Pulling out her phone, Miranda began texting someone. "We are still going to need more help." She'd led us to the garage, over to her car.

Not wanting to wait for her, I climbed into the driver's seat. Miranda went with it, climbing into the passenger side.

"I'm such an idiot," I berated myself as I pulled the car out. "I should have searched Seth's hotel. I was so focused on following him. Of course, that cocky asshole would leave Amit out in the open where everyone could see. The balls on this guy are massive. Huge. We could use one of them alone to replace the hot-air balloon on that Paris-themed hotel. And boy, I can't wait to kick him square in those bulbous cajones."

"First off, gross," Miranda said. "Second, how are we going to get this massive crocodile to Sinopolis? They can't move Grim, and I don't think we can strap this frozen god to the roof of my car."

"Aren't you head of Sinopolis security? Don't you have access to all his toys? I bet he's got trucks or someone who is in charge of moving things around for Sinopolis."

Miranda shot me the stink-eye. "Are you angling for my job?"

I held a hand up while pulling out into traffic. A horn blared at me as I whipped out in front of someone. This was no time for traffic laws or speed limits. "Hey, it's not my fault you aren't used to having resources at your old job. If I've learned anything about Grim it's that he can get anything at the snap of his fingers."

Miranda said, "Touche," and started texting again. "Don't kill us, or crash my car."

Screaming honks followed us as I jerked out of the way of an oncoming car. My vampy senses made me perfect for driving. My reflexes were heightened far past my old human ones.

When we jumped out of the car at Seth's hotel, Javier was already there and out of the car. Miranda had gotten us a kind of backup.

"I don't think they are going to take kindly to us taking what is rightfully Mr. Scarapelli's," I said, for Javier's benefit. "And this isn't something that can wait. I'm going to be real with you. Shit may go down, but the number one thing is we need to get that crocodile out and back to Sinopolis."

Miranda pulled out a gun and checked the magazine. Javier must have been one hell of a poker player, because he didn't even lift an eyebrow. When Miranda met his eye, she gave him a curt nod.

"We can't tell you what's going on. It's as much for your own safety as it is of classified nature. But she's not kidding. Shit might get real in there."

"So you in or out?" I asked, all but ready to tear off the doors and get in there.

Javier looked back and forth between us before walking back to his car.

A snort blew through my nose. At least we knew what he was about. I turned to go inside, but Miranda held an arm out to stop me.

Sure enough, Javier returned from his car, carrying his own piece now.

"If you say that's how it is, that's how it is," he said.

So much for the two of them playing by the letter of the law.

With that, I threw open the doors to the restaurant. The dramatic bang of the doors caused the whole place to silence. Indeed, right at the center of the restaurant was a glass box display that showcased a giant petrified crocodile under bright lights amongst lush green foliage. Son of a bitch. Seth really was a showy asshole.

And if to prove my point, I found Seth sitting at a raised booth, surrounded by impossibly young women fawning over him. The intensity in his flashing green eyes could have been surprise, but in a moment, he'd regained his cool demeanor. He made it appear as if he'd planned for me to barge in. But Grim was right. Seth spent so much time strategizing how to distract us, he never expected us to show up where he'd stashed the prize. Seth probably thought we were still dealing with my uncle or Grim imploding. Guess again, douche nozzle.

Two of the servers stiffened, and I recognized them from the security footage. Past them, I met the eyes of the short blonde woman through the cutout to the kitchen. The blonde narrowed her mean eyes at me. A third Asian man stepped out from the back kitchen, the fourth thief. It didn't show up on the security footage, but all four had a distinct green glow about them. Just like the gunmen, except far stronger. In the air, with sizzling steak and chicken, soy sauce, and garlic, was the same lime scent I recognized belonged to Seth.

"If everyone could remain calm. There is a gas leak, and

we need everyone to exit in an orderly fashion." I announced.

The server to my right wasted no time. He threw his serving tray at me, food flinging off it in every direction. Shrieks broke out as people ran for the exits.

So much for calm and orderly.

The women dispersed from Seth's side, but he remained in his booth, arms along the backs as if preparing to watch a Vegas show. Oh, I'd give him a show alright.

The attack was quick, but I blocked the tray with my forearm. As people fled the restaurant, the tray-chucking server hurled himself at me.

The man was trained in combat, but so was I. I met him, blow for blow. Whatever the green glow was, I was sure it strengthened him. Our skill was matched, but I surpassed him in strength. Then he made the fatal mistake. He threw a kick, and I caught his leg. Ha! Chump move.

The four thieves hissed in unison, "Hail to Set, bringer of chaos." All four people glowed green, as if powering up. A sparkling energy emanated from Seth's eyes, as they worshipped him. Bast said taking worshippers was a big no-no. Seth deserved a spanking and I planned to be the one to give it to him.

The glint of steel followed a **snicket.** Again, I intercepted his attack with my other arm. Then I lunged forward and sank my teeth into the man's throat. Sucking heartily, I drained him until he collapsed. I hadn't tasted human blood since drinking from Grim. Indeed, it had no hold over me. Licking the side of my mouth, I could taste the tang of Seth's power. The server was majorly juiced up.

The restaurant had cleared out, but the remaining three thieves shuddered. Their bodies contorted and rippled with the sickening crackle of bone. Flesh roiled and turned over into scales as they expanded and lengthened. Soon, we were facing three massive snakes at least ten feet long. The two men were now a muddy green color, while the woman turned the light-yellow color of her hair.

"Holy fuck." Miranda said the words that Javier's face made.

Forked tongues shot out, tasting the air. A shiver of revulsion went through me. Fucking snakes.

If Seth's followers could turn into snakes, no wonder the fingerprint key on the lift to Amit's habitat was a cinch. If they could grow scales, they could melt away their own fingerprints.

The one to our left slithered toward me with surprising speed. Javier and Miranda's guns cracked in succession as they shot at the massive snake. All too soon, the clicking of empty chambers stopped them from firing. The snake collapsed, blood gushing from the many holes now riddling its body.

"Javier," Miranda cried out as the other green snake shot forward. Javier barely turned to face the snake before it was upon him. Jaw slackening in horror, he faced the massive, unhinged jaw, about to swallow him.

I blurred over, putting myself between the snake and Javier at the last second. Grabbing a top fang while stomping on the bottom of its jaw, I held the snake at bay.

"Get out of here. I'll handle this," I yelled to Miranda and Javier. This was supernatural business, which made it my responsibility. I wouldn't have either of them die on my watch. The snakes were dangerous. Seth, even more so.

"No way," Miranda shot back, though fear glazed her eyes.

"Just secure transport for Amit." She needed a job? I'd

give her one. It was damned important too. But I needed the mortals out of here.

Seth still sat, untouched, like a king residing over gladiator games. Even if I fought off the snakes, I couldn't kill Seth. I needed to make sure Grim got Amit no matter what happened to me. I'd tie up the snakes and Seth as long as I could to give Miranda and Javier time to grab the croc god. If anybody could complete the mission, it was those two.

Warm blood spilled over my hands as the fang sliced my palm. Still, I held on.

The body of the snake recoiled in a sickening slither before it jerked back from me. If it weren't for my vampiric sense of balance, I would have tumbled ass overhead. Instead, I fell back into a fighting stance. The snake lunged at me in a striking move. I dodged it. The next four strikes had me jumping over tables and chairs to get away as the snake knocked them over to get to me. I was fast, but so was this souped-up serpent.

If I'd brought a gun or three, I could have finished this one off. Or even a sword or knife. Fangs were my only weapon. I could bite the snake, but blech.

The glint of steel caught my attention. Of course. When in doubt, use what's around you.

By now, the golden snake had slithered its way out of the kitchen, entangling itself with the green one. Now, two hissing sets of fangs snapped at me.

The way snakes moved made no sense to me. The way half of their body seemed to slither one way while it really moved in the opposite direction...not only did it give me the willies, I struggled to anticipate its next move. I dodged out of the way by a hair's breadth from its fangs and the coil of its body.

Moving faster than I'd ever pushed before, trying to put

everything between me and the oversized snakes, I ran for my life. I didn't know what would be worse. Having one of those massive, needle-sharp fangs plunged into my body, or being swallowed whole and slowly digested alive. Either prospect put speed on my heels until I could position myself just right behind the massive hibachi table.

The green snake knocked over another table, jabbing at me. At the last second, I flipped the heat knob all the way up with one hand and in the other, grabbed the bottle of alcohol, squeezing it onto the blazing hot metal table. Flames whooshed up, and the snake's nerve-grating screech pierced my eardrums. Then, grabbing the sharp knives behind the counter, I alternately threw and jabbed them into the flayed head. The razor-sharp knives cut through the thick hide. Thank god for competent chefs who took care of their tools. When the sixth knife found its way into the snake's eye, the massive head dropped to the cooktop. A sickening stench, equal parts fishy and oily, filled the restaurant as the snake's chin burned up.

For the first time since I arrived, I noticed Seth lean forward with intent interest. No doubt he was surprised some lowlife bloodsucker could do this much damage to monsters under his command.

Despite having killed, or at least disabled, the green snake, the long, slinky yellow body shuddered and slithered over the unmoving green scale of the other.

Crap. I'd lost sight of the head. How did one lose sight of a massive snake face?

Wet spittle and an angry hiss came from behind me. I whirled around. As I turned to face the yellow snake, the long body encircled me, coiling and constricting before I could react. My arms trapped at my sides, the snake coiled around me two, then three times.

I cried out in pain. My bones crunched under the impact as slick scales pressed against my skin.

I caught a glimpse of Seth. He'd relaxed into his chair with a smug smile. Then he did the most insulting thing possible. That sonofabitch pulled out his phone and began to scroll. The god wanted me to feel as worthless as possible. It wasn't even worth looking up from his stupid social media feed to witness my death. *Rude.*

If I'd needed to breathe, I would have been suffocating. In no time, I realized it was useless to try muscling my way out from its hold on me. The snake regarded me, tongue flicking out, hitting my cheek with a disgusting, fluttery impact.

Maybe Miranda would come back with more bullets? Maybe I could bite my way out from the inside of the snake if I lived that long. Dread filled me, as I knew neither was likely.

My stomach dropped as the snake reared back its head, preparing to bite me in two. The moment of anticipation was all the more terrifying. Then it struck.

Facing the unhinged jaw of fangs, all I could do was scream. "Stop!"

The snake stopped cold.

One second, then two seconds passed, and it still didn't move.

I stared into the pink maw, fear clouding my senses and vision. It took a second before I absorbed what happened.

This time, in a hoarse voice, I commanded, "Release me."

The pressure gave way almost immediately and my feet found the floor again. The snake closed its mouth.

Holy blood bags. It obeyed me.

I'd been so busy trying to avoid being controlled by

Grim or anyone else, I'd forgotten I had mental powers of persuasion on my own. Master vampires could control vampire peons and regular humans. I'd done it once before, but dismissed it from my arsenal of abilities because of how much I hated being controlled, and because I figured the blood bond with Grim would have changed that.

Grim.

Shit, I needed to get back with Amit before it was too late.

I sunk power into the command I gave the snake. "Eat Seth."

With lightning speed, the snake turned around and struck. Weightless for a moment, having been released by the snake, my body then smacked against the floor with bruising impact. The dumbfounded Seth didn't even have time to drop his phone before the massive jaws closed around him.

Lifting my cheek from the floor, I glowered at the lump in the snake's throat. "Update your status now, asshole."

Then my head fell back down as I heard the rhythmic beeps of a truck backing up. Miranda and Javier got a truck. Good. I pumped a victorious fist into the air from my horizontal position. Now to save the world.

22

Sure enough, Miranda and Javier had gotten ahold of a moving truck and a cart large enough to get Amit loaded up. The restaurant was already trashed, so they backed the truck up right through the front doors, up to Amit. After pulling myself off the floor, I broke the glass enclosure around Amit's petrified form, so we could slide big boy into the back.

As I heaved and hoed, pushing the croc god into the truck, I swallowed back the fear the leathery-skinned god wouldn't wake up and try to eat all of us. Though Amit was petrified, I could feel his eyes watching us as acutely as I sensed his rage.

And to complicate matters, I didn't know what to do with the massive magic snake who had a lumpy Seth caught in its throat.

When I called the oversized serpent over, Javier bolted over to the dumpster behind the restaurant, Spanish streaming out. My Spanish was rusty but I caught a number of curse words and I think he was either asking a nun to make a sandwich, or asking god, 'why him?' Miranda simply held up a hand and said, "Nope, too much." Then stalked around the truck to get in the front.

With a shrug, I directed the snake to get in the truck too and coil in the back corner until I could figure out what to do with it and with Seth. The lump was still moving, but more sluggishly now.

Javier made good time driving us back to Sinopolis, though every moment felt like an eternity. I jumped out of the truck's cab before it even stopped, running around to the back. I threw open the rear door.

"Fuck me sideways."

"What now?" Miranda said, coming around the back.

"The snake and Seth are gone." It was true. Only Amit stood inside. No trace of the snake.

How the hell it could have gotten out, I had no idea.

Miranda sneezed. "Oh god, what were they shipping in this thing? A herd of cats?"

A tremor shook the ground under our feet. Right, snake-Seth problems later—save Grim now.

There were several oversized carts with wheels stationed by the lift for transporting who knew what down into Amit's habitat. The three of us made quick work of moving Amit onto one of the carts and into the lift. Javier didn't protest when Miranda sent him back to the office to make sure the building was secure. There was a deeply perturbed look in his eye as he left us to it. I didn't have time to either enlighten him or ease his mind. Grim was somewhere in his antechamber on the verge of total destruction.

Before I tugged closed the bay doors, a manicured hand stopped me.

Bracing myself for another fight, it surprised me when the door reopened to show Bianca. Dressed in white and pink, she stepped inside, her fashionable stilettos strangely noiseless against the metal flooring. "I figured you'd need some help waking up dear Amit." She walked to the petrified god and cooed, "There, there, dear. I know, it's been quite an ordeal, but you are almost home." Bianca smoothed her hands over Amit's bumpy hide. Then over her shoulder, Bianca said to Miranda, "I'm glad you know now. Your allyship is of most importance."

Miranda only nodded back, but her eyes remained wary.

I shut the doors this time, pressed the button, and we began our descent into the secret depths of the Sinopolis Hotel. Miranda only tightened her jaw when we found our way into the underground jungle. Leaving Bianca and Miranda to finish with Amit, I ran through the lush foliage into the antechamber. I trusted Bianca to keep my friend safe. Because I needed to see Grim. Make sure he was okay.

Grim had been on the edge of destruction and all he seemed concerned about was what would happen to me. Grim wanted to make sure I was safe and protected when he was gone.

He'd lost sight of the damage he would inflict when he saw my uncle, only focused on punishing someone who had harmed me. For someone who grew up locked in her room a lot, without dinner, for embarrassing others by being herself, Grim's actions rocked my world.

I'd spent so much time making sure I never got too close to anyone. I could act however I wanted to, but I still wouldn't let anyone close in case I disappointed them. I didn't want to be punished for being me. And while in the beginning, that was all Grim seemed to do—vampires are bad, you dress too crazy, blah blah blah—it wasn't long before I realized the most judgemental being on the planet had changed his mind about me.

Worst yet, Grim confirmed Galina's assessment. If he

died, the blood bond would break, and I'd be a free agent. A couple of days ago, it was all I wanted. But now all I wanted was for Grim to be okay.

When I entered the massive antechamber, at the center was a rectangular stone sarcophagus with ancient, ornate carvings. Grim lay atop it, with only a white and turquoise wrap around his waist. Black veins ran along his face and entire body. A darkness surrounded him. Above the writhing smoky darkness lay a shield of light-blue magic, sparkling and glistening, as if it were containing the darkness. On closer look, I could see millions of tiny glyphs in the energy field. It was the same magic I'd seen from Timothy, and the blue color was a perfect match to the color of Fallon's eye.

As I searched the room for Fallon and Timothy, I found them. But not as I'd known them before. I recognized Timothy's suit rather than his face. He stood in one corner of the room. His head had morphed into an elegant crane's the color of pure snow. His beak curved down into a needle-sharp point. A traditional ancient Egyptian headdress of blue and gold sat on his crown and above that a swirling orb of orange power hovered. On the other side of the room, a frightening half-falcon, half-man beast stood. His shirt had been divested, leaving a bare black chest and light gray wings exposed. It was Fallon. Like Timothy, he wore a similar headdress and the glowing orb above his head was blue, like his glowing eye.

The need to tug on them and ask them *what now* was overwhelming, but I couldn't interrupt whatever trance they both seemed to be in. Either they were in deep concentration to protect Grim, or protect the world from the darkness surrounding him, or both.

A mighty roar akin to that of the T-Rex from a *Jurassic*

Park movie tore through the place, shaking dust off the columns and ceilings. I coughed and wiped my face and hair.

Sounded like Bianca successfully woke up Amit, and he was a hangry boy.

Standing near Grim, I waited for him to do his thing. Nothing. He continued to lie there.

"Grim," I said loudly. "You need to let the souls go now. Amit is ready."

Still nothing.

Frustration and fear mounted in me. Hesitant but determined, I reached out and touched the magic barrier. My hand slipped right through the blue light with only a slight tingling sensation. Pressing on, I walked into the forcefield until I reached the layer of Grim's power. The overpowering scent of brimstone mixed with his spicy scent nearly choked me. My eyes watered. Something was off about the air in here. The darkness hungrily lapped against my skin.

My vampirism and diamond-hard soul were immune to whatever was in here, but the darkness was alive. It searched for souls, life, to feed and pull into its oblivion. If the magic membrane around Grim broke, I knew it would expand and reach for all the souls it could before pulling them into the massive black hole of death Grim had become.

"Grim," I said to him again, touching his cheek. I feared my presence would break the magic membrane, but it would anyway if I didn't get Grim up and purging souls. The energy in here was intensifying with every second.

"Come on, Grim," I said, giving his cheek a sound smack this time. "Snap out of it. Amit is here. Dump those souls and give him a good meal."

Grim remained unresponsive. He stared up at the ceiling, unseeing. Faces and hands pressed against his stomach from the inside, as if trying to push their way out from his body. His stomach began to blacken, like rotting flesh.

Cupping both sides of his face now, I said, "Grim, you've got to wake up. You've got to do this." Then I kissed him. It had worked the first time, but his lips remained stiff under mine.

The blood bond will break. You'll be free.

A reminder of what Bast and then Grim had told me popped up. If Grim died, another god of the dead would be named. With my skills and Echo's resources, I could disappear, go underground. Get as far away from Vegas as possible and pretend to lead a semi-normal existence drinking pig's blood.

Since I was a kid, living with my aunt and uncle, I'd dreamed of being alone. Living on my own terms, with no one getting close enough to hurt me again. But then I'd lost my memories, and all I did was search for the people who missed me. My heart broke a little when I realized there was no one.

But there had been Grim. I now had memories of horsing around with Grim in his pool, chasing each other around, and dancing in his club. He fought for me no matter how many vampires or gods came for me. The way he listened to my childhood traumas, never pushing, letting my pain exist as it was. He treated my friends with the utmost respect and generosity.

I sank my fangs into Grim's neck, but this time, instead of being transported onto cloud nine, my entire being dropped. And I went straight to hell.

23

I found myself in a pit of writhing, angry, evil souls. They tore at me and I screamed and tried to fight back, but there were so many. They wanted to feast on me, soil me, make me one of them. The torment of being torn to pieces for those few seconds felt like an eternity of pain.

Then the frenzy slowed as something approached. The air around me resonated with the heavy steps of a being even more terrifying approaching. The souls dispersed, leaving me lying on onyx lava rock. Pushing up on my elbows, my face covered in tracks of dirt and hot tears, I looked up at the shadow cast over me.

It was Grim in his god-likeness. The towering black jackal had a mix of scales and thick fur, while death and fear rolled off of him in waves. I'd thought the tainted souls had fled in fear, but I realized Grim had called them to him. And they rushed to feed off Grim. They stuck to his back and arms, clawing, biting, screaming, and sucking all of his power.

I pushed myself up to my feet and stumbled toward him.

"No, get off him," I screamed. The moments I had of pure agony...Grim had been down here enduring it for far longer. His strength far surpassed mine, but his fangs dripped with saliva and his own blood as crimson tears slid from his eyes. They were destroying him.

Grim reached toward me, then contracted his arms with a growl of pain. I ran to him and reached up to cup his face in my hands. Pleading with those glowing gold eyes, I said, "Amit is here. He is awake. You need to let go of the souls so Amit can eat them now."

"I can't." His voice was as monstrous and bone-rattling as his appearance. But I didn't fear him. He wouldn't hurt me.

"You can. You're a freaking god. A god of the dead. Now show them who is boss."

A dark soul feasting on his shoulder sprang up and dove toward me. Grim raised a hand to shield me, and the soul re-latched onto Grim's flesh. The howls and moans of agony and anger of the souls whipped through the air like a tornado.

"Perhaps this is for the best." Grim said, running a clawed thumb down my cheek. "When the blood bond is broken, Timothy can help you go into hiding. You can live out the rest of your existence on your terms."

The knot of fear in my belly doubled. A week ago, I would have jumped at the chance. But now. My entire world had changed. I couldn't walk away from this fight, no sooner than I could walk away from Grim.

I laid a hand over his, pressing my cheek more firmly into his palm. "Why me?" I echoed the question he'd said before.

He closed his golden eyes and a rush of blood seeped from them. "Because you touched me."

With his other hand, he pressed the pad of his thumb to

the center of my forehead and I was jerked through time. It was like standing on one edge of a piece of paper that had been folded to bring me to the other edge in an instant.

The car was a smoking wreckage, but I managed to crawl out of it. When I got to my feet, my hands and legs were scraped and bleeding, and my head hurt. Rubber from one of the tires littered the road like a popped balloon.

My parents were still in there, and I was too small to lift the car. No one cried for help. A man in a black suit stood in front of the car. Something told me I should have been afraid, but I'd been hit on the head really hard, making it hard to think, to react. The man turned, and he had the most beautiful golden eyes.

"Who are you?" Though his expression hardly changed, he seemed to be surprised I spoke to him.

He gave me a hard stare for a moment before answering. "Someone who happened to be passing by."

Before I could think, I ran up to him and touched his leg. "Are you going to help them?"

A jolt shot through me at the touch.

People ran out of their cars to the upturned vehicle, but no one seemed to notice me or the tall man.

He continued to study me for a moment. "Yes, I'm going to help them." He reached down and took my hand in his.

A warmth spread through my chest. Sadness and fear still vibrated through my being, but a reassurance and overwhelming sense of eternal love wove into the other feelings.

Then the man reached in through the car and pulled up my dad and then my mom. They stood there, a sad smile on their faces.

My mom looked straight into the suited man's face and said in a matter-of-fact way, "I'm scared."

She always said what she was thinking or feeling and taught me to do the same.

The man's eyes glowed brighter. "You don't need to be. I'm here to walk with you."

I didn't understand, but somehow, I knew I wouldn't be going with them.

My mom gripped my dad's hand, and both visibly relaxed. "Thank you."

A couple of black dogs approached, unnoticed, as the frenzy of people surrounding the car continued. Sirens wailed in the distance, growing closer. The man turned to the two dogs and shook his head. They paused, then turned around and went back in the direction they came.

My dad leaned over and kissed me on the head and murmured everything would be alright, and my mom crouched down to give me a hug that crunched my bones, in the good way. She told me to be a good girl, and to always follow my heart.

"Where is he taking you?" I asked.

My mom spared him a glance. "He is going to walk us to heaven."

"But I don't want him to." Emotion grew like a bubble in my chest until I feared it would burst.

"Now, now." My mom wiped my tears away. "It's very nice of him. He's making sure we won't get lost or feel scared on our trip. Isn't that right?" She looked up at the man.

He nodded, squeezing my hand. Another flood of warmth spread through me, allowing me relief from the painful bubble.

"And one day he will come walk with you and bring you to us. He'll make sure you aren't scared then either."

I observed the suited man. He communicated his love

for humanity through our joined hands. He would protect my parents, me, everyone, for all time.

Still, I sensed a deep sadness in the man.

"But..."

"What is it, baby?" my dad asked.

"Who walks with him?" I asked.

A strange emotion flickered over his face. My parents seemed to wait for him to answer.

"No one," he answered.

"Doesn't that get lonely?" I asked him. "Mommy and Daddy have each other to walk with, but you are alone."

My parents exchanged a wary look. Maybe I wasn't supposed to be talking to the man, but I was already holding his hand. The man seemed to be thinking. He made the same intense face other kids in my grade made before answering one of Mrs. Hartley's hard questions. They wanted to make sure they got it right.

"Yes," the man finally admitted. "It does."

I squeezed his hand this time. "Okay, well, I'll walk with you, and we can visit Mommy and Daddy sometimes. But they have each other."

Something sharp zinged through our joined palms. A slight smile lifted one corner of his lips. I could tell he didn't believe me, but I always kept my word.

"It's time to say goodbye," he said gently. My parents hugged me one last time.

When the man released my hand, everything went black.

Later, I woke up in a hospital, fuzzy from drugs, unable to remember what happened. I cried for my parents, but was told they couldn't come for me. They'd died in the car accident and my aunt and uncle were coming to take care of me.

Time split, like a piece of paper unfolding again, and I was back in hell with Grim, being eaten alive by all the angry souls.

"You marked me," he said.

A fresh wave of tears fell down my cheeks. I didn't remember any of that after I woke up in the hospital, but I remembered it now. Grim asked why me. Because I volunteered. No matter how bullheaded or serious he got, I wanted to be the one who was there by his side. "I don't want you to die."

"You can be free now."

"I don't want to be free. I want to be with you." It was true. Since I'd turned into a vampire, everything had been insanity. But with Grim, I was anchored. I trusted him. He'd earned it. I didn't care if we had to deal with all this godly bullshit, as long as we got to make cupcakes and passionate love in between.

My mom had asked me to follow my heart, and it was leading me right to him. I'd struggled and tried to fight it, but faced with the choice of eternity with or without him, I chose with.

I took several steps back, forcing him to release me. Then I called out to the hungry souls. "Hey suckheads, it's all you can eat at the vampire café."

Some of the wiggling, feasting souls paused to regard me.

Grim's eyes widened. "No, don't do this."

I raised my arms. "Come get it."

Then they all bucked off Grim and crested over me. Towering over me in a quivering dark mass, I sensed their insatiable hunger and pure evil.

"Vivien!" Grim's monstrous yell barely penetrated the screaming mass. They crashed over me in a blinding wave of pain. My screams bent back, circling around each other as I became the center of pain and suffering itself.

Eternity after eternity stretched, and I begged for it to end, but it never did. Hell was real, and I was the piece of meat thrown into the pit.

24

I blinked. The cold of the stone sarcophagus seeped into my back and blood trickled down my neck from fresh puncture marks, but Vivien was gone.

While my essence had separated from my physical being, leaving my body here, Vivien's body and soul were melded together. She'd willingly stepped off this plane to free me from the dimensional prison I'd been sucked into. She had taken my place.

Panic exploded inside me. Stuck in that hellish plane, the dark souls were torturing, eating her alive. I had to save her.

Amit roared from his private enclosure. He was home, and he was hungry. Vivien had managed to bring him home.

Summoning all my power, I called forth my reapers. The supernatural jackals appeared in the antechamber. Hundreds, thousands of them. With a resounding roar, I directed them into hell. They charged, jumping between the space between dimensions, into the pit.

Protect Vivien, I ordered.

The horde of hounds dove and went to work attacking and dragging the feasting parasites off Vivien. The dark souls fought back with fangs of their own. Canine growls and whimpers mixed with unearthly screams.

Harnessing my power, I reached into the pit, grabbing as many damned souls as possible. A massive dark ball formed in front of me as I gathered as many as I could. But I could not send the energy to Amit. The forcefield Timothy and Fallon conjured prevented me from feeding Amit.

"Release," I commanded, my voice sonorous and layered.

The glowing orbs above their heads flared as their eyes snapped open at my command. The forcefield dropped and both collapsed. They'd spent all their energies containing me.

I hurled the ball of dark souls through the open stone door, tossing it to Amit. The growls and roars of satisfaction came, but in moments, he was ready for more. Into hell I reached again, pulling the souls up toward me. They had weakened me, but I couldn't allow myself to stop or rest.

Again and again, I amassed the souls into balls I threw to Amit. The god grew stronger with each meal I fed him.

I could still see my reapers fighting for Vivien, doing their best to keep her safe, until they'd formed a protective circle around her. She lay prone at the center.

With the last batch I hurled to Amit, my essence separated from my body and shot down back into the pit so fast, fire chased me all the way down. Fear and fury fueled me with impossible speed. Vivien lay on the scorched ground, her skin an ashen hue, her glow extinguished.

My essence split and shifted as I turned into my god-likeness. I howled and the hellish plane shook with the raw release of my pain.

No. No. I would not accept this. I couldn't lose her. I needed Vivien and if I had to tear the world apart to get her back, I would do it.

I scooped Vivien's prone body up from the hellish pit, then careened back upward to the mortal plane with her in my arms. I needed to get back to my body. If she drank from me, she would be alright.

My astral form rejoined with my body on the sarcophagus. My skin prickled and my bones vibrated from the intensity of my fear and power spilling over. I bore down against the sensation, refusing to let my body shift into my god-likeness. Still, my essence remained in jackal form, a ghostly layer over my human body.

Vivien now lay in my arms, and I searched for any glimmer of her light. Nothing. My hand brushed back the hair from her face, as I held her against me.

"Vivien. Wake up. Wake up, for me."

My energy was nearly drained, and my vision blackened around the edges as exhaustion threatened to take me under like it had Timothy and Fallon. But I would not give in.

I let one human finger morph into a sharp talon. I sliced the skin open on my other wrist and held it to her lips. I'd let her drain me dry, if it would mean she'd wake up. My blood trickled down into her mouth, but she didn't swallow or latch on to me. I continued to squeeze my life force into her mouth for several more minutes before lowering my arm.

"Come now, don't be so dramatic," I whispered, hugging her against me. "I know how you love to tease me, but I need you to wake up now. I promise if you do, we'll make cupcakes. I'll even wear a silly apron just to make you laugh."

The memory of meeting Vivien as a child had been so innocuous it hadn't been worth remembering, until our connection brought it from the recesses of my mind.

My lips brushed against hers as something warm fell from my face onto hers. I wiped my cheek, stunned to find a tear. Then a second. They were my tears. I hadn't cried for thousands of years. But my grief howled inside. It was as though my insides were ripped from my body. One dropped to her lips, sliding down the way of my blood.

Now I knew why it had to be Vivien. Vivien had volunteered to walk with me through eternity so I wouldn't be alone anymore. Though she had been young, her commitment had been pure and true. The promise she made to me as a child sent a ripple through fate, binding us together in a future neither of us could have predicted.

Or perhaps fate bound us sooner? Why else had I been on the spot to reap her parents? The coincidence of being so near to hear the call of their deaths was as rare as it was unlikely. I was too old to believe in coincidence.

When I'd bound Vivien to me in those underground tunnels, it had almost been as if I were completing a task left undone. As if all the events conspired to bring us to that exact point, so I could fulfill my part.

Vivien had likely forgotten her commitment as well. If she remembered it at all, she would have written it off as a dream. But fate had brought us back together and sealed that promise.

Despite our rocky, confusing start when I discovered this woman was a vampire, I'd learned not only to trust Vivien, but realize there was a place in this everlasting life for me to love too. Love didn't have to tear me apart. There was no choosing between my duty and my love. Vivien was in this with me, and wouldn't ask me to tear myself apart to serve her ego.

I couldn't lose her now. There were so many things I wanted to show her. I wanted to show her the world, take her to the cradle of life, do anything to see her smile. And, of course, make sure she was always warm by either my blood or an outrageous coat that resembled a Muppet.

A wry laughed choked its way out at the thought.

"Can we use rainbow sprinkles?" Vivien's voice cracked. Her fingers wrapped around my waist, clinging to me with what little strength she had left.

Pure joy and relief rocketed through me. I kissed her again, deeper this time, until Vivien melted against me, and I could no longer feel anything but her all around me.

Then, wrapping my arms around her, I said, "Of course. Whatever color sprinkles you like."

Her glow reappeared, but it was no longer a bright light. It was as if an inky blue galaxy surrounded her, dotted with bright shining stars. A new strength and power surrounded her. At one time I would have been suspicious, even scared, of the unknown element, but now, I didn't care as long as she was with me.

Nuzzling into my chest, she sighed. "And I know what apron you should wear."

"Oh yeah?"

"One that says, *I kiss better than I cook*."

Smiling into the top of her head, I said, "You've only sampled one of those things, so you may want to reserve judgement. But I'd do anything you ask of me right now.

And yes, I realize what a dangerous position that puts me in."

The curve of her lips against my chest made my heart pound faster. "Well then, I better get my requests in now, while you're weak and pliable."

"Go ahead." I still couldn't stop smiling.

"When we bake, you can wear the apron, but nothing else."

My laughter rocked both of us as I curled my body around hers.

When I pulled back again, she lifted a hand up and I realized she wasn't touching my human skin. Her fingers danced along my essence that still glowed around my body in jackal form.

"You're beautiful," she whispered.

For the second time, since that day on the road when I reaped Vivien's parents, I felt seen. Truly seen in my truest, complete form, intermixed with all my power and vulnerability.

I wasn't a reflection of her deepest, darkest curiosities, or a death wish. Vivien truly wanted me for me. The truth and reverence in her eyes rocked me to my core.

Death finally had a wish of his own. To keep her by my side for the rest of eternity.

We fell asleep for only a short while, but when I came to, Timothy and Fallon were gone. They let us rest. Reinvigorated by the rest, as well as the comfort of having Vivien in my arms, I made quick work of taking her up to the penthouse and tucking her into my bed.

With my strength fast returning to me, I got Vivien to drink deeply from me before she fell back asleep. She'd already drunk more than a reasonable amount of my blood. I should have worried she was reaching a dangerous level of power, but my concern for her welfare overshadowed my fear of Osiris.

Vivien's glow continued to intensify as she strengthened, a magnetic galaxy swirling around her. It was a miracle I managed to leave her side, I was so mesmerized by the beauty of her power.

While Amit had fed on the souls of the damned, I still retained those that needed judgement. My duty was not quite over, so I returned to my antechamber to finish the job.

Many long hours later, when I returned to the penthouse, emptied of all souls now, I found Vivien in the kitchen. Surprised, but not disappointed, I found her in nothing but a pair of panties and a tank top while she pulled a pan of cookies from the top oven. The white spray from a fire extinguisher decorated the lower oven, and flour and sugar covered every surface.

Such chaos would have sent me into an apoplectic fit before, but now I welcomed any evidence of Vivien in my life. There was no controlling her, and I was learning to lean into riding the waves.

Vivien pushed her hair back with her forearm, smearing more white powder around, and smiled at me.

"I think I'm getting better." When she handed me one of the already cooled crispy rounds, I braced myself before biting into it. The crack of my teeth confirmed they were burnt.

I nodded in approval, but set down the remaining cookie. I rounded the counter to where she stood, in all her enticing glory. Copper hair mussed, and a sheen over her body from the heat of the oven.

"I thought I'd find you sleeping," I said, dipping my head to kiss her neck. The noonday Vegas sun was hot and bright outside.

Vivien pushed my jacket back over my shoulders before attacking the buttons on my shirt.

"I know, right? Ever since I binged on your blood, my energy level has been way up. We should bottle your blood up and sell it as a miracle drug. We'd make millions."

Kissing my way up her neck, making my way to the spot I knew would make her lose control, I said, "We already have millions." A hell of a lot more than millions, in fact, but I didn't see the need to get technical.

"Maybe you do," she said, running her fingernails down my bare back. It felt incredible. "But I don't."

"Of course you do. What's mine is yours."

She stilled under my ministrations, but I didn't stop. "We aren't married."

"No," I agreed. "But blood eternally binds us."

"There is that," she agreed, but I could still tell her mind was mulling things over.

"I've accrued more wealth than I could spend, even with giving away masses of it to charities and causes." Framing her face with my hands, I said, "Not to mention I'm head over heels in love with you and would give you anything you desired. You need only ask."

"How about a diamond as big as my fist?" She skated right over my declaration of love and curled her fingers into her palm.

"If you desire it."

"How about a mansion with a ton of secret doors and tunnels?"

"Remind me to take you to my home in Egypt. My

temple is connected to the pyramids, and there are doorways to other universes."

Her eyes glazed over with wonder. And I regretted being so free with my information. She got into enough trouble in this realm. No need to terrorize any others.

She chewed on her lip. I knew she didn't want a diamond or a mansion, but she was trying to get in her creative mode to figure out what she really wanted.

"Can I have a motorcycle?" she chirped. "And oh! A puppy!"

In a swift, smooth motion, I pulled her up onto my hips, her legs wrapping around me. "Like I said, anything you want. But are you sure you don't want to go back to bed right now?"

She sobered. "Not yet. There are things I need to do, and they can't wait." I knew what she alluded to, but I wouldn't push her about her family. Her uncle and aunt were in the hotel still. I'd had my staff keep tabs on them, and had told her so.

"Not to mention with Seth on the loose..."

Vivien explained how Seth had taken worshippers. They'd used his power for transmutation to become big snakes. The snake Vivien learned to control had escaped along with Seth. I could only imagine how livid he was at having his own weapon used against him. He'd caused trouble before, toying with us. But his wrath was near volcanic when evoked. I'd no doubt he was somewhere plotting revenge even as we recovered. But Seth would be handled.

"Seth has crossed a line and Osiris will not stand for such actions. Seth's punishment will make Qwynn's look like a vacation. You need to focus on recovering."

She frowned whilst playing with my hair. "I'm not tired. I feel like I have unlimited energy."

As I carried her to the bedroom, I said, "Again, that's the blood. But I imagine the effect will wear off. And I didn't have sleep in mind."

An evil grin curled her lips before it stalled, then fell. "Wait, did you say you love me?"

My eyebrow rose. "Is that what I said?"

The next thing I knew, she was kissing me passionately, pulling at my hair, grinding against me.

I laughed into her mouth at the sudden, enthusiastic reaction.

She stopped kissing me, tripping over her words. "I also...I mean, this is happening so fast...and..." She took a deep breath. "I want to say it." She shut her eyes tight, as if bracing herself.

I brushed a thumb against her cheek. "You don't have to say it back," I assured her. "But to me, you stick out as a bright sun in what has been eons of gloom and heaviness. I can wait for as long as you need to sort out your feelings."

Then she stumbled on. "It's only because this is all new, and there have been a lot of intense situations. And I've never said it to anyone before. Plus we have eternity, which is really intimidating because that's a long time to be with someone and not get bored."

She left no room for me to say there was no chance of boredom being an issue. I pulled her tank top up and over her head, revealing those beautiful breasts. I dropped my head to worship the right one with my tongue and tiny nips that made her jump. I'd learned the right one was more sensitive than the left and used it to my full advantage.

"Shutting up now," she said, her words breathy.

Not bothering to pull down her panties, I moved them to

the side so I could play with the fast-dampening folds there. Between that and the attentions I paid to her breasts, Vivien was soon panting and begging for more.

I pushed her back onto the bed, and undid my belt, sliding it out from my pants. "Like I said, whatever you desire."

25

Death himself offered me anything I desired. Turned out, I had a lot of desires that needed to be met. In all kinds of positions, all over his penthouse. He wasn't kidding about the BDSM accoutrement, either—not that we'd gotten around to whips and handcuffs, but I was nearing the prospect with a healthy dose of curiosity.

The elevator pinged from the next room. Grim was in the shower, so I jumped out of bed and grabbed one of his shirts, buttoning it over my breasts. It fell to my mid-thigh, making me semi-decent enough to step out to see who was there. The doors had slid open, but there was no one. Taking another step, I found a box sitting in the elevator.

"Hey Grim, there's a package here," I yelled out. Before the doors could close again, I grabbed the box and set it on the kitchen counter. Maybe it was a new toaster? Nah, it was heavier than a toaster.

There was no mailing address of any kind.

Grim padded out, wrapping a towel around his hips. I

had to work at not licking my lips like a hungry tiger. His bronzed skin and dark hair were still wet from the shower.

"This was in the elevator," I announced, while ogling his sculpted torso.

"In the elevator?" He cocked an eyebrow.

I shrugged. "Maybe it's from Timothy and he's too afraid to come up here. What with us banging it out like animals."

His amused expression softened his features and gave him a boyish charm that made my toes curl.

Instead of grabbing a sharp object, Grim's finger lengthened into a claw and he slashed the tape open.

"Are you showing off for me?" I asked.

"Why, are you impressed?"

I came around the counter to the chair next to him and sat on my knees so I could see into the box too. "Maybe a little."

Grim pulled back the flap. He recoiled at the same time. I jumped off the seat and back several steps.

"Holy motherfucking hell, what is that?"

Any boyish expression was wiped from Grim's face. In its place was the expressionless mask the god of death wore when dealing with nasty business. "It's Seth."

I crept forward a few steps to confirm. Indeed, the god's face was in the box, face up, eyes open. My hand covered my mouth to keep from hurling. Disturbing didn't even begin to cover it.

"Is he...?"

"Yes." Grim's voice, a low rumble now, said, "He's dead." He pointed to the neck. It was a clean slice, but the skin had blackened at the cut point. His nose, ears, and lips had also blackened.

"I thought you said gods couldn't be killed."

"A god has not met a true demise for many hundreds of

years." Closing the flaps of the box again, he turned to face me. "There are, in fact, only two weapons I'm aware of that can end a god's existence. One was a sword of divine smite that disappeared in the medieval ages, but it appears as though it's resurfaced." He gestured to the box.

I couldn't disagree. Based on the clean cut at the neck, it looked like someone hacked Seth's head off with a sword.

Thank you *CSI*, *NCIS*, and *Bones*. And people said you couldn't learn anything from television.

"You said there were two weapons that could kill a god. What's the second?" I asked.

Grim's dark eyes settled on me. "The other weapon is standing next to me in her panties and has a penchant for baking."

Oh, fuck me.

With a deep breath, he went on. "It is forbidden to disclose such information to you, but Idris all but told you. Should you consume enough of my blood, you will become infinitely powerful until you are matched if not superseding that of a god's power."

I reached for a stool, steading myself. This was bad. This was very bad.

"I could kill a god?"

"If you drank enough of my blood, yes."

What he suggested seemed as impossible as me as being told a couple years ago I would one day be turned into a vampire.

Grim went on. "It's why the other gods both fear and covet you. Some believe you are a weapon they can wield, like a tool, and others believe you will be the end of us all. And now that your powers have grown from feeding on me, and we can't hide it, they will only grow bolder in their pursuit."

Jenkins, did you hear that? She's got a target on her back.

Sir, I heard. We are royally screwed. What are we going to do about it?

Hit the lever to switch her focus. Get it onto anything else. If she thinks about it too long, her head will pop, and we'll be out of a job.

Roger that, sir.

Following the lead of the men in my head, I turned to a more solvable problem. "Who would do this to Seth, and why would they send it to you?"

Grim spoke slowly. "There are only two reasons I can think of. Either someone wanted to prove their fealty to me, by handing over the head of my enemy..."

Then I saw the piece of paper taped to the side. I plucked it off the box and read it out loud. "It's a quote. *You can't go back and change the beginning, but you can start where you are and change the ending.* C. S. Lewis."

"It's not over," Grim said, a storm moving in over his brow. "Whoever is trying to upset the balance amongst the gods is sending a message."

"Yeah, that Seth wasn't our guy, and to taunt us that we still don't know who it is," I said.

"Or why," he mused.

"Having been around your lot more in the past week, I'd say there's no limit to why. Hardly anyone seems happy that Osiris won't let them take worshippers, and that they must serve humanity. Not to mention the imbalance of power within the ranks has also made for a few sour grapes." We still hadn't even had time to deal with Idris yet. He had a pounding coming for him, though, after bleeding me out.

Grim only let out a dissatisfied hum.

Overwhelm swept over me. It was all too much. Conspiracies, divine weapons, and the information I could be a god killer. No, never mind, I didn't want to kill anyone. The gods were going to corner and browbeat me, no doubt. They needed better hobbies. Maybe the next god who came after me would be amenable to some baking lessons. Or maybe I needed to find out who killed Seth before Grim was next.

"I need to go back to my suite and change," I said, needing to do something even though all I could do was put on combat boots to prepare for what was coming.

A hand stopped me. I didn't resist, as Grim drew me up against him, leaning down to kiss me. Pressed against his hard, wet body, my thoughts were driven out of my brain and off a cliff like so many dodo birds.

Grim said against my lips, "While I agree we must begin our search for a god killer who could threaten my brethren and all of humanity, I must insist that you stop this madness." Wet hair fell over his forehead, into his dark eyes.

"Can you be more specific? I subscribe to a lot of modes of madness." While I was disturbed by Seth's head showing up in a box, and that killing a god was suddenly possible, Grim and I would handle whatever was thrown at us. I was strong on my own, but with Grim, nothing would get past us. We would figure this bitch out, and then if Osiris came for me...well, one problem at a time.

"The madness being you living in a separate suite. While I respect your independence, I think it's better if we stick together."

Despite his distracting fingers pushing up the shirt I wore, skating along the skin of my back, I stepped back, out of his reach. "Make your case."

He paused, but recovered quickly. "You have to come here for all your meals anyway, the kitchen is perfect for experimental baking, my closets are far bigger, allowing for even bigger, fluffier or spiky jackets…" He trailed off, as if expecting me to jump at his first offerings.

"Keep going," I goaded, crossing my arms.

"I need your protection. Seeing as someone is killing gods, I could use a bodyguard." By his placating tone, I knew he didn't believe I'd be able to protect him, but the point struck a chord in me.

I narrowed my eyes in suspicion. "This feels like another ploy to control me."

"You know, there are benefits to my having control over you." His mouth curved upward in a devilish smile. For a moment, his skull mask flickered through. Death was teasing me.

Maybe he'd stop when I stopped loving it.

I let out a wry laugh. "Benefits? You mean you get the benefit of winning any argument by commanding I agree with you."

Rounding behind me, he ran his hands along my arms until I uncrossed them. "You know I would never do that." He dipped his lips to the space between my neck and shoulder, dropping soft, lingering kisses there. My brain turned into fuzzy static in a bowl of melted butter.

Between kisses, he said, "The blood bond can be used for all manner of purposes; much of that reflects the inventiveness of the god wielding it. The benefit would be as much yours as mine."

Though I tried to remain flippant, my words came out breathy. "Good thing you aren't cryptic. But sure, I like benefits. Are we talking medical? Vision? Dental? Fang care is no joke."

"You're right." He kissed up my neck, pulling me against his body. "It would be much better to demonstrate." Then he leaned in, the curve of his lips pressing against my ear as he commanded, "Come for me."

In the moment it took me to realize what he was using his power for, my brain short-circuited as my body shot off the edge of a cliff. In the throes of blinding, bone-melting pleasure, shudder after bone-wrenching shudder of pleasure overtook me. Heat pounding through my drenched, aching core. Even as my pleasure was wrung out of my body, I desperately wanted Grim to fill me.

Grim caught me in his arms, still wearing that devilish smile as I convulsed in his arms, crying out.

Okay, maybe I could get on board with this codependence thing.

EPILOGUE

Grim left to inform the others of Seth's demise—a trip I did not envy him. I offered to go with him, but he said it was godly business. So instead, I made my way back to my suite.

Like I'd told Grim...there were things I needed to see to that couldn't wait any longer.

I'd agreed to move into the penthouse with Grim, but I needed to get back to my rooms.

Once in my suite, I made my way to my closet. I hadn't bothered putting on shoes, only cinching a belt around Grim's shirt, which I still wore. Maybe it should have been strange walking around Sinopolis barefoot, but it was fast starting to feel like home.

Later I planned to meet up with Miranda. Since I could stay awake during daylight hours, I could bug her even more. It also did not suck having a friend who knew what was going on.

"Hello Janey," came a voice behind me.

Uncle Phillip stood in the doorway, blocking my exit. The smell of expensive cigars and stringent spearmint gum made me sick to my stomach. Still, I controlled my rioting emotions.

"How did you get in here?" The hotel rooms automatically locked when they shut, and the door definitely closed behind me.

"Money, of course. It's what makes the world go round. The front deskman was most accommodating once I padded his pockets. He even offered to let me know when you returned to your rooms."

I took a step back.

"It can only be explained as fate. You and me ending up here, at the same time," he said with a smile that didn't reach his eyes. There was an unerring focus in his gaze. He blocked the doorway of my closet with the same look he always got whenever he cornered me as a girl. It was like being transported to another time.

I'd learned then, it was better not to fight. He'd only make things worse.

"I must admit, you were always an attractive child, but now..." He sucked in a breath. "Something has changed about you. Seeing you again has made me feel like a young man."

"Who is the girl?" I asked.

A smug smirk pulled his lips. "You mean Allison? She's a foster. After our adopted niece died of a heroin overdose, despite all our attempts to save her from temptation, god granted Delilah and I another chance to save another young soul." He placed a hand over his heart, feigning anguish at my fake death.

I wasn't surprised my uncle and aunt told everyone I died. If I didn't fit the picture, might as well axe me from the storyline and make themselves look even more like bleeding heart heroes. Little did they know, I actually died.

My uncle slid his hands into the pockets of his overpriced suit jacket. "I'd hoped you would have been more well-behaved when you lived under our roof, more cooperative...like Allison. But now I find myself missing your spirit more often than not." Those keen gray eyes took me in from head to foot, assessing with predatory consideration. When his hands emerged again, one held a bottle of liquid, while the other gripped a rag. The numbing sting of chloroform hung in the air.

I took another step back, my shoulders hitting the hangers.

"And since fate has brought us back together, I would be remiss to take advantage of our reunion." Uncle Phillip took another step into the closet.

I threw my hands up in surrender. "But first, I have one question."

A dark eyebrow arched. "Oh?"

I straightened, dropping the cowering flower act. "How does it feel to know that as we speak, Aunt Delilah is being arrested for child abuse, and Allison is being taken by social services?"

My uncle gave me an unsure smile. "Don't be ridiculous. Even if that were true, we are friends with many judges who know family is everything to Delilah and me. Your aunt would never even see the inside of a jail, and we'd have Allison back in hours."

"The appearance of family is everything to you," I said, my voice cold as ice. "And not this time."

Once we had Amit back in the house, I went to work making arrangements for my aunt and uncle. Grim offered to take care of them for me, but he respected I needed to do this myself. With Miranda's help, I'd been able to inform the hotel staff they would likely be approached by my uncle with a bribe. They were instructed to take the money, then I would have them alert my uncle as soon as I was in my suites.

The entire staff was already completely devoted to Grim, and Miranda was fast earning their fealty as well. The moment it happened, I got a text from John, one of the front desk employees. He was more than enthused to help me.

Meanwhile, Timothy volunteered to help find Allison a new foster home, one with people who would actually care for their ward. They might not be the richest family, but they were adept at taking in emergency fosters who had undergone a lot of trauma. Grim insisted I let him cushion their bills to provide for Allison, and I conceded that one.

"But as for you...as you pointed out, fate has a different plan for you."

In a movement so quick, my body blurred. The door shut behind Phillip with a bang, causing him to jump.

"You were right about one thing." I shot him a wicked smile, my canines elongating. "I *have* changed."

The bottle and cloth dropped from Phillip's hands as his eyes widened. He stammered, "W-what the hell?"

"Say hi to Amit for me, uncle."

Want a bonus epilogue where Grim gives Vivien a surprise gift?

Visit www.hollyroberds.com and download it now!

WANT A FREE BOOK?

Join Holly's Newsletter Holly's Hot Spot at www.hollyroberds.com and get the Five Orders Prequel Novella, The Knight Watcher, for FREE!

Plus you'll get exclusive sneak peaks, giveaways, fun lil' nuggets, and notifications when new books come out. Woot!

A LETTER FROM THE AUTHOR

Dear Reader,

Thank you for reading!

I loved writing this story and have so much more in store for Grim and Vivien as they discover the cancerous root amidst the gods and learn the limits of trust and love.

Loved this book? Consider leaving a review as it helps other readers discover my books.

Want to make sure you never miss a release or any bonus content I have coming down the pipeline?

Make sure to join Holly's Hotspot, my newsletter, and I'll send you a FREE ebook right away!

You can also find me on my website www.hollyroberds.com and I hang out on social media.

Instagram: http://instagram.com/authorhollyroberds

Facebook: www.facebook.com/hollyroberdsauthorpage/

And closest to my black heart is my reader fan group, Holly's Hellions. Become a Hellion. Raise Hell. www.facebook.com/groups/hollyshellions/

Cheers!

Holly Roberds

ABOUT THE AUTHOR

Holly started out writing Buffy the Vampire Slayer and Terminator romantic fanfiction before spinning off into her own fantastic worlds with apocalyptic stakes.

Recently relocated to New Hampshire from Colorado, Holly is exploring the possibilities of become a witch (as one must consider when living in New England) and is hard at work implementing the word "wicked" into her vernacular.

She lives with her husband whose handsome looks are only out done by his charming and wicked supportive personality.

Two surly house rabbits supervise this writer, to make sure she doesn't spend all of her time watching Buffy reruns.

For more sample chapters, news, and more, visit www.
hollyroberds.com

Printed in the USA
CPSIA information can be obtained
at www.ICGtesting.com
LVHW022155290524
781384LV00012B/535

9 781960 961037